JUDITH SKILLINGS

DRIVEN TO MURDER

AVON BOOKS
An Imprint of HarperCollins*Publishers*

This is a work of fiction. Names, characters, places, and incidents are products of the author's imagination or are used fictitiously and are not to be construed as real. Any resemblance to actual events, locales, organizations, or persons, living or dead, is entirely coincidental.

AVON BOOKS
An Imprint of HarperCollins*Publishers*
10 East 53rd Street
New York, New York 10022-5299

First Avon Books paperback printing: February 2006

Avon Trademark Reg. U.S. Pat. Off. and in Other Countries, Marca Registrada, Hecho en U.S.A.
HarperCollins® is a registered trademark of HarperCollins Publishers Inc.

Printed in the U.S.A.

10 9 8 7 6 5 4 3 2 1

The deadliest sport . . .

Reaching into the cockpit, she forced Peyton to step back out of her way. She tugged on the catch of the six-point safety harness. It kept the driver securely in place, released with one flick in case of fire. She waited bent over for the engine to light off. It rumbled. Seconds later, it smoothed. She gave Ian a thumbs-up and patted the cowling.

Halfway to standing, she heard the gunshot.

Heard the high-pitched whine. The crack as Plexiglas shattered. A thunk as the bullet impacted the asphalt.

The crew kid shrieked as the gas can flew from his grip, landing upright a few feet away. Her head jerked in response. She saw the small round hole where the bullet entered the gas can, scattering flecks of macadam where it bit into the tar after exiting. Twin streams of gasoline spurted like a cheap wine from a fountain on an Italian buffet.

She felt her own scream—a low animal howl— begin deep inside her belly, swell and explode . . .

Books by Judith Skillings

DRIVEN TO MURDER
DANGEROUS CURVES
DEAD END

This book is dedicated to

J. R. Frawley

For thirty-one years and too many reasons to count.
Some of them have to do with racing.

Acknowledgments

Without my Indiana connections, this story would not have been possible. Because of Freida and Jonathan West's warm hospitality, we've attended every Formula One race held at the Indianapolis Motor Speedway and enjoyed them in great company. Thanks to Freida also for being such an energetic researcher, and to Natalie West for naming the squirrel. Thanks to Tom and Marylu Delph; Senior Trooper Eric J. Dunn of the Indiana State Police; Julie Weaver and Kevin Forbes of the engineering department at IMS. (Please forgive me for removing the catch fence.) And the dozens of friendly fans whose names I never knew; you provided the background.

Closer to home, my fond appreciation goes to Annette Farrell, Hannelore Kahles, Mermie Karger, Rick Mullin, Pam Perkins (and Alex), and Julie and Steve Sokoloff, for sharing their professional expertise. Hugs to Bert and all the guys at the shop for the continued support.

To my editor, Sarah Durand, and Dominick Abel, my agent: thank you so much for keeping me on track. It's been a fun ride.

Special thanks go to Johannes Willenpart, owner of both the Lotus 49C and the Arrows FA-1 at the time this book was being written. His enthusiasm for the cars and his generosity in sharing materials made this story the one it is. I will always cherish my photograph in the cockpit and thank him sincerely for introducing me to Michael Oliver, author of the definitive book on the Lotus, and to the Argetsinger family, founders of the superb International Motor Racing Research Center at Watkins Glen.

Author's Note

In September 2002, twenty-five historic racers took to the track at the Indianapolis Motor Speedway as part of the festivities preceding the Formula One race. The cars belonged to Historic Grand Prix, a group of more than fifty owner-drivers of authentic Formula One cars that raced from 1966 to 1983. The group stresses historically correct presentation and on-track performance. While they did not race that day in Indiana, these spectacular vintage racers can be seen competing each season on tracks throughout Europe.

DRIVEN TO MURDER

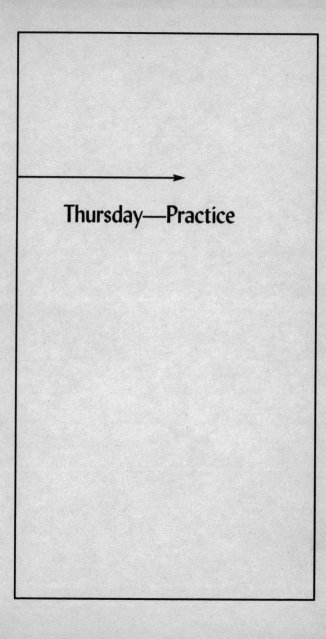

Thursday—Practice

One

It could have been a perfect New England autumn day. A childhood memory of Indian summer painted in primary colors. Blazing red sugar maples. Titian blue skies. Puffy white clouds pushed along by a breeze tinged with the hint of frost. The day her mother—Pauline—had taken the three kids for an outing to the Brookfield Orchards. Rebecca closed her eyes, raised her face to the warmth of the sun. She imagined she could smell the tang of fallen apples, hear the hum of yellow jackets lured by putrefying pulp. Imagined that if she stretched out her arms, her fingertips would brush the branches of gnarled trees laid out in rows by eighteenth-century settlers.

Ridiculous. The flashbacks were becoming a nuisance.

It was the twenty-first century. She was standing on fresh blacktop opposite turn twelve of the road course at the Indianapolis Motor Speedway. Gasoline fumes and the stench of burning brakes hung in the air. The pervasive whine came not from insects, but from 3-Litre engines accelerating hard onto the front straight at the most famous racetrack in the world. She was playing mechanic, twisting wrenches to improve the performance of a rich man's toy.

Admittedly, it was a teenage fantasy come to life. The chance to be a part of Indy, to brush shoulders with the most famous names in open-wheel racing, had enticed her away from home and business. Her crush on racing was sophomoric and not easily explained to her pragmatic friends, so she hadn't tried. When she'd been offered the three-week stint, she'd waved off their objections, packed her tools and flown west.

Behind her someone called out, "Rebecca. Moore." She sighed, opened her eyes and turned. The car's owner, Peyton Madison III, wagged his fingers for her to come closer.

Ian Browning, their driver, was straightening the shoulder harness before sliding into the cockpit of the Lotus 49C, touted by race pundits as the most exquisitely designed race car ever. Peyton murmured last-minute encouragements. Ian avoided eye contact. He was focused on the race course, as if he were already strapped in, moving the car through the gears, gliding around the turns. They barely had time for two more practice laps before the track was turned over to the Formula One cars.

The kid on the crew picked up a canister of gas to top off the tank. When he grinned, acne scars formed a half moon on his cheek. Rebecca watched him uncap the gas, then turned and braced Ian's arm as he raised his leg over the flexible housing and settled in. She lifted the Plexiglas windshield into place and began tightening the bolts on her side.

Uncomfortably close, Peyton pressed his thigh against hers, picked at the corner of a Shell decal with his thumbnail. He offered her a Southern smile, charming and as short-lived as a firefly passing through. Then reminded her that he was counting on a lap under a minute, twenty. Fast enough to put the Lotus on the front row during tomorrow's qualifying session. If it happened, she would be a hero. If not—

Peyton touched her arm. "Clouds are building."

Her mouth twitched into a demi-smile as she explained that clouds were good. They ensured cooler track temperatures. Peyton nodded as if he understood. He didn't. He knew less about racing than she did. At least she'd arrived with a firm grasp of auto mechanics as they applied to vintage cars. The variables of racing—track conditions, down force, tire adhesion, driver fatigue—were challenges she enjoyed mastering.

Reaching into the cockpit she forced Peyton to step back, out of her way. She tugged on the catch of the six-point safety harness. It kept the driver securely in place, released with one flick in case of fire. She waited bent over for the engine to light off. It rumbled. Seconds later it smoothed. She gave Ian a thumbs-up and patted the cowling.

Halfway to standing, she heard the gunshot.

Heard the high-pitched whine. The crack as Plexiglas shattered. A thunk as the bullet impacted the asphalt.

The crew kid shrieked as the gas can flew from his grip, landing upright a few feet away. Her head jerked in response. She saw the small round hole where the bullet entered the gas can, scattering flecks of macadam where it bit into the tar after exiting. Twin streams of gasoline spurted like cheap wine from a fountain on an Italian buffet.

She felt her own scream—a low animal howl—begin deep inside her belly, swell and explode.

Two

"Jo, I yelled like a demented fishwife. Knocked one of the crew into a tool chest. Kicked the gas can as if it were a soccer ball headed for goal. They thought I'd lost my mind. Most hadn't heard the shot. Had no idea what was going on. The owner gripped my shoulders. Glared down his nose, offended like I was an hysterical Southern belle who forgot the manners her nanny taught. He ordered me to leave the track. He'll probably fire me."

Jo Delacroix cradled the phone, directed his energy through the line. It was the first time he'd heard from Rebecca in nearly two weeks. She should have sounded relaxed, full of trivial news. Instead, notes of panic rippled along like a tidal undercurrent beneath the surface of her ranting. She'd been strung too tight when he'd put her on the plane for Indianapolis. He hoped the time away would calm her, that she would get some rest. Not be shot at. "Rebecca, last May you watched a man burn to death when a bullet ignited gasoline fumes—they are a deadly combination. Of course you reacted."

"How could I have been so unprofessional?"

"Don't worry about the job. If Peyton Madison fires you, I'll sue him."

No response. The receiver echoed with the scrunch of her boots on loose gravel. Jo assumed she was trudging away from the track, jostling the cell phone with each step. He imagined her turning tight circles on the shoulder of the road, slender legs giving vent to her frustration, occasionally kicking a stone into the gutter. His favorite client was an expressive pacer, her body unable to stand still when her mind was racing.

Racing. That was what had taken her away.

Jo sat back and folded the *Last Will and Testament of Cyrus Borden.* He slid it into the center drawer then extracted a newspaper guide to the Indianapolis Motor Speedway that Rebecca had mailed him. *Historic cars* was written in black marker in the margin. An arrow pointed to the infield near the Hall of Fame Museum. Before leaving, she'd patiently explained that she would be prepping an actual Formula One car that had raced in the seventies and eighties. Many of the competing cars had been driven by world champions. Technology had changed, but not the thrill of seeing these cars navigate a road course.

Her enthusiasm was wasted on him. It did nothing to soften his disapproval of her being in Indianapolis. Still, he recognized that Rebecca had to try. She needed to be accepted by people she let get close. Her aloofness was simply a shield against rejection. Today, she'd lost her composure in front of a group of men who held her in begrudging respect and she couldn't stop kicking herself. Concern about the gunshot was secondary.

Jo stretched forward and lifted a pen from its holder. Whether the bullet had been intended for her or not, she could have been killed. "Rebecca, why would—"

"It was idiotic, Jo. As a reporter, I met informants under deserted overpasses. Tracked them through ghettos where no one spoke English and everyone was armed. On a sunny day in Indiana, I lose it over a stray gunshot that did no damage. It doesn't matter that I had cause."

"Doesn't matter?" He slapped the pen on the desk; momentum carried it off the edge. "Of course it matters. You're human like the rest of us."

Did she think it would just go away? That she could erase it and start again with a clean sheet of paper? She'd been wounded when a killer fired a gun at her, burned when she tried to smother the flames to save him. Jo had witnessed the aftermath. Inhaled the stench of charred flesh, seen the burnt bones denuded of skin. Smoothed ointment on her blistered hands. Brushed waves of hair from her cheek, come away with the strands stuck to his fingers.

He couldn't forget. How could she? The horror of the event might have faded like a sepia print, but he was certain it still kept her company during sleepless nights, a ghost rocking in the corner. He ached to eradicate her pain. But at this minute, his fear for her safety was inching toward anger. "Maybe you're refusing to accept the obvious: You attract dangerous miscreants. Why not a homicidal mechanic?"

The boots stopped scattering gravel. She breathed into the phone line, but didn't respond, biting back a retort. He should have kept quiet as well. She didn't need to be reminded that she was a magnet for lunatics.

He'd known her less than a year. Already, Rebecca had survived close calls with fire and water. In mythological terms, there were only two more elements she had to battle. Two more confrontations he had to guard her against. More and more, he felt like a member of some ancient tribe, who having saved her life, was responsible for her forever.

Not an unpleasant task, if she would stay within reach. Which she wouldn't.

For much of September, Jo had tried to discourage her from taking the job at Indy. He insisted that she knew nothing about race cars. Predicted that by leaving her automotive restoration business in Head Tide unsupervised, she was inviting financial ruin. Vintage & Classics had been close to bankruptcy when she'd inherited it from her uncle. It could go there again, if she wasn't careful.

She'd tossed a quart of oil to Frank, then turned on Jo. "Nonsense, they don't need me. Ask them. It's the end of the touring season, so the workload's easing up. The shop will be fine. Besides, I consider mingling at the Brickyard a strategic business move. The race crowd is worth cultivating. They're often as besotted by classic cars as they are by their racers."

She'd been less articulate dismissing her obligations to family and friends. Reminded him that her tattered relationships were none of his business. Maybe they weren't. Or maybe she was simply over-

whelmed by the number of loose ends suddenly need-
ing attention.

Or, maybe Rebecca was running away again.

Jo pushed back the chair and retrieved the fountain
pen, pulled the newspaper section closer. He con-
sciously softened his voice. "Where did the shot come
from?"

After a second, she answered. "From the stands
across the track. The bullet clipped the edge of the
tent, splintered the windshield of the car, then pierced
the gas can on a downward trajectory. I'm guessing
the southeast vista near the VIP suites."

He smoothed the map. The pits for the F1 cars were
shown along the front straight. The historic cars' paddock was relegated to the tarred infield, sharing space
with the vendors selling official team merchandise
and souvenirs. Twelve teams were housed under four
long tents lashed together. Rebecca had drawn lines
representing the tents, doodled a flag on a center pole
and placed an "X" to mark her slot.

Behind the stands at turn twelve, Jo added a stick
figure with a rifle aimed at the tent. The pen tore
through the newsprint, gouging the blotter beneath. He
lifted the pen tip from the paper and set it down. "How
could someone smuggle a rifle into the track? Isn't
there security?"

She was walking again, rustling dry leaves. "During the pre-race week only a few gates are open,
manned by hired security. The guards do cursory
checks. Look for someone or something that blatantly
doesn't belong. Mostly they collect autographs and
try to make dates with race groupies."

"Sounds all-American."

"That's all that's American. The spectators, like the race drivers, are mostly European, Asian or South American. So the guards tread softly. If FedEx delivers a cardboard box long enough to contain a rifle, and it's labeled as a replacement axle shaft, the guards are willing to believe it's an axle shaft."

"You're saying minimal security. Could the shooting have been an accident? Kids playing in the stands, targeting birds, perhaps?"

"Like Little Cock Robin? I doubt it. The shot nearly clipped the three of us—driver, mechanic, owner. Ian was in the Lotus. Peyton and I were huddled next to it."

"Sitting ducks. But all he hit was the windshield and a gas can?"

"The bullet grazed Johnny Evans who was holding the can. Minor scratch. He blanched when he realized what had happened. Then turned macho and refused to have it bandaged. Ian Browning, the driver, joined me in having hysterics. Certain he was the intended target, that a rival team was trying to throw him off his stride. Peyton pulled Ian aside and calmed him down.

"Something's funny there, Jo. The owner refused to report the shooting to track security. Insisted that the team wasn't in danger. Puffed all up and said that if an elusive gunman was out to kill, one of us certainly would be dead."

"What? He views it as a dramatic form of intimidation?"

"I guess. But he won't say who's supposed to be intimidated. Or why."

Three

Rebecca hung up and stashed the cell phone in her backpack. She hadn't told Jo about the earlier mishaps. Maybe there was no need. Her teammates had scoffed at her, swore they were just racing accidents. Given the past year, it was possible that she was overreacting, being overly morbid. Hell, it was more than possible, it was likely.

If you overlooked the gunshot.

The bullet had been real. It could have been deadly.

At the edge of the road a Canada goose pecked in the grass for something edible. A Camaro, radio blaring, sped by with a parcel of laughing teenagers looking for mischief. It was still a magnificent day and the drone of high-powered engines said the track was still in use.

Was she really going to let a self-impressed twit like Peyton Madison spoil her time at the Brickyard? She'd been expelled from the Lotus pits, not the track. There was nothing to stop her from returning to watch the F1 cars practice. She'd grab a hot dog and sit high up Stand J, cheer Schumacher and Montoya through the hairpin turns.

She settled the backpack on her shoulders and retraced her steps, replaying the conversation with Jo as the noise from the track grew louder. Normally, Jo Delacroix's voice could sell salvation to an atheist. That was the main reason she'd called him. To let his voice slow the pulsing adrenaline, sooth away her humiliation. He'd calmed her, but something was off. Even in her distracted state she sensed, what—anger, concern, disappointment? Definitely tension.

Jo Delacroix was her lawyer, that was how they'd met. It was no longer how she thought of him. In her new life, he was her closest friend. Also her savior—literally and emotionally. He was the intellectual thoroughbred in the one-horse town of Head Tide, Maryland. A graceful athlete disguised in summer-weight worsteds. Tall, with mocha skin, mellow amber eyes, generous smile, sensuous walk. Piano player fingers.

More frequently, as the pre-dawn stars faded over the fields out back, she wondered what it would be like to make love with him. They might have been headed in that direction—before Mick Hagan, her renegade cop, had moved into town. Hagan's compass was firmly fixed on her. His intensity had derailed Jo, caused him to pull back. Left her stalled at the intersection.

Practice finished up just before five. She trotted down the stands as the voice on the loudspeaker reminded fans that the gates would open at eight o'clock tomorrow morning for historic F1 car qualifying. She didn't need to be reminded, though she wondered if there would be a message on the answering machine telling her not to bother showing up.

She paused just inside the gate, scanned the faces of the exiting crowds. She wasn't searching for anyone in particular. Just observing. Hoping, as she had in grade school, for a half-smile, the hint of an invitation to walk home in the company of another child. That was a long time ago, at a school with walls and regular hours. Today she was returning alone to the house Peyton had rented for his senior crew members, a sixties ranch located north of the track on Patricia Street within easy walking distance, which was its only charm. It was a bland brick house with three bedrooms, two baths, a patio surrounded by stockade fence, neglected vegetation and on-street parking.

Peyton wasn't staying there. He had a room in the city at the Canterbury Hotel, *the* place to stay if you wanted to be seen. A hotel frequented by celebrities like Mick Jagger and Elton John, and the infamous, like Mike Tyson and Michael Jackson. On race weekends, it was home to those wanting to rub shoulders with the automotive elite. Peyton also had a motor home the size of a Trailways bus parked just outside the track, handy for afternoon naps. His transporter, which would hold four cars, grazed in a lot with dozens more just like it.

The front door was open when she arrived, only the storm door separating the sunshine from the dust motes. Clearly Ian had hurried home after the last practice lap. Evidence of his presence was strewn throughout the living room. Keys in the brass fruit bowl on the bookcase, a magazine open on the sofa, racing shoes kicked in the direction of the fireplace. He, however, was missing from his usual spots. Not in the small kitchen. Or outside lounging in the last few minutes of sun. Ian Browning, her driver and roommate, was in her bedroom, flipping through the clothes in the closet.

Rebecca pitched her backpack at the bed. "Find anything you like? The purple knit would be good with your complexion."

He had the decency to blush. "I was making sure you hadn't packed up and split. That's all. I was worried about you. Where have you been? I cut out after my last run. Told Peyton I couldn't concentrate with someone taking potshots. What if his aim improved?"

"I thought moving targets were harder to hit?"

"Not funny, Reb. Shower and dress. I'm starving. Luis y Maria's awaits."

Burritos and beer sounded like the perfect pick-meup until she took a good look at Ian. Scowl lines scored the flesh at both sides of his mouth. His eyes flitted around the room like frenzied birds before a storm. Normally, he was an undemanding dinner companion, content to talk about racing and turn in early. Right now, he was not acting himself.

Not that she could define normal as it applied to Ian. They'd met a scant two months ago at the Washington Vintage Grand Prix. He'd flashed an impish grin, quizzed her on engine parts. When she could tell a distributor from a fuel pump, he'd squeezed her shoulder and whispered in her ear. "Lass, you're the answer to my mechanical prayers."

The head mechanic on his race team had been diag-nosed with prostate cancer and wouldn't be around to work the race at Indy. Somehow Ian had bullied the team owner into offering her the job. Then he'd per-suaded her, a newspaper reporter turned classic auto mechanic, to accept it.

The scuttlebutt among the crew was that Ian's influ-ence over Peyton involved money, a necessary com-modity in a rich man's sport. He was old enough to have climbed halfway up a corporate ladder, yet bragged he'd never worked a full-time job. He just raced. And while he was young for a vintage racer—mid-thirties versus the average age of forty-five—he was too old to make the leap into competitive racing, which paid its drivers in earnest. Ian seemed to be one of life's lucky few who had no obligations other than to indulge his whims. Tom summed up what they were all thinking. "Ian's got to be a trust fund baby, or blessed with very indulgent parents."

Rebecca shooed Ian from the room, followed him down the hall. In the bathroom she dropped her team coveralls on the floor and luxuriated in a shower as hot as she could stand it, lathering her hair twice to wash away the stench of exhaust gas. She donned a short print skirt, knit top and sandals, ran a comb through the damp waves. They would air-dry into curls before she finished the nachos. As an after-thought, she added a touch of makeup—armor against the day's humiliations—and snatched up a sweater on the way out.

Luis y Maria's Cantina was a hole-in-the-wall on the strip eight blocks away, wedged between a defunct hardware store and bustling video rental. It was nowhere as dingy as it looked from the parking lot. Colorful piñatas hung over each of the eight tables and mariachi music played through speakers in the four corners. The non-English-speaking wait-staff came in a variety of sizes and closely resembled each other. Most importantly, it had killer salsa and beers cold enough to freeze your teeth.

It also had Peyton Madison and Wayne Evans seated in a booth at the back.

"Surprise. Surprise?" Rebecca flipped a look at Ian.

He shrugged in response, whispered, "It's time to kiss and make up."

Before she could retreat out the door, Peyton spotted them, hailed them like long-lost cousins on his mother's side. Ian placed a hand on her spine and pushed her forward. She had to move or trip.

The crew chief's back was to the door. He didn't bother turning around. Seated, Evans appeared to loom over Peyton: a head taller and half a foot wider. Standing, he had only an inch on his boss. His short legs and a low slung belly gave him a fortuitous center of gravity for working on open-wheel racers. His hair was prematurely gray; his face permanently creased from scowling at the crew in the sun.

Peyton slid over, patted the bench for her to sit beside him. While they read the menus, he nattered on about Ian's chances to put the Lotus on the pole the next day. Chatted away like the gunshot had never occurred, like no harsh words had been exchanged, like he hadn't expelled her from the track. Acted like her outburst had been forgiven, if not forgotten.

When he asked the driver a pointless question about the car's handling, Rebecca closed her menu. Tuned out Ian's answer. In profile Peyton just missed being good-looking, though she doubted he shared her assessment. A small, well-shaped head, chin narrow and thin, pursed lips. The dark brown eyes would have been alluring if they weren't usually glancing over your shoulder in search of someone more significant to suck up to. The whole package exuded pampered frat boy, the kind who thought nothing of cheating at cards or welshing on bets. Catching him at it would reveal your low character, not his.

Two hours later, the tacos were reduced to a smear of red sauce, and Dos Equis bottles littered the table. Peyton still hadn't mentioned the gunshot. Two hours of chitchat and no one had said a word about it or the other mishaps around the pits. No one had mouthed the word *sabotage*, though she was willing to bet she wasn't the only one thinking it.

Less than a week ago, the car she'd been hired to work on, an Arrows FA-1, had been damaged when a brake line gave way, spraying brake fluid on the front tire. The line hadn't broken—it had been cut nearly through next to the end fitting. Pressure from hard braking in turn six had separated the line and sent the car headfirst into the retaining barrier. Ian was bruised but unhurt. The suspension of the car was bent beyond repair. A replacement couldn't be shipped to the track in time for the race.

Demonstrating his membership in the more-money-than-brains club, Peyton had lowered the ramp of his transporter and pulled out the Lotus 49C. Rebecca had stood with the crew, dumb with awe. While the Arrows—once raced by Ricardo Patrese— was an expensive toy, the Lotus was an historic work of art: the epitome of classic racer, sleek, low and very sexy. It had been driven by Austrian legend Jochen Rindt shortly before his death and sported the number 3, as it had at his victory in the Monaco Grand Prix in 1970. Automotive writers who tracked such things put its price tag at close to a million dollars. It was a car to be displayed in a museum, not raced around the Brickyard.

But Peyton was determined to race, and to win.

Switching cars had resulted in long days for the crew. By Tuesday the Lotus had been ready to produce competitive laps. Topping it off, Evans discovered that a spare gas can was filled with water instead of fuel. He caught it before it damaged the engine, but they lost precious track time draining the tank and checking the systems before refueling.

Then, Wednesday morning, the left front wheel had fallen off on the first practice lap. It was as much luck as skill that enabled Ian to steer the Lotus into the grassy infield, away from the barrier walls, and avoid his second crash in under a week.

Evans had been furious. "Damn splines are worn. Can't keep the hub on. Too much stress from hard turning at high speeds."

Peyton agreed, waved it away as normal wear, metal fatigue or something. Something that should have been noticed by the tire changer. Hunkering down, Rebecca had pointed to the shiny surface on the threads, insisted that someone had filed the studs down recently. Intentionally.

No one bought it. They raised a communal eyebrow at the dumb broad butting in again and told her to find replacement studs.

She'd rocked back on her heels, counted to ten. Yes, she was female, and having a woman in the pits changed the chemistry and everyone's comfort level. They had to watch what they said, how they said it. Chet Davis, the tire changer, communicated through grunts and only then if she asked a direct question. Tom's sidelong glances said he was way too conscious of her figure under the one-piece track suit. The crew kid, Evans's nephew, was straight out of vo-tech and showed off for her at every opportunity, not caring that she was old enough to be his mother. Evans just glowered. Bided his time, prayed she'd make a major mistake. She might know her way around an engine, but that didn't stop him from branding her as a jinx, as unlucky as any hoop skirt on the deck of a sailing ship.

Peyton squeezed her knee, edged her from the booth as he rose to pay the bill. Ian stood to let Evans exit for the men's room, then sat back down, wiping orange grease from his fingers. Rebecca threw down her napkin. "Stay here."

In the dim hallway she caught up with Evans, pulled him around to face her. "Did Peyton tell you about the gunshot?"

He tugged his belt into the ridge below his gut,

dropped his fists to his side. A contender ready for the bell. "Yeah. So?"

"So, he didn't report it to security. What's going on?" His eyes narrowed. No response. "The shot could have set the pit ablaze. You would have known that, if you'd been there when it happened. Where were you?"

Evans shifted his belly, crowding her against the wall. "I was where I belong, Moore, doing my job. What's yours?"

She cocked her head. "What are you getting at?"

He checked that Ian was still seated out of earshot. "You're the mechanic. You say the brake line was cut. Then why the hell didn't you notice it before sending the car out? Likewise, if the wheel studs were filed down, who did it? Not one of my guys. I say that old nicked file in your bottom tool drawer could have shaved the threads off real slick. It's got fresh filings. Guess you'll say someone could have borrowed it, right? Done the job, put it back and you know nothing. Say whatever you want. We never had problems before you showed up."

Evans reversed direction, left her dawdling by the men's room door. He tossed a wad of crumpled bills on the table and followed his boss from the restaurant.

Rebecca felt her face flush. *How dare Evans accuse her?* One minute he swears the incidents are accidents, next breath he's pointing his finger at her. Any file could have damaged the threads. Any utility knife could have cut the brake line. There were three loaded tool chests in their area alone. Dozens more under the tent. Who knew how many along pit road. All of them contained—

She jumped when Ian snapped his fingers in front of her face.

He tapped at the end of her nose. "I know what you're thinking, my lovely. Leave it alone. If Peyton suspected sabotage, he'd be screaming bloody murder. You know he'll do anything to give us an edge. Complaining to track management would assure us sympathetic press. That would be his style." He draped the sweater over her shoulders. "It must have been an accident. Another bit of Peyton's bad luck. What's to be gained by ruining a small team like us?"

It was an excellent question, one that consumed her on the short ride back from the restaurant. Motive was the mystery. Who would gain if the Lotus team was unable to compete? They had a good chance of winning, but so did at least three of the twelve. Unlike demonstration runs, this was a race for money. The winning team would take home $100,000. Though not a fortune, it was an unusual perk for vintage racing. Normally the teams spent a tremendous amount of time and money. All they got in return were bragging rights and a small mention in a magazine sidebar.

For this, the inaugural race at the Brickyard, a group of investors had decided to raise the bar. Lure the best from Europe to compete and spark U.S. interest in the road racers from the late-sixties, seventies and eighties. The backers were businessmen who shrewdly realized that Americans love competition and demand to see it rewarded. The larger the purse, the more media interest, the greater chance of establishing a new series, or at least an annual event at Indy.

If Team Lotus pulled out, the race would still go on. Eliminating them couldn't be the saboteur's goal. *So what was?*

Four

They circled the block twice before Ian found a space on the curve. He let the car rumble to a stop. It was a 1957 Corvette he'd borrowed for his stay in Indiana from an enthusiast who got free weekend passes in exchange. It was an all-original car in need of major exhaust work. Ian preferred to park it in sight of the house, but a rental car had taken his favorite spot.

Retrieving her purse, Rebecca slid her legs over the sill. "You'll qualify the Lotus tomorrow as scheduled?"

"Stop fretting, Rebecca. I expect you to be there. I need you. Peyton's just being pissy. Call it pre-race jitters. Or bad press." He fished behind the driver's seat, reached for her hand. Into it he smacked a rolled-up copy of *AutoWeek*. "Seems Peyton has a nasty habit of rattling cages. Derek Whitten may be trying to shake him up. He's a smelly beast, rumored to have lethal fangs. No matter what he says, his Brabham can't compete with the Lotus."

"Whitten? The shooter?"

Ian slammed the car door. "No? Well how about an unsubtle warning from Peyton's bookie? It says on page eighteen that our team owner has a gambling habit. Wagers *beaucoup de* pocket change on all types of sporting events. According to the snoops, his cash out exceeds his cash in. I know how much faith you put in reporters' accuracy."

"Occasionally, they get it right. If he's strapped, how's he footing the bill here?"

Ian shrugged. "Who cares as long as he does? He's boasting about entering a car at Le Mans next year. And plans to invest in an F1 team. In either case, I wouldn't mind hitching a ride." He draped an arm over her shoulder and hugged. "So, my sylvan wrench monkey, let's keep the shooting to ourselves. If the boss says there's nothing to worry about, I say we agree."

She didn't, but she let the subject drop along with Ian's arm.

They walked back to the house discussing nothing more serious than the weather predictions for the weekend. Their steps echoed on the cement sidewalk. The street was eerily still, country dark. Rebecca started when a cat hissed at something invading its territory then darted into the underbrush. Ian laughed at her, but moved closer.

She was glad of his proximity, which annoyed her. Her nerves were stretched too thin by the events of the past months. She'd hoped a few weeks away would allow her to regain equilibrium. That solitude might yield a better perspective, help staunch the slide into depression. Instead, her view was darkening as she was becoming more withdrawn.

Breathing deeply, she tried to relax. *Hey, sure it was dark, damp and too quiet, but at least there was no body of water to drown in.*

There was no reason to be jumpy. The stillness was easily explained. Many of the squat houses were empty, vacated by owners who'd fled town during race week. By Friday, they'd be overflowing with fans. If you didn't follow racing but lived near the track, renting your house gave you enough cash to vacation away from the noise. Which was how Peyton landed their house. He'd intended it to accommodate Ian, Evans and Rebecca. The second night in town, at a country-western bar, Evans had found himself a more agreeable arrangement. So only Ian and Rebecca were in residence.

That was another cause for whispers in pit lane. Totally unfounded. Ian held her hand lightly as they strolled, but there was no chemistry between them, just companionship. Maybe they were too similar: male/female versions of the same model. Ian was an inch taller, twenty pounds heavier. Although his hair was brighter red than hers, it too waved and glistened with highlights in the sun. Both had long lashes over light eyes. Ian's were more gray than green.

She wondered if he'd noticed her at the Grand Prix for the same reason Narcissus jumped into the river: too fond of his own reflection.

They crossed through the beam of a street lamp about thirty yards from the house. In a falsetto whisper, Ian improvised a racing limerick. He was on the third line, struggling to find a rhyme for *transaxle* when he cut off abruptly. He jerked Rebecca to a halt and nodded toward their bungalow.

It was dark. As dark as the empty neighbors to each side.

There should have been a light.

The porch light had burned out earlier in the week, so she'd switched on the lamp next to the front window before they left. Ian had parted the drapes to help them find the keyhole. Now the drapes were closed and the lamp was turned off.

As she stared, the living room curtains fluttered. The filtered glow of the nightlight in the hall was visible briefly. Someone was inside. *Evans?* That was unlikely. He would have told them at dinner if he planned to move in. Besides, he left the restaurant the same time they did. He couldn't have arrived ahead of them. Same for Peyton. He might be low enough to come snooping, but he'd do it when he wouldn't get caught.

The shooter? Having missed his target at the track, was he opting for hand-to-hand combat? If the shooter had come calling, did that make Ian the intended target? Or her?

Ian pulled her forward, propelled her toward a sturdy elm. Flapped a hand indicating she should stay put. He scampered to the bushes beneath the picture window, cocked his head to listen. In the distance a car revved its engine. Nothing else.

She watched him crab-walk toward the gate in the fence, each step announced by the rustle of fallen leaves. Halfway there, he froze, squatted in the dark, dwarfed by the shadows from the house.

Could he hear someone inside, waiting in the dark, straining to hear him approach?

In the silence, her pulse pounded in her ears, rapid and shallow. She ached to be closer, to help if Ian needed it, but she remained welded to the trunk, the bark cutting ridges in her palms.

Suddenly, Ian jerked forward, inched along like a creeping shrub. A foot from the gate, he raised his arm toward the latch, teased the bar up with his fingertips. Once unlatched, he could access the patio. The sliding door into the kitchen would be unfastened. Neither of them ever locked that door—as the intruder had probably discovered.

The bar had just cleared the hasp when the gate burst open.

Ian toppled backwards.

A pygmy clothed in black flitted around him and bolted across the lawn, running full tilt, hugging the tree line. The shadow darted within an arm's reach, then skidded left into the street. Too startled to give chase, Rebecca spun, stared feebly at the intruder's back.

As the form passed under a street lamp, she glimpsed a dark ski mask obscuring the face, heard impossibly small feet slapping the road.

Five

"Son of a bit—"

Mick Hagan cut short the profanity as he hit the ground on all fours. *What the hell had tripped him?* He pushed up, leapt to standing and sprinted across the lawn. The street was empty in both directions. Nothing but a weak moon and the grating of crickets. Nothing to indicate which way the midget had turned before disappearing into the night. *Damn.*

Around seven, he'd arrived at the house where Moore supposedly was staying. No one answered the door. Since she wasn't expecting him, he didn't blame her for being absent. He would have faulted her for being dead in a back bedroom, so he entered through the kitchen and checked the place for bodies, warm or cold. Finding none, he liberated two beers from a puke green refrigerator. Drank one, trying to deciding if it would be prudent to leave his suitcase in the car until he talked with Moore.

It was full dark, just an inch left in the second beer

when he heard someone scurrying around on the patio off the kitchen. He called out. No answer. He opened the slider, looked out in time to see a shadow ease through the gate and blend with the dark. Too big for a cat. Too stealthy for a stray mutt hunting leftovers. Someone with opposable thumbs who'd left the gate ajar, maybe intentionally.

Curiosity piqued, he'd shut off the interior lights, pulled the drapes, feigned going to bed. Then he'd stashed his gun in the windbreaker pocket and snuck onto the patio. With nothing else to do, he'd waited under a shedding tree with strained thoughts of Moore for company.

An hour later, the intruder returned. Just as the bantam weight tiptoed within arm's reach, some yahoo arrived and spoiled the nab.

Mick wiped a bloody palm on his jeans, glared at the cut. The short stuff had scratched him, kicked him in the knee before bolting, but that wasn't what rankled. Fingering the gun in his pocket he started toward the figure sprawled on the lawn. He hoped the guy who tripped him was a convicted felon on the run. He felt the urge to shoot somebody.

Until he saw Moore.

Bare arms and long legs, her skin was iridescent white against the bark of a tree. He couldn't see her gray-green eyes, but he bet they were blazing. She didn't like surprises. Especially his.

She pushed off from the trunk and started toward him, mouth open, ready to let him have it. Then shook her head, changed her mind and direction. Brushing past him, she retrieved a sweater from the lawn and spoke to the lawn ornament who was picking twigs from his pressed khaki slacks.

"Ian, the man who accosted you is Mick Hagan. A suspended Washington, DC, police officer who has no possible reason for being here." That said she stormed to the front door and let herself in. Didn't even scratch the lock inserting the key in the dark.

Mick released his grip on the gun. Shooting her in the back would be hard to explain to strangers.

The boy scout offered a weak apology for tripping him. Gave his name as Ian Browning. Moore had mentioned the race driver before. They'd met at a Grand Prix when she was trying to elude a shady nightclub owner. As he shook Browning's hand, he noted that the driver's wavy hair was thinning on top. Mick wondered how Moore was going to explain Browning's presence in the house.

Of closer concern, he wondered how he was going to explain his presence in Indianapolis, assuming he got inside before she bolted the door. He leapt up the steps, caught his knuckles in the crack, pushed the door open smearing blood on the door frame. He leaned against it, sucked at his scratched hand. "Blame it on Delacroix."

Moore spun from switching on a lamp. "Jo suggested you rush to Indiana to protect me from night crawlers? I don't believe it."

"He asked Zimmer if he knew a policeman in Indianapolis who could keep an eye on you. I overheard. Since he didn't, and I have lots of free time, here I am. At your service." He punctuated it with a mock bow.

She returned a scowl. "Great. Teach me to confide in my lawyer. I'm not in any danger."

"Since when?"

Browning had squirmed into the house. He stood to the side trying to decide what was going on and what his role was. He slipped over to Moore and placed a hand on her arm. She shook it off.

"It's all right, Ian. Hagan is here to protect me. From what, I haven't a clue."

Browning blinked in his direction, unimpressed, but trying to be polite. "Shall I—"

Moore didn't let him finish. "Would you mind spending the night in the motor home? You need a good night's sleep for tomorrow. I'll be perfectly safe."

Without comment, Browning left to collect his gear. He exited by the front door.

That was fine. More than fine. It was the first good news all night. One fewer complication to deal with. That left only Moore. She looked uncomfortable. Possibly guilty, or maybe just annoyed. He wasn't sure which was preferable.

At the moment, he regretted rushing to her rescue. It had seemed a quixotic thing to do at the time. As impulsive as a college kid, he'd thrown a handful of clothes in a bag, grabbed three Tom Rush CDs, caught a flight out of National, rented a piece of crap car and driven into the sunset over some of the flattest land he'd ever seen to come to her aid. Had he really expected her to be grateful?

When she turned her back on him and headed for

the kitchen, he followed. She rooted in the refrigerator and produced two cold Millers hidden in the vegetable drawer next to an oozing tomato, one place he hadn't thought to look. Taking the beers, she exited the kitchen through the sliding door. Outside, the air was as cool as her demeanor, which if you combined the Old French and Middle English definitions, had to do with leading by governing yourself, as in keeping one's temper under control. His own temper, however, was heating up.

It had been an irritating day precipitated by Moore's call to Delacroix about a sniper shooting up the pits. When he'd volunteered to keep her alive and out of trouble, the lawyer had nodded once, then slammed the door on his way out of the sheriff's station. Clearly not happy, but mollified that someone who understood Moore and carried a gun would be on the scene. The sheriff had guffawed that it would take more than one slick city cop to keep her from attracting undesirable attention. "Beginning to understand how you got yourself suspended from the force, Hagan. Spend more time away from the job than doing it."

When the gum-snapping travel agent had insisted that there were no seats available on any flight going into Indianapolis, he'd settled for flying to Dayton, Ohio—a city he had never considered visiting. The Pollyanna had chirped that it would only take an hour longer to get to the track in Indy. Rates were way cheaper. Probably an easier drive than poking along in freeway traffic from the Indianapolis Airport.

She'd exaggerated on all accounts. It had been a boring drive to an empty house and a cool reception.

Moore stood by the open gate, scanning the empty front lawn. Above white legs, her body blended with the shadows. He sensed her tension. "You left the gate open."

She turned. "So?"

"So? Moore, someone's taking potshots at you. Yet, you leave the gate and the sliding door to your house unlocked. Is that smart?"

"No."

"Are you trying to get killed?"

"There are easier ways."

She set down her beer and left the patio. Left him standing in the dark wondering if she would return or if she'd turned in for the night. What would he say if she did return—offer to go to a motel, or back to Maryland? How long would it take to drive? Twelve, fourteen hours? He should have brought more CDs.

Before he could decide on a course of action, Moore slipped through the gap in the slider, pulling a sweater on over her skimpy top. Pity, but at least she planned to talk to him long enough to get chilled. She sat at the warped redwood table lacking a center umbrella. He remained standing, waiting as she picked at the label on the beer, pulling off shreds of soggy foil. She wouldn't look up. "I'm sorry Jo's worried about me. I shouldn't have called him. I overreacted."

"Speak into the microphone, please. We'd like that admission for the record."

Rolling wads of foil on the table, she ignored him. "I'm glad you cared enough to come."

He waited for the *but*. With Moore there was always a "but."

"But, I don't want you here."

"Why not?" He sat.

She pushed the bottle away. "I'm floundering. The race community is the ultimate good old boys' club. Most of them don't think women should exist outside the kitchen or the—"

"I know what women are good for."

"You think you do." She flicked a foil ball at him. "I enjoy the challenge of working on the car, Mick, just not the ancillary baggage. How will it look to the crew if I suddenly show up with my own police bodyguard?"

"Like you're smarter than the rest of them." He reached for her beer. "They don't have to know I'm a cop. Aren't you allowed to have a male interest who doesn't carry wrenches?"

He thought he'd slipped that in pretty smoothly. Walking into the unlocked house had alarmed him on several levels. His search of the premises turned up too many male items to ignore: razor, splash-on cologne, silky men's bikinis. The good news was that they weren't intermingled with Moore's lingerie or discarded under her bed. It looked like she and her driver had separate bedrooms and baths. But he'd like it spelled out.

Moore continued to mutilate the label into confetti. "We were gone only a couple of hours. Out to eat. Even if I'd thought about the gate, I'd have left it unlocked."

"That's asinine." She didn't snap back at him. She looked sheepish. He set down the beer. "You were expecting the intruder?"

"Sort of." Again she left him dangling. He heard a kitchen drawer slide open, shut. When she returned, she dropped a handful of glossy photographs on the table in front of him, standard 4" × 6" snaps developed at the local CVS. "You're the detective. Give me your impressions."

They were long-distance shots of what he assumed was Moore's pit area at the track. The top one showed a slender driver being helped into or out of the cockpit of the car. He focused on the curve of the driver's rear where the race suit was pulled taut, willing to bet the person under the helmet was Moore. Next photo confirmed it; she was fluffing her hair after setting the helmet on the hood of the car. Grinning like a cat with feathers on its chin.

"You know how to drive that thing?"

The racer was sleek pod, red over white, with a pointed gold nose. It had a roll bar behind the driver's head and four fat wheels attached by thin struts, i.e., it was one teensy step up from a go-cart.

He shook his head. Cars were tools designed to carry you from point A to point B. Occasionally necessary for chasing bad guys, they required enough bodywork to sustain a crash, windshield to fend off rain, doors that locked to keep a perp inside. Why would a sane person scream around a track in a flimsy open car at unimaginable speeds just for the thrill of it?

Moore grinned. "For my twenty-first birthday, Uncle Walt gave me lessons at Bertil Roos Race Driving School in the Poconos. It was a rush. Probably the most beneficial few days of my life."

She got positively dewy-eyed reliving her hours of training on the track. She described easing a skid car with a broken axle through a slalom course of cones;

braking without spilling wine from the gimbal-mounted goblet; sliding out of a curve, fingernail-close to the wall. Talked about the importance of hitting the apex of a turn, not lifting in corners, relying on peripheral vision to focus as far down the track as possible.

Wasn't his idea of fun. It might not have been Moore's either, if her uncle hadn't instigated it. Mick had heard enough Uncle Walt stories to realize that Moore would have jumped off tall buildings without a chute to win his approval.

The remaining pictures were close-ups of the exposed engine or parts of a car, like a detached steering wheel sitting on the hood, or a tire leaning against a low concrete wall. He flipped through them, raised an eyebrow at Moore. "Your intruder left these? Not the usual stalker shots."

She said nothing. Waited like this was a pop quiz and he was heading for an "*F*."

He went through them again, turning each one over to stack it in order. On the backsides were questions printed in fat crayon. On the one of the steering wheel were the words, *Comes off—why?* On the shot of Moore cradling a helmet was written, *You race?* The handwriting was loopy and childish, big open circle instead of a dot under the question marks.

"Purple crayon?"

She turned the pictures face up, one at a time. "He's been leaving two sets of photos every day for over a week, one set with a caption. I arrive home from the track and the pictures are on the table, wedged under the pot with the dead geranium. Peanut shells scattered on the table. I reply to the questions and leave the second photograph for him to retrieve."

"Any idea who your fan is?"

"A child who should be in school, not hanging around the racetrack. I was hoping to find out tonight. I'd written my name on the last one. He might have replied."

At first it had bothered her that a stranger was taking pictures from the distance. The presumption was annoying. There were enough people intruding in her life. She refused to make room for a curious child she'd never met. Then, as she started feeling isolated from the team, she began to look forward to the next installment. That's why she wouldn't lock the gate. Days like today, the intruder seemed to be her only friend in Indianapolis. The one person who didn't think he knew more about cars than she did. A young person eager to learn. She was touched by the implied adulation.

She pulled her legs up onto the seat, stretched the sweater over her knees. Only her fingertips peeked out from under the cuffs.

"When I was about eight, a spring snow storm closed school early. No one was home when I arrived. Dad was at work; Mom was out with the twins; Mrs. Bellotti was stuck somewhere shopping. The snow was glorious. Fat flakes mounting up quickly, reducing vision, melting on my face, muffling the city noises. I rebelled at staying inside the empty, dull house, so I pranced through the drifts to the Boston Public Library feeling like Sir Hillary conquering the Pole. Stamping off my boots, I dropped my coat near the door and marched into the main reference room.

"I'd only been there a few times before, never by myself. It was so quiet. There was one other person besides the librarian. A man, who looked elderly, was bent over a table, half his face lit by the lamp. His hooked nose nearly touched the paper. He was scribbling as fast as stiff fingers would allow. Brazenly, I went over and sat opposite him. He kept writing. I pulled out a fat volume from the row of reference books and pretended to read. He continued to write. I looked down, turned a page, then more. Realized I couldn't understand any of the letters.

" 'Read Greek do you?' He threw out the question. I nodded, but he wasn't looking. He repeated it louder as if he thought I was dim. Instead of admitting my ignorance I asked him what he was writing. He said it was none of my business. I asked if he was taking a test? That riled him enough to set down the pen.

" 'Young lady, the written word is man's single most significant achievement. It separates us from animals. It joins people together by expressing that which we feel in common. If you should ever grow wise enough to have something worth saying, you too shall know the magic of words.' With that, he slammed shut his notebook and stood up, towering over the table."

Mick swigged his beer, wishing her face weren't in shadow. "He walked out on you?"

"No. He gave me a scratch pad and sat me on the floor in front of the *Encyclopaedia Britannica.* Said, pick a topic, any topic, look it up, read about it and start writing. I asked what I should write. 'Whatever moves you,' he said. 'Don't stop writing until your hand cramps or your pencil breaks.' "

Mick laughed, he couldn't help it. The old guy knew how to get rid of a pesky kid. "Tom Sawyer lives. Or was it Huck Finn who handed over the paint brush? I'm surprised you ever wrote another word."

Moore dropped her legs back to earth. "Because of that stranger, I became a reporter."

"Okay, okay. Strangers can influence an impressionable kid for the better. Sometimes." He straightened the stack of photographs. "But how do you know this kid isn't the gunman? He's obviously fixated on you. Spends his days watching you from a distance. Maybe he upgraded his toys, switched from a camera lens to a high-powered rifle."

"To shoot me? The pictures aren't threatening. Just inquisitive."

"True. But you admitted to Delacroix that you don't know where the bullet was aimed. Maybe your fan has decided to eliminate your playmates. Take out your driver, your boss, or both."

Moore was shaking her head before he finished the sentence. "He's a photographer—a watcher not a doer. I'm more concerned that he might have *seen* the shooter. He doesn't seem to miss a trick."

She grabbed the photographs from his hand and turned over the one of the hub missing its wheel. "He witnessed an earlier mishap. See what's written on the back. 'Why did the nuts fall off?' Perceptive question. I'm positive the bolts had been tampered with. None of the studs were bent; all the nuts came off at the same time."

Mick set down his beer, focused on her with one eye. "You're saying the bolts holding on the wheel on this high-speed race car were intentionally stripped? Your driver could have been killed."

Her guilty expression was affirmation. He pushed back from the table. "That's great, Moore. Really great. And you say you're not in danger. Any other life-threatening episodes you want to share with me? I mean, as long as I'm already here."

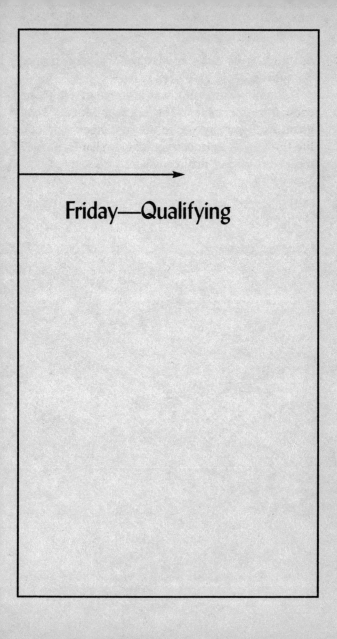

Friday—Qualifying

Six

The night had gone downhill fast from there. Rebecca couldn't remember what started the argument. Something in Hagan's tone as he quizzed her about the idiocy of racing, the lack of security at the track, the crew's antagonism toward her, the number of men on the team, the man living in the house with her. He'd called Ian a self-centered fop. Asked what kind of tools she was sharing with her driver.

Some of it, all of it, had chafed.

In another place, at another time his prying might have been obliquely flattering. She might have dismissed it as Hagan having had a long day, a boring trip, too many beers. But her day had been pretty damn lousy as well and his presence rankled. She didn't want coddling or sexual antagonism. Or the painful memories he brought through the door, clinging to him like the smell of skunk on a wet dog.

The inquisition ended when she'd rummaged in the linen closet, dropped a blanket and sheets on the sofa and flung a pillow at his head. "The spare bedroom is at the end of the hall. You can use it, or the sofa."

From his actions this morning, he felt as contrite as she did. The linens were folded and stacked. He'd fetched the *Indianapolis Star* from between the doors and separated out the twelve-page race section. Placed it on the counter as a peace offering. He'd even made a pot of decent coffee, which she considered an essential talent in any man sharing her living space.

The clouds were building. It would be overcast by afternoon. Right now there was enough sun to make it pleasant on the patio. Hagan was out there pretending to read the *AutoWeek* she'd carried in last night, waiting to assess her mood. She wished him good luck; she wasn't sure of it herself.

Hagan had appeal. He was—in the consensus of the regulars at Head Tide's only diner—a hunk with an edge. Black Irish: dark hair, brilliant blue eyes, tight jaws and tighter glutes. He was also trouble. As the diner's owner quipped, "Man's got an edge sharp enough that a girl could cut herself and bleed to death without noticing." When he'd moved to town, Flo sent her a box of gauze bandages.

Unknown to the gossipers, Hagan was also a closet intellectual, who masked his intelligence for use only behind the scenes, on an as-needed basis. She'd caught him a few weeks ago in her living room flipping through the *OED,* lips moving as he pronounced *jaup* or *jawp*. Chortling over the definition: "to dash and rebound like water with splashing of the vicinity; to move with splashing; to make a light splashing sound." The noun meant the splash of water that landed against a surface, a spot of mud on clothing. Hagan was one person she wouldn't challenge to a crossword competition. *Who was she kidding?* She wouldn't challenge him to any kind of competition, if winning was important. They'd butted heads before.

She squinted at the clock on the stove. Barely enough time to toast a bagel before heading to the track. She had work to do. What was she going to do with Hagan? The most practical move would be to take him with her, let him check out the players, scout out where the shot came from. But she'd be embarrassed if the other crew members suspected he was there to baby-sit her.

On the other hand, Ian already knew he was in town. He would think it queer if she hid Hagan away. If Ian didn't tell them differently, the guys would peg Hagan as a boyfriend. Or a groupie trying to hog reflected glory by hanging around the pits. *Right*. Hagan who drove a ten-year old SUV, which he could barely keep on the road.

The bagel popped. She tossed it onto a plate. "The cars are qualifying this morning, so I'll be busy. It's interesting to watch. I can fill you in on the walk over."

"How about filling me in on the crashed Arrows and a windshield that's 'priceless beyond rubies'?"

She raised her eyebrows. Hagan gestured to the glossy magazine open on the table. He had been reading after all. She slathered cream cheese on both halves while she gave him more background than he wanted on Arrows Racing. The British team had operated from the late 1970s to the early 1990s. It had been formed by defectors from the old Shadow Racing, who splintered off, taking the car design with them. The first five cars Arrows produced were forfeited when they were sued by the original designer. Peyton's was an early car, the third one constructed according to Arrow's own, very complicated design. "If I remember correctly, their claim to fame is being the longest existing F1 team that never won a Grand Prix."

Hagan reached for a half of the bagel. "The brake line was definitely cut?" Rebecca nodded. He chewed. "By someone on the crew?"

"Not necessarily. Anyone inside the track during off-hours could have done it. Fifteen seconds with a Swiss Army knife. It had been sliced partway through from the bottom, close to the fitting. It wouldn't be noticed unless you were looking for it. I wasn't."

"Why?"

"At that time, I didn't know someone had it in for the team."

Hagan held up a hand. "No. Why do it? What's gained because of the crash? What did it change?"

She broke off a bite, licked at the cream cheese before answering. "If Ian had been hurt or killed, the team would have pulled out, probably. Though Peyton might have found another driver."

"Anyone knocking at the door?"

"Not that I know of. As it happened, only the car was put out of commission."

"But, conveniently, Peyton had a spare. A very expensive one, according to that article. One that someone tried to fill with water instead of gas, filed the bolts on a front wheel, and shot at with a high powered rifle—according to you."

She nodded. "The only good news is that the bullet shattered an aftermarket windshield, not the original. We only install the 'priceless' one for photographs."

"Sure your boy Browning doesn't have a sworn enemy stalking the stands?"

"Am I positive? No. But the evidence contradicts it. The bolts on the Lotus were stripped so smooth that the wheel came off at the first bend, i.e., early in the morning when he was driving on a near-empty track, before the car was up to speed. Similarly, judging from the depth of the cut, the brakes on the Arrows were intended to fail the first time he applied them, at turn four. Ian's frugal with braking, so they didn't go until turn six. If they'd let go earlier, the car would have spun through the grass, not into a wall. The water would have annoyed the engine but not hurt Ian. And, as you know, the bullet missed. Q.E.D.—he's still alive."

Hagan pushed his plate away, folded his paper napkin and laid it on the dirty plate. "Okay, we'll scratch the driver as the target, eliminate murder as the motive. How about financial ruin? By switching cars, Peyton's still in the game, but poorer."

"Way poorer."

"So, the pressure's on to produce a good finish."

"He needs a victory."

"Right, per the article he has betting losses to cover and the wrecked car to repair, even if only to sell it. The nickels add up."

She nodded. "Plus he has a personal stake: besting Derek Whitten. Another idle son of the very rich, but with a difference." She wetted her fingertip, used it to pick up sesame seeds that had fallen on her plate. "Peyton is obsessed with buying his way into F1. I assumed he was rolling in the necessary dough. Ian says no. Thinks he's living off a limited trust.

"Whitten, on the other hand, has already inherited the family manse and the funds to maintain it, and still has plenty to fritter away. His wealth really irritates Peyton. It's like he believes they were switched at birth. He should have been the one raised in the castle."

"They're related?"

She laughed. "Only in temperament. Both are self-impressed manipulators. Each is so busy pushing other people's buttons, he doesn't realize he's being backed into a corner until he bumps into the wall."

While she took the plate to the sink, Hagan wandered outside. When she followed, he was inspecting the gate latch for a way to lock it. She pulled at his elbow. "Please leave it open. I'd like to find out the intruder's name, even if I never meet him."

Hagan's gaze was so intense she wanted to take a step back. She swayed forward instead, brushed the back of his hand. He let out a short whistle. "Okay. The gate stays open, but we're locking the slider. And give me the front door key. I'll have a copy made. In exchange for my being so accommodating, you'll call your buddy Peter Hayes at the *Post* and have him run a background search on your boss, Peyton Madison III. I want to know his every flaw."

Seven

Mick turned his back to the crew, lowered his voice. "Swiping tools, Moore? I'm not swiping them. I'm not even pilfering. I'm borrowing. Once I lift the prints, you can return them."

He crammed his hands into his jeans pockets to keep from shaking her. His jacket clanged as a small wrench belonging to the crew chief bumped against a socket from the tool chest of the tire changer, or maybe a Phillips from the smiling Black's stash of screwdrivers. Moore wasn't stupid, but she was a fool for blindly trusting her teammates. Any one of them could be an escaped homicidal maniac with recidivistic tendencies. With pseudo annoyance, she slammed binoculars at his chest before banishing him from the pits.

He grinned. She was probably just jealous of his dexterous prestidigitation and his access to a fingerprint lab.

"Where was the shooter when he fired?"

A car screamed past as Moore mouthed something

about turn twelve. She tried visual aids, both hands holding a program map steady against the wind. He noted the spot then snatched the map to take with him.

The road course snaked through the infield of the oval track, which looked like a rectangle with rounded corners. For some reason, they raced the road course going clockwise, but the oval counter-clockwise. The road course used two straight sections from the oval connected by a series of thirteen turns, so apparently road racers weren't superstitious.

From the infield to the stands was a regular "you can't get there from here." He had to cross under the track via a tunnel that deposited him at the backside of the stands. Then cut through a narrow aisle between stands, tromp up a short flight of steps set sideways before he could start climbing. Once halfway up, the stands were open, the view unobstructed. Not ideal for a sniper, but if he laid down in the foot well between the bleachers, he wouldn't have been visible from the infield.

Smuggling the rifle in and out of the track wouldn't have been much of a challenge. Especially if it were broken down. Every other person was lugging something—cases of sodas, cartons of souvenir T-shirts, racks of hot dog rolls, coolers with beer. All going about their business, no one looking like a sniper. Or expecting to bump into one. Given the options, he would have rolled a fully-assembled rifle in one of the four-foot-by-six-foot Ferrari flags. About 60 percent of the fans had a red banner with the prancing horse slung across their shoulders.

Mick selected a seat midway along and focused the

glasses on the track. Per Moore, the cars would qualify one at a time. He'd asked if that was normal.

"It is for F1. It's better. No other racers on the track warming up their tires, spinning out of control, slowing down or generally getting in the way. The qualifier takes a few practice laps, gets the green flag, does three laps at speed. Timekeepers average the times. At the end of the day, the fastest car gets the pole."

Fans could see the whole show on eighteen huge video screens placed in the infield; hear it over the loudspeaker. Announcers gave the times, told the scattered spectators if a driver was over or under the current pole sitter's time at an intermediate stage. Or predicted the outcome of the lap just by listening to the lift in the corner, whatever that meant.

He stretched out his legs. *Just like Dad and baseball.* Mick smiled.

Patrick Hagan couldn't have seen most of the games he'd watched. He was too busy jotting down strikes, balls, errors and RBIs. Each spring, he had walked to the corner drugstore and bought a kid's composition notebook with the black and white marbleized cover. In Magic Marker he scribbled the year on the front. He took it to every home game he attended. Had it on his lap as he listened to endless, butt-numbing away games. More boring to his son than watching paint dry.

"You're missing the point, Michael. Any major league player can throw a perfect strike. It's how consistently he can do it, and against which hitters that makes baseball fascinating."

Mick never did get the point. He hadn't watched a

game in years. But the day they buried Patrick Hagan with full police honors, he'd wrapped the cardboard-covered notebooks in tissue paper and packed them away in an old suitcase. They were in his mother's attic, next to the carton with his Erector Set.

The loudspeaker announced an open half-hour practice session. Mick shifted on his haunches and leaned forward, scanning for the Lotus pits. When Moore's face leapt into view, he felt a little like Jimmy Stewart in *Rear Window*. He'd always empathized with Hitchcock's laid-up photographer. It gave him a charge to watch others when they didn't know it, for reasons that they didn't suspect. Hence his fondness for undercover work.

He could easily imagine some kid haunting the stands, taking telephoto snapshots of Moore. She might not be as glamourous as Grace Kelly—no ensembles designed by Edith Head—but she was worth staring at. It sounded like something he would have done as an adolescent. Or would do as an adult. She was driving him crazy, and spying on her was a turn-on. What he should be doing was viewing her objectively—like a witness he was protecting.

He slouched back, adding a few inches of distance, widening his field of focus. From what he could see, Evans ran a tight team. The men interacted smoothly, each knowing what was expected without being told. The chief frowned a lot at Moore, but it seemed to be out of habit rather than at anything she did or didn't do. She looked professional swapping tools and trading places as she fiddled with the car. Waiting for

Browning to bring it in from a trip around the track, however, she stood on the fringes. Not physically removed, but emotionally shut out.

Chet Davis bent over to check front tire pressures. Wiry, around forty-five, he sported an oversized mustache equal parts brown and red. He didn't say much; his face conveyed less. Every now and then, the mustache would twitch enough to convince casual observers that there was life behind it.

Tom, of no last name, was a hip Black in his early thirties. His hair was a mass of springy kinks on top, one thin braid at the nape of his neck. He had a scar on his left cheek, souvenir of a bar fight with a broken bottle or jailhouse shiv. He was the most talkative of the group. Correction. He was the one who conversed most coherently. The kid, Johnnie Evans, never shut up. He was a nephew to the crew chief, which was obvious. The kid alternated between being obsequious and pouting to the point of surliness. Behavior only a near-relative can get away with. Typical horny teenager, he never missed a chance to rub against Moore.

As if sensing his gaze, she looked up, squinting so hard into the sun that the irises were invisible behind her long lashes. A vertical crease, however, was prominent between her brows. He thought it was less deep than it had been in the months since she'd found the dead body of a rival in her shop, which happened about the same time he'd tracked her down to settle an old score. He hoped so. His interference then had made the situation worse. His reluctance to accept her innocence nearly got her killed. Right now, he wanted to see her smile. Wanted her to sense his presence in the stands and smile for him.

He waited.

She didn't. She turned her back and disappeared under the tent.

Eight

Since he couldn't spy on Moore, Mick moved the glasses down the row of competitors. All the teams were going through the same motions. Each cluster of mechanics was dressed to match the car. Each of the cars varied in shape and paint scheme; maybe they were all different models. Every one of them an invitation to a quick death at an early age.

Halfway along the row, he stopped at the black and gold car that Moore said would be the Brabham. It belonged to and was driven by Derek Whitten. Through the glasses, Whitten looked as superficial as he had in the *AutoWeek* photo. A playboy engaged in noble pursuit of speed. About six feet tall, he wore wraparound reflective sunglasses and a custom-tailored race suit. His straw-colored hair was thick: too long and too evenly streaked. One temple was trying to recede; Rogaine was working on the other side. A tropical tan contrasted nicely with the almost-perfect white teeth. One incisor bent inward a bit, adding boyish appeal to the carefree image. Rolled-up sleeves revealed a clunky wristwatch that winked whenever the sun came out. It semaphored a message into the stands as Whitten waved to one of the crew and pointed in the direction of the infield. When the guy nodded, Whitten strolled off. Probably going to lunch; it was time.

Mick lost sight of him between the Mercedes/West tent and a wagon selling official track merchandise. He inched the glasses along trying to spot him again. Got sidetracked when the glasses stalled on a Latina's bare midriff, tattooed in bold script—probably *Screw me,* though it looked more like *Schume.* Maybe it was Portuguese for "Go team go."

Luckily, Whitten also stopped, though not to admire the tattoo. He was hugging the back side of a tent, talking to a big guy with short legs who looked like, and turned out to be, Evans.

That might not mean much, if anything. Moore had complained about being the odd woman out. "The teams are an incestuous bunch, Mick. They travel to the same races, hang out with the same crowds, vacation on the same islands. Swap mechanics and pit crews back and forth. They've known each other for decades."

So, Evans and Whitten could be good pals. They might be conferring about the best vendor for a cold draft, or bitching about the distance to the press boxes. It was possible. *Sure thing.* Except that they worked on rival teams. One of which was being plagued by potentially dangerous mishaps, which might benefit the other.

The men split, went in opposite directions.

Through the glasses Mick followed Evan's beefy shoulders back to the Lotus pit. No sign of Moore. Peyton, however, was lounging on the concrete wall. In his silk tweed jacket and dark glasses, he was posing as the man at the helm. Smooth olive complexion, marred by stingy lips and a weak chin. Moore had pegged him: A pampered rich man's son with nothing going for him, but in possession of everything he could want. Or was he? His type was rarely satisfied. They'd been introduced that morning— thirty seconds of exposure was more than enough to figure him out.

It was time to take a break from spying. If a sniper was lurking in the stands, he was well hidden.

Mick stood, rotated his neck. The metal benches clanged with each step as he clomped down the stands. He'd take one more leisurely trip around the perimeter of the infield then call it day at the races. Maybe Moore could break away for a quick bite.

Six rows down, he noticed another spectator glued to binoculars—a tall figure standing in the shadow of the VIP suites: red baseball cap, silver sports jacket, jeans, black sneakers. Could easily have been a fan come to study the historic cars as they qualified. Only the fan wasn't watching the track, or the pits. The fan's glasses were aimed laterally along the stands, pointing in his direction.

Pausing, Mick raised his own binoculars and stared back. The image that filled the lens was nondescript. Shapeless clothing. Reflective sunglasses and the binoculars obscured the face. Baseball cap was pulled down, hiding the hair; jacket collar was turned up to meet it. A narrow strip of Caucasian skin showed along the jaw line. From the angle of the glasses he decided that the voyeur wasn't interested in him. He was focused in the distance, lower down. Turning slowly, Mick panned the stands behind him.

Fifty feet away, maybe ten yards below, a pint-sized form was wedged, belly down, in the foot well between bleachers. Faded jeans, bleached-black hooded sweatshirt. Same attire as last night's intruder. Arms extended, he gripped a digital camera equipped with a telephoto lens.

Mick let go of the glasses, sidled quickly between the bleachers aiming for the closest aisle.

When he was still twenty yards away, the photographer felt him coming. Without looking back, he popped up and ran, sprinted to the aisle, clambered down the flight of steps, hit the pavement at the bottom and fled under the stands.

Mick took the shortcut: hopped up on a bench, clanged to the end of the row. One hand on the railing, he vaulted over the side, dropped twelve feet onto the path. The pygmy was just rounding the corner into the light.

Binoculars banging, Mick tore after the fleeing figure. He caught a break when the kid clipped the edge of a cart selling Dove bars, stumbled for a heartbeat before regaining his balance.

Mick lunged, snagged the pointy hood of the sweatshirt with his fingertips. Lost it again as his prey sprinted forward. The limp fabric slipped out of his hand, flopped onto skinny shoulders revealing tight corn rows fastened with black and white polka-dot barrettes.

Barrettes. What the—

"A little young to be your girlfriend, I think."

Mick whipped around. The fan with the field glasses stood a scant yard behind him, catching her breath. Beneath the unisex clothing, she was a feminine, middle-aged woman: poised, curious, seemingly open. Head cocked, she waited for an explanation.

He wasn't sure she deserved one, even if he had enough breath to spit one out. He sucked in air and mumbled, "Disobedient daughter."

She laughed.

He turned away and set out at a jog. The woman didn't follow.

There was no sign of the girl; he didn't expect there would be. She ran like a prairie wind and could fit through small cracks. *A girl. A wraithlike, petite African American girl.* He shook his head, consoled himself with the fact that the kid hadn't been carrying a gun, just a camera. So, maybe it really was a case of long-distance hero worship and she had nothing to do with the shooting. Maybe she wanted to be a mechanic when she grew up and was taking pointers by studying Moore through a camera lens. Whatever. The kid had been put on notice that someone was watching out for Moore.

Maybe more than one somebody. He stopped.

Stupid. Some detective he was. He should have quizzed the fan with the field glasses. For all he knew, the woman was an undercover security guard who'd been tailing the kid all week and could tell him if she was a theat or merely a pest. The woman hadn't look like a rent-a-cop though. She'd grinned like an amused tutor when he took off to pursue a cold trail.

Mick rolled up his shirtsleeves, scanned the crowd as he continued walking. At a white and red food wagon, he bought a fat hot sausage sandwich with fried onions and sauerkraut and a five-dollar beer to wash it down with. He passed on the thirty-two-ounce souvenir plastic cup for two dollars more. He ate sitting on a patch of grass not far from turn ten. Clusters of people were strolling by in both directions, jabbering in a variety of foreign languages, including various American dialects. The kid could have attached herself to any of them, evaporated into the crowd like an ant in a colony.

He upped his beer, taking a deep swallow. When he set it down, he spied a familiar figure lolling behind the emergency medical center—Derek Whitten. Again. The guy certainly spent a lot of time away from his pits. He didn't look like he needed medical attention, more like an ad for Rolex. Blond in a black driving suit leaning against a light building.

Whitten checked his watch twice in the same minute, then looked up as a middle-aged man in a gray suit jacket scurried over. The visitor had the air of an insurance adjuster who'd eaten too many meals on the expense account, none of which he'd enjoyed because he had to justify them to his accountant. He'd gone bald from rubbing his hand over his brow just thinking about it.

Whitten peeled away from the wall and extended

his hand, then listened in arm-folded silence. The man gesticulated smoothly, as if laying out numbers on a spread sheet. Maybe the guy was an insurance salesman trying to justify Whitten's premiums. He seemed mildly interested.

When it was his turn, Whitten picked at an offending bit of dirt under one nail, began spinning a tale. The pasty-faced stranger got whiter, rocked back on his heels, looked around as if the Indians were closing in. Whitten patted the guy on the arm in a reassuring manner.

Mick waited for them to split up before standing and pitching the beer cup in the trash.

Not really tailing the bald man, he meandered along in the same direction. Which meant he left the track without telling Moore. She was probably too busy tinkering with the race car to care, though she'd be miffed that he hadn't stayed to see her boy do his stuff. She'd get over it.

Despite Delacroix's concern, Mick didn't think Moore was in imminent danger. By leaving now, he could cruise down Georgetown Road and locate a shipping store. He'd transfer the prints from the borrowed tools and overnight them to Zimmer to search for a match. Then go back to the house. After a balmy day in the full sun, he felt a nap coming on. Maybe he'd stretch out in a lounge chair on the patio. That way, he'd be on hand if the petite paparazzo reappeared.

Hanging back about twenty feet, Mick kept pace with the man in the gray suit—past the garage area, the pagoda, the media center, the tower suites. They were just entering the tunnel at gate seven when the woman from the stands slipped into the crowd along-side the man he was following. Mick almost stumbled when they stopped walking. She bent her head close to hear over the din echoing in the tunnel, nodded encouragingly. Then took his elbow, spurred him on past a couple with too many kids, too young to be inflicted on the public.

Mick hugged the inside path, letting them get well ahead. It had been a foolish oversight to leave his stash of toothpicks in the glove box of the Jeep. He needed something to chew on.

In the last hour he'd seen Moore's crew chief in deep discussion with the rival team owner. Then the rival team owner had exchanged input with a nerd in a gray suit, who was something other than a race afficionado. The suit, in turn, reported to the woman with the binoculars who'd been spying on him and/or the little Black girl who, presumably, had been taking pictures of Moore. It was indeed an incestuous group.

What were they involved in? And was it all connected?

Up ahead, the couple he was following sidestepped to huddle near the perimeter fence. Mick lingered in the shadow of the stands. Bought an ice cream from a girl decked out in parka and hat even though it must have been close to seventy. He'd taken the first bite when they moved out and crossed the street. At the corner of the parking lot, they split.

The man disappeared down a road running between blue industrial buildings. The woman entered a parking lot and unlocked the driver's door of a white-paneled van. Ford, at least five years old, totally nondescript.

She got in and shut the door but didn't start the engine. She was looking down at something in her lap. Could have been consulting a map, reading a book, writing in her diary.

Mick ambled on past street vendors selling everything from ear plugs to signed automotive art originals. He slowed at an Indy Girl trailer and checked out the skimpy tops. He was contemplating a midriff-baring yellow sweatshirt for Moore when the white van pulled out of the lot. It turned onto Georgetown Road, rolled by him, then went right at the light on Twenty-fifth Street. Halfway down, it pulled over and sat idling on the shoulder of the road not far from gate ten.

The driver's head was down again when Mick walked by on the opposite side of Twenty-fifth. He turned north on Hulman, resisted the urge to look back to see if she had raised her eyes and was watching him.

For whom was she waiting?

Could it be the kid? Both females had been checking out the infield through lenses. It was possible they were in cahoots. If so, then maybe she hadn't been chasing the girl, rather protecting the tot from him, following him to make sure he didn't catch the girl with the camera.

Nine

With the prints shipped to Zimmer, Mick walked back to the empty house. He'd seen six or seven white vans on his travels. Most had men slumped over the steering wheels, swearing at red lights, looking forward to punching out for the day. None of them driven by his friend from the stands.

Once inside, he headed toward the patio to check for a photograph under the plant pot. The answering machine beeped as he passed, as if his footsteps had triggered it. A voice started to leave a message. *Peter Hayes.* Mick snatched up the receiver, waited for the machine to figure out that it could stop recording, shouted Hayes's name.

Hayes jumped in first. "Hagan? What are you doing there? You're the last person I'd have figured for a race fan. I can't imagine Becca invited you. Or maybe I can. She's known for her deplorable judgment regarding men."

"Makes you want to weep, does it?"

"I wouldn't go that far. But speaking to a real voice, even yours, is enough to make me swoon.

For his part, Mick was mollified that Moore had contacted the reporter as promised.

Hayes hummed. "Where to start? Tell Bec I unearthed a mother lode on a Peyton Madison II. Kept tripping over him. Assumed he must be the father. Some kind of petrochemical bigwig and amateur philanthropist. Son is less lofty, which means less press. Most of his mentions are fairly recent and have to do with his trying to worm his way into the professional race scene.

"I e-mailed a handful of articles, plus a dozen bibliographic citations to Becca's computer. *Life* magazine ran a human interest story on Madison in March 1974. I didn't bother scanning it. They do have public libraries in Indiana, don't they?"

"Can't swear to it. You know cops can't read."

Hayes snorted. "Too bad. Becca was asking about the son, but you might be interested in Daddy. Intriguing cuss, mainly because he came out of nowhere."

Reading from his notes, Hayes said PMII first surfaced in the media in the mid-1960s. At that time, he was thirty-eight, head of PLM Chemicals, which was relocating from New Jersey to South Carolina. Company had one success after another: ground-breaking patents led to government contracts and the like. Madison took it public in the early 1980s. Now, at seventy-eight or -nine he still goes to the office five days a week. Not so for the profligate son, who was listed as the only child of a second marriage and titular head of the Madison empire.

"Nothing on the old man's early years. No birth, schooling, parents. Nothing on his first marriage. No birth or death records for the wife; no society column mentions. Nada. Have Bec call me if it's vital. Figured it wasn't, since she only asked about junior. See you."

"Don't hang up. If you haven't already, see what you can ferret out on the son's financial standing, any bad habits or unacceptable playmates."

"Other than Rebecca, you mean? Will do. Just call me your pet ferret."

Hayes laughed and clicked off. Mick had no chance for a smart comeback, which was too bad since he liked sparring with the reporter. Hyperactive in V-necked sweaters and flimsy glasses, Hayes was a thorough researcher and a quick wit, an old friend of Moore's from her days on the newspaper.

Images of Moore flitting around DC, notepad in hand, deadline looming amused him as he headed for the patio again. He wished he'd known her then, when she was cockier and liked herself better. Before she'd learned that being right could make someone else dead wrong.

He had one foot in the kitchen when the doorbell rang.

Ten

Rebecca elbowed Evans in the rib, grinned as she smacked Tom a high five. *What a difference a day makes.* The team had eked out another few horsepower. Ian's last practice run had broken the field record for historic racers. Clouds were building off to the west and moving in fast. Once they arrived, the track would cool and speeds improve. Ian had the next-to-last qualifying slot and a solid shot at taking the pole. The team could smell victory the way a shark smells blood.

She made the final adjustments to the carburetors per Ian's input, straightened, stepped away from the car. Now it was up to him.

As Ian pulled the Lotus onto the track, she allowed herself to think of something other than the components of an internal combustion engine for the first time in hours. She wondered if Hagan was still hanging around. She hadn't seen him since she'd caught him pilfering tools. He'd thought she was too engrossed in her phone call to notice. Her annoyance had been mostly an act. She was curious if any of her compatriots had criminal pasts, which might explain what was going on, and glad that Hagan had the resources to lift fingerprints and have them run through law-enforcement data banks. Assuming Hagan still had access to those resources.

Two months ago, when she got into trouble over the death of an exotic dancer, Hagan had disobeyed orders. And had been a tad trigger-happy. For those infractions, he'd been put on two months' administrative leave. Instead of vacationing in Cancun or painting his mother's shutters, he was taking a busman's holiday—assisting Zimmer, the Blue Marsh County sheriff. That placed him a stone's throw away from her home and business. Much too close for comfort.

Or not close enough?

Strands of feelings for Hagan intertwined with her more rational thoughts. They either knotted up or slipped through her fingers. Never stayed smooth and straight enough to weave into whole fabric. There was intense sexual attraction between them. If she could shut down her brain, erase her memory bank, she had no doubt what their relationship would become—in a throbbing heartbeat. But the synapses kept firing: The old memories remained vivid, the potential with Jo beckoned.

Emotions had never carried her away. Even as a teenager, with Bobby Lamont feverishly pawing at her in the backseat of his brother's Pontiac, her eyes were wide open, alive to the folly of the act and questioning the attraction. It wouldn't be like that with Hagan. There would be no time to heed her father's warnings of trading a few minutes of pleasure for years of regret. No time to think, no breath to protest with. That scared her. It was another reason she'd jumped at the chance to get out of town fast.

Then he'd followed not far behind. And tonight—

"Moore." The team owner tugged at her elbow with warm, moist fingers. "Rebecca. Didn't you hear? Look."

He pointed at the mammoth scorekeeping tower. She squinted up, grin widening as the Lotus's amber number three appeared at the top, next to the white number-one position. The remaining car numbers shifted downward. Peyton drawled with as much urgency as the Southerner can that Ian had done it. He'd taken the pole.

Peyton didn't praise her—she would have been suspicious if he had—but at least his smile looked genuine. That was something positive. On the negative side, he continued to stroke the skin on the inside of her forearm below her rolled-up sleeve. It was an almost unconscious motion: slow, sinuous, wrist to elbow. His touch made her cringe. He was attractive, single and reputedly wealthy, but too smug about all three to be appealing.

She collected her tools while the rest of the crew welcomed Ian back to the pits, slapping his back and repeating his time over and over. As a teenager, she'd felt the same pang of exclusion standing back from the wharf as the family welcomed her twin brothers home after they'd won the Nantucket Regatta. She was an expected participant in the event, but not a part of it.

Had she really been excluded then? Was she now? Or did she prefer to stand on the fringes, watching?

She wiped the last wrench and stowed it. They had tomorrow off while the Formula One cars qualified. Before Hagan showed up, she'd planned to spend the day at the track. Her uncle had introduced her to F1 the first summer she'd lived with him in Head Tide. Sunday mornings at seven they'd munch doughnuts in front of the television as the cars competed on courses like Monza, Hockenheim, Silverstone. Walt had rooted for top teams—Ferrari, Benetton, McLaren, Williams—as they battled for the constructor's cup. She'd worshiped the greats: Prost, Lauda, Damon Hill, Villenueve, Mansell as they whipped at 200 mph through hairpins bearing the names of the dead. When Ayrton Senna hit the wall at Imola, she'd frozen cross-legged in front of the screen, disbelieving, inconsolable. Like fans around the world, she wailed in anguish for the fallen hero. The kid in her still couldn't believe she was just yards away from the most sophisticated racing machines in the world and the men whose names were legends.

She helped push the Lotus into the tent. A corner of the duct tape had peeled off the windshield, revealing a spiderweb of cracks—reminders of the gunshot. Ian claimed he didn't mind the tape. Said it was a good-luck talisman, a badge of survival.

The crew were closing up the paddock, giddy over their driver's success. Tom yelled over, "Join us for a pitcher, Rebecca?"

"Can't. But thanks."

She might have enjoyed partying with them tonight, a little bonding to soothe her wounded ego. Regrettably, she had a command performance elsewhere, which she'd neglected to tell Hagan about.

Before calling him, however, she wanted a word or two with her lawyer. She plopped on a low concrete wall, sprawled her legs along the top, pulled out her cell phone and dialed Jo's number. She understood he was worried about her—and maybe that accounted for his agitation—but sending Hagan to baby-sit was out of character. Why had he done it?

She wasn't going to find out anytime soon.

His secretary, Edna, said her boss was in a meeting across town with a client and wasn't expected to return to the office. She knew he'd be sorry to have missed her call.

Maybe.

She pushed the end button then dialed the house on Patricia Street. Six rings, no answer. Hagan had to have returned to the house; where else would he have gone?

Ten rings.

Why wasn't he answering? He was much too nosy not to answer a phone in someone else's home. Especially hers. She frowned, waited for the answering machine message to kick in, unsure how to phrase her message.

Before the recorded voice could ask her to leave a number, Hagan growled into the phone, out of breath, or angry. "Moore? Was this monkey suit your idea? What the hell are you thinking?"

She paused, wondering what Hagan was thinking. What did he imagine the tuxedo was for? "Does it fit? I had to guess at your in-seam." She had to guess at all his measurements. The clerk who took the call at Mr. Tux giggled at her approximations. Apparently they'd delivered it on schedule.

Hagan snorted. "Yes, it fits. You going to tell me what it's for?"

"Tonight's champagne reception. Peyton and several other team owners are hosting it to thank the sponsors. It's an excuse to invite the media, get some face time, which could translate into future backing. Nothing like glitter, good food and top-shelf brands to seduce unsuspecting race fans into opening their wallets."

The black-tie affair was being held at St. Elmo Steakhouse in downtown Indianapolis. They'd rented the bottom floor, complete with wine cellar and tasting room. Ian and Rebecca had been ordered to be there, center stage, looking glamorous. Peyton was convinced that the sight of a lovely female mechanic coupled with the dashing race driver would prove a photo op no paper would pass up.

That morning she'd tried to beg off, using Hagan's arrival as an excuse.

Peyton had wagged his hand. "Nonsense, Rebecca, bring him. Doll him up, persuade him to say little and keep him in the background, out of the photographs. All will be well."

Rebecca did not repeat his comments to Hagan. Hagan hadn't liked Peyton on instinct. Peyton didn't like anyone but himself. Already they were like two alpha dogs circling.

"The party's at seven. I have an errand to run. Ian's

letting me use the car. He'll ride over with Peyton. I'll swing by the house around six and pick you up."

"You'll come now. I'm going with you."

"No you're not. The errand is personal. Female."

"Yeah, well so's your photographer."

"What? My photographer, what—"

"Stuff it, Moore. It's a waste of time trying to protect you. If you want to know what I've learned, you come get me now."

She was tempted to suggest that if he felt he was wasting his time maybe he should leave town. "I'll be back before six, I promise. You can fill me in then. And I'll bring champagne. Ian qualified on the pole."

"Whoopee."

Rebecca stuck out her tongue at the phone, then flushed at her childishness.

The errand was none of Hagan's business, although it was his fault. With him on the scene, the faded black knit dress she'd shoved in the suitcase at the last minute seemed inadequate. It would have done when she was going as one of the crew. Now that she had a date, she wanted something more, more what? More flattering, more provocative?

She should have her head examined. She loathed herself for doing it, but she was heading to Nordstrom's to buy a dress to impress the man she had fled town to avoid.

Eleven

Rebecca answered the phone before Jo heard it ring. He nearly dropped it. *Could she feel him thinking about her? Or are cell phones telepathic?* The sales rep hadn't mentioned that.

He'd left work early and was sitting on Rebecca's patio. The air was warm and still, a few streaks of cloud broke the monotony. Her uncle's cat, Maurice, leaned his black bulk against Jo's ankle, licking his belly. The new kitten pawed at a cricket already minus a back leg. The cricket lunged for the grass at the edge of the flagstones. The kitten bounded after. It was so tranquil Jo had felt calm enough to call Rebecca and apologize for being churlish. Or leave a message. He didn't imagine she would answer. "Expecting an important call?"

"Yours. Did Edna give you my message?" Before he could respond, she flung the real question at him. "Why did you send Hagan to keep an eye on me?"

Rebecca: direct and to the point. Jo understood her

annoyance. He marveled at himself for encouraging Mick Hagan to travel to Indiana and move in with Rebecca at a time when, admit it or not, she must be feeling vulnerable. It was not in his best interests, but it couldn't be helped. "Let it go, Rebecca. It's done. He'll keep you safe until after the race and you return home."

She started to argue, then did what he asked and dropped the discussion.

Flipping through a *Road & Track* magazine, he half-listened as she told him about Ian's qualifying on the pole, explained more than he cared to know about the difficulty of passing on road courses. He'd take her word for it. He was searching for a catchy race driver name.

Rebecca was calling the black-and-white kitten Mike. She liked the way the cats' names went together—Mike and Maurice; Mo and Mike. Jo and Frank thought it sounded too much like Mick, so they were competing to come up with an acceptable replacement. They didn't think Rebecca would change the cat's name, but they were amusing themselves researching a new one. So far they had rejected Panis (sounded too wimpy), Andretti (too Italian, the cat would crave pasta), Carpentier (he'd have to join the woodworkers' union). While Rebecca nattered, he scanned a profile of Paul Tracy, a Canadian driver in the CHAMP car series, who began his career as a wild man behind the wheel, crashing four cars in his first season. Fondly known as P.T.

As Rebecca ran out of race chatter, Jo noticed a catch in her voice. "Something else I should know about?"

He envisioned her shaking her head, setting the waves dancing, hair still moving as she responded. "My imagination's working overtime, Jo. That's all. Too much on my mind."

If it concerned Hagan, he didn't want to know about it, so he accepted her dismissal. He slipped a creased letter to mark his place in the magazine and turned the conversation to the banal happenings in Head Tide. He told her that Cyrus Borden had died and it looked bad for his middle son, Elton, the one most recently disinherited. Rebecca would remember Cyrus. She'd first heard of him when hiding out in the law office while the sheriff tore her shop apart, searching for evidence to explain the murders of a local husband and wife. Sheriff Zimmer had been salivating in anticipation of arresting either Rebecca or her head mechanic, Frank Lewes. Frank had lost that round.

For the past seven years Cyrus had regularly cut one or more of his sons out of the will. He didn't mean much by it, it was his form of recreation. He enjoyed ranting, even if he had to pay for the lawyer's undivided attention. Jo suspected that Elton was Mr. Borden's favorite. He admired the boy's stubbornness, his willingness to be different and develop his artistic streak.

"I've requested a meeting with all three sons prior to the reading of the will to discuss a more equitable settlement. It shouldn't be a problem, the boys get along."

Jo omitted the second chapter in Cyrus's story. That one was guaranteed to give Rebecca a migraine. It would not be easily settled. He hoped it could wait until she returned home. Until he could explain it to her face, soften the blow.

He switched to gossip, benign chatter to keep her on the line. "Flo is up in arms. A bagel shop from Waldorf has bought Carole's Beauty Shop on First Avenue. Flo's convinced that her breakfast customers will desert her diner for a trendy new place."

"What? And pass up on their daily infusion of artery-hardening cholesterol?"

"Unlikely, isn't it? Frank needs you to call him. Someone dropped off a car, simply parked it in the driveway last night after closing. 'Like those folk think we got nothing else to work on but their precious car.' He wanted to check with you before he calls the owner and threatens to have it towed away."

"What kind of a car?"

"One that's spelled like a hat?"

"Derby Bentley. Cute, two-seater with large headlamps?"

Jo said he thought so. Cars tended to look alike to him, a product of growing up on an island where few people drove. Certainly, no one drove anything resembling a classic.

"Despite his grumbling, Frank hopes the car needs lots of work. It would make a good winter project. Of course, Frank's assuming the shop will remain open. You're planning to return, aren't you?"

Rebecca sighed.

Yes, he was needling her. He didn't have the time or inclination to cajole her. She was running away with no regard for those she left behind. Selfishly, he needed her to face it, come home and mend bridges.

And do it soon. "I spoke with Dorothea Wetherly earlier this week. Have you called her?"

Rebecca said nothing.

He continued. "Or your parents? Have you at least phoned them?"

Again, dead air. He let it hang, gave Rebecca enough time to count to ten. It didn't dissipate the annoyance in her voice. "Don't bully me, Jo. They've had thirty-seven years to discuss the situation with me, but they haven't. I'll call when I'm ready."

Rebecca felt betrayed by her family, but she was letting one deceit overshadow all the good that had come from it. She'd lost nothing. She'd gained an additional grandmother. Few people were as lucky as she was when it came to family. Why couldn't she accept her good fortune? At the moment, she wasn't interested in his advice. She was curt when they said good-bye.

Jo held onto the phone. Staring into space, he saw her face: green eyes flashing, the left corner of her mouth twisted down into a stubborn frown. Gradually, the face softened, faded to be replaced by a playful temptress from his youth, twisting long dark hair into a clip, winking over her shoulder at him. *Angelica.* His first love. She'd been haunting him a lot lately. *Why not?* Because of him, she'd died much too young.

He crossed to the back door to herd Mo inside. The kitten followed, running full-tilt into the leg of a chair. He bounced back and blinked his eyes at the affront. Jo scooped him up and massaged his tiny face until he purred. He set the cat on the counter and smiled as he penned "P.T.?" on a yellow Post-it note. The kitten pawed at the pen as he wrote. A good sign. He affixed the note to the front of the refrigerator along with the other suggestions.

Before shutting the back door, he gazed across the fields. They'd been recently mowed. Rounded mounds of hay dotted the landscape. At the edge of the woods the shadows inched forward, swallowing up the sunlight in their path. Peering into the darkness, his mind conjured up Rebecca's white body floating as still as death, another nightmare he could not shake.

He turned away, snatched up the car magazine and retrieved his letter. Held it tucked under his chin while he bolted the lock. He didn't know why he was still carrying it; every line had been committed to memory. A cousin, the child of his mother's youngest sister, had written in an upright hand on lined paper that Thomas Levy was in the cancer ward where she helped out. He was in a bad way, asking could anyone find Jo Delacroix?

I didn't tell that I knows where you is. Mama kept your address. She say you want to see Mister Levy is your business. None of our affair. She guessed we had to tell you. No one else would.

So true. No one would. No one other than a bitter aunt and her immediate family.

He dropped the door key in an ashtray on the counter, crushed the letter into his pocket.

Twelve

Mick would admit to being marginally competitive, though not in the macho way expected of cops. He could care less if the new rookie scored higher on the firearm quals, ran a faster mile or sank more free throws than he did. But he liked to be in the know. Have more information than the yokel in the next seat, or the woman sharing a candlelight dinner with him.

Ergo, he'd been unsympathetic when Moore told him about the old man inspiring her in the library on a snowy day. She rarely offered vignettes of her life as a youngster, so he should have been flattered. He should have been more encouraging. He would have been, if Moore hadn't crept too close to his personal territory. Libraries were his secret weapon.

The town's public library had lured him in at an early age. The quiet, the sense of history, realization that knowledge on any subject was waiting on the shelves had been more seductive than the playground. As a teenager, he'd been way too cool to admit his addiction to books. When kids from school caught him skipping down the steps, he'd roll his eyes, grouse that he was running an errand for his mother.

After his dad died, Mick had haunted the high-ceilinged reading room, flipping through magazines on subjects from antiques to zoology. When basketball became too painful because he expected to glimpse his father watching from the doorway, he quit the team and hid out every afternoon in the stacks. There he'd pull out a book at random, read for a while then re-shelve it and wander until another title snagged his interest.

He didn't tell his mother, afraid she'd chide him for being a quitter. Or worry that he was a fag to prefer the solitude of books to the jostle of the basketball court. When she'd surfaced from mourning, she'd noticed he wasn't bringing home wrinkled uniforms and smelly socks to be laundered. He'd mumbled that he was just hanging out with some guys. That made her worry about drugs. Finally, guilt compelled him to confess that he was a bibliophile. She'd laughed with relief and tried to hug him.

There was a phone book stuffed in the top shelf of the bookcase. Mick looked up the address of the nearest public library: the Eagle branch of the Indianapolis Public was just a few streets away.

He locked up, ambled north on Falcon, then along West Thrush Street. Didn't see either a falcon or a thrush, just knots of waist-high kids squealing as they scooted along the sidewalk. Many of them were heading in his direction, up Brewer to the library. He nodded and followed along. Breathed deeply. It was an open, inviting kind of town. A good place to begin a lasting relationship, without nosy neighbors or competing suitors.

Inside, an African American woman with her hair straightened then frozen into a flip gave him the once-over. Peered at him through scratched lenses of over-sized bifocals. She didn't smile, but concluded that being a cop he could be trusted even though he didn't have a city library card. She directed him to the periodicals archives before resettling behind the reference desk. "Computer access to the Internet is in the room through the arch." He nodded without turning, sought out a vacant table.

Hayes's research on Peyton Madison was locked inside Moore's computer. Mick had no urge to duplicate it; he could wait for a few hours to read it. But he was curious about the profile in *Life* magazine. The rag was famous for its photography. Good chance there'd be a family snapshot and that it would be revealing. That was one lesson that had stayed with him from undergraduate days at RISD. Really good photographers revealed more than a frozen second in time.

The magazine was rumpled from being packed in a cardboard archival box along with other reminders of a happier period. He blew dust from the upper edge, flipped the pages over until he found the article, "Peyton Madison: Southern Gentleman and Master Chemist."

The first page was a collage of photos featuring Madison II with various business associates. Businesslike with good posture, he kept a slight distance between himself and fellow workers. The casual shot in a chem lab looked staged: boss getting chummy while approving underlings' efforts. Another, more formal pose in the boardroom finished off the page.

Page two was dominated by an eight-by-six-inch black-and-white family portrait. Beneath it was a lengthy caption. It identified Madison and his new wife, Teresa Maria, née Ignacia, holding their infant son, Peyton Madison III. They were posed alfresco in a spacious suburban yard with their even more spacious home as backdrop. The write-up mentioned that this was his second family. His first wife, Ingrid (née Thierman), and son, Karl, had died while on vacation in the mountains above Rio. Friends felt that the tragedy had prompted Madison to move to America for a fresh start at life. Given his second wife's coloring and her surname, Mick was willing to bet that Madison had brought her along from South America as a souvenir. The strain around her mouth indicated that it might have been a difficult transition.

After obtaining a grainy photocopy, he pulled out a seat in front of a computer terminal. Unleashing Google, he brought up the search engine and typed in *Browning*. That produced entirely too many hits. He added, *Ian*. That linked the two names in 12,036 articles, each of which contained an Ian or a Browning, which was often a gun. Switching the names around to *Ian Browning* and dropping the comma resulted in a more manageable eight hundred and ninety-six references. Most concerned a duffer by that name who was a monthly contributor to *Fly Fishing and Tackle Mag-*

azine. Another Ian Browning distributed self-help motivational CDs, DVDs and videos with titles like: *Do It For Yourself, By Yourself*.

He scrolled page after page of the same irrelevant drivel. Mindless torture. Before signing off, he jumped to the last page of entries, the oldest ones. Sort of like reading a magazine beginning at the back cover, which he did, suspicious that the important news was slipped in where casual readers would overlook it.

Almost all of the older citations referred to articles by or about some Irish banker, Robert Browning, a heavyweight in the world of finance. The items were published in an impressive cross section of international business magazines, but it didn't seem to help much until one headline mentioned that the banker had a son. Ian didn't speak with any discernable accent, but he could have been born in the British Isles and not live there. Farther down, a second article named the son: Ian Browning. *A direct hit.*

Mick clicked on the link and found himself reading a 1982 article from the *Irish Independent*. It dealt with the shocking death of Katherine Browning, fifteen-year-old daughter of prominent banker, Dublin financier, Robert D. Browning. The girl had been discovered dead at a house party on May 22nd. According to the newspaper article, she'd attended the party with her brother, Ian, who was helping police with their inquiries. It was feared that alcohol and Ecstasy had played a role in her tragic death.

A few days later, *The Economist* confirmed that the

untimely and tragic death had resulted from a reaction to the recreational drug. Her brother admitted knowing that the drug was circulating the party but was unaware that his sister had consumed any. He was not charged with any drug-related offense. The between-the-lines tone berated him for not being more vigilant in watching over his sister. A small photograph showed a thin-shouldered adolescent leaving the police station flanked by two upstanding businessmen in fine woolen overcoats.

Thirteen

Rebecca fumed all the way to the city, south down Sixteenth Street to Meridian, then straight to Circle Center Mall. Jo's conversation, his solemn tone, echoed inside her head. She heard loud and clear the scolding he hadn't quite delivered. Jo was irritating because he was right. She knew he was; she accepted that. But it didn't fully explain why he was so annoyed with her.

Yes, she should call her parents—Robert and Pauline—but not yet, not from Indy. The conversation hanging over the three of them was like a thundercloud that wouldn't go away. The humidity was impossibly high, air alive with thunder and the threat of lightning. She needed to be in the heart of the tempest when it broke, not hundreds of miles away. She didn't want the impact diluted by distance, muffled through the phone wires.

She should also call Dorothea Wetherly. Her newly

acquired grandmother adored her. Irrationally, Rebecca blamed the woman for most of her pain and confusion.

The clerk at Nordstrom's helped distract her from fretting over Jo, Mrs. Wetherly and her parents. She was a well-preserved sixty, dressed in a fitted charcoal dress with three-quarter-length sleeves, sensible leather pumps and a name badge that said *Mrs. Lacey*. When Rebecca hesitated, trying to explain about the party and justify her immediate need for a new dress, Mrs. Lacey grinned wickedly and said she had just the thing. She would be right back.

She returned to flaunt a shimmery wisp of nothing in a color never matched by Crayola. A shade somewhere between champagne and copper mesh, it glowed like the highlights in Rebecca's hair. She ran the cloth through her fingers and disappeared into a changing room.

The neckline skimmed her chest, dainty cap sleeves hugged her biceps. Cut on the bias, the fabric clung to every pound of her, from breasts to knees, before flaring out and down to skim the floor. Mrs. Lacey handed her a pair of neutral pumps so she wouldn't step on the hem. When she moved, the dress stretched and flowed like it had a life of its own.

"Just the thing indeed."

"Indeed. Did you notice the embroidery?"

She'd been too busy staring at the sex kitten in the mirror to take in the finer details of the dress. Over the past weeks she seemed to have slimmed down while filling out in all the right places. Maybe she'd been wearing coveralls so long she'd forgotten what her body looked like.

Mrs. Lacey pointed out a discrete lotus flower embroidered at the center of the neckline. It had been hand-applied in matching silk thread. Its stem curved down across her left rib cage, circled lower around her waist to her right cheek then slithered down to end just above the knee. The skirt was slit from there down. *Like it needed to be any more seductive*. The dress would get a reaction from a statue. Even Hagan might take note.

She couldn't bring herself to look at the price tag; she'd probably need smelling salts. The cost didn't matter, she was taking it. No other dress could possibly look this good or make her feel so fabulous. Jo, if he were here, would encourage her to buy it. Or maybe not—under the circumstances. Of course, if he were here, the circumstances would be different. She might be buying it for him. And Jo would appreciate it. He would even know the significance of the lotus flower.

In the mirror, the tissue-thin cloth shimmered along her body. Her face was lightly tanned, which was becoming. The frown line between her eyes wasn't. Why was she scowling? Because Jo wasn't in Indianapolis; or because Hagan was? She should be glowing, reveling in the anticipation of an elegant evening out. Champagne, four-star fare in the company of beautiful people. Being courted by the press. Ian on the pole. Hagan in a tuxedo.

She rubbed at the crease next to her right brow, well aware of the mounting insecurities that caused it but still wishing it would go away. Broadly put, she worried too much over past mistakes; fretted over future ones. Her grandmother had a similar crease, a crack that would deepen to a gash then suddenly vanish. Had it been etched on her brow by the same kind of doubts, by mistakes she'd made regarding her daughter? *My real mother.* Rebecca stretched her neck, relaxed her shoulders, smiled at the mirror. Then laughed, watching the line dissolve as the tension ebbed. Totally erased by a flicker of joy. She should smile more often.

She should be smiling now about her grandmother of two months. Dorothea Wetherly was a woman of intelligence, spirit and tenacity, to whom she genuinely liked being related. It was repositioning the rest of the family tree that was troublesome. At thirty-seven, how do you cope with learning that the couple who raised you aren't your parents? Relatives—a biological uncle and an aunt by marriage—but not the parents you always assumed they were.

What hurt most was that Uncle Walt, with whom she'd spent nearly every summer of her life, had known and never said a word. It must have been hard for him to lie to her, even by omission. He was honest to his own detriment; she had the tax records to prove it. Yet he'd never told her that Jamie, his youngest brother, was her father, and Nicole Wetherly, Dorothea's only child, was her mother. The couple had died just when their lives were beginning.

Her throat constricted. The damn crease returned as her eyes misted over. She squeezed them shut, sighed to release the tightness. When they blinked open, the dressing room was suffused in deep blue, as if the sea that had claimed her parents' lives was encroaching, washing over her. She sniffed, shook her head, watched the wall of waves sparkle with reflected light.

Then it spoke. "It needs a bit at the neck. I have just the thing."

She jerked around. Standing behind her was a stranger wearing an electric-blue Shantung silk dress with long sleeves, a short skirt and the price tags still attached. The woman could have been anywhere between fifty and sixty-five. She stood at least five foot ten, without an ounce of fat. Her hair was pure silver, cut in a pixie fringe to frame large hazel eyes. She had a generous mouth and plump cheeks in a narrow face. A network of what her mother called "character lines" crinkled around her eyes.

The woman tugged at the cowl neckline draped low on her chest then twisted around. The roll of cloth vanished behind, leaving her back bare to the waist. It was a back worth exposing. "What do you think?"

Rebecca nodded. "It looks fabulous."

"It's not too youthful?"

"No youngster could have earned the right to wear that dress."

The woman regarded her quizzically in the mirror, then laughed. "You may be right. I have earned this. Here, let me show you what I have."

She rummaged in her handbag, pulling out pens, lipsticks, mini-tapes, leather cigarette case, Day-Timer. Dumped them all on the corner bench.

By the time Mrs. Lacey returned, the stranger was dangling a delicate chain loosely around Rebecca's throat. Thin strands of gold and silver were twisted like DNA into half spirals linked together. Its airy feel suited the dress. Mrs. Lacey agreed that it was quite the perfect finishing touch. The stranger nodded, said that it was settled, clasped the necklace in place and started to walk away.

Rebecca protested. "Wait, please. I can't accept it, how would I return it? I don't even know your name."

The woman in blue stopped. "How rude of me not to introduce myself. I am Elise Carlson. You're Rebecca Moore. We're attending the same party tonight. You can return the necklace afterward."

Rebecca felt herself flush.

Elise patted her arm. "Don't fret. We haven't been introduced. I saw you at work in the pits. A female mechanic is something of a novelty. Even for other women. We'll talk more tonight. Ciao."

Fourteen

When Moore emerged from the bathroom smelling of gardenias and looking like a Hollywood goddess Mick's first thought had been that Edith Head must still be alive and designing. Okay, that was his second thought. His first thought stalled between *Oh, my God,* and an instant jolt of testosterone. The lame comment that won out was, "What did you do with Moore, the mechanic?" It did not win him points. Walking to the car, he ached to pull at the bow tie suddenly choking his throat. Maybe rip off additional items of clothing while he was at it—starting with the gold dress.

On a bad day, clad in stained jeans and a work shirt, Moore was too sexy to be ignored. Not that she tried. He was intoxicated by her. Why else would he be in suburban Indianapolis decked out in a rented tuxedo going to a pretentious party with a gaggle of car nuts none of whom he knew? The scene was a blistering reminder of stuffy cotillions he'd been forced to attend at the country club every holiday season after his father was killed. His grandparents ceased inviting him the year he joined the police force. That was the same time they rescinded their offer to pay for graduate school and he took up smoking.

Mick helped Moore lower herself into the car, tucked the flimsy fabric under her warm thigh, enjoyed a glimpse of cleavage, before she zipped up the Orvis waxed hunting jacket. Even that incongruous wrap didn't mar the effect. He smiled, reflecting that he might enjoy the evening after all. She was no homely, teenage airhead with a trust fund. He was no longer a tongue-tied gawky adolescent.

He blamed his lack of finesse with women on his father. Patrick Hagan had the insensitivity to die when his son was barely fifteen. Bereft of male guidance, Mick had spent his formative years—those pustule-prone days when boys start approaching girls for more than help with their homework—with no role model. There was no harried male to shout "Darling, I'm home" each evening. No man in the house putting cool moves on his mother, making her moan in the dark on summer nights. No father to coach him, feed him lines he could try out on the neighborhood girls. He'd done his share of dating, before and after his brief marriage, but had never given the art of seduction much thought. With Moore radiant in the passenger-side bucket seat, it was difficult to think of anything else.

The glow lasted for all of the thirty-minute drive to the restaurant, probably because they didn't talk. They'd left the rental heap on the street and taken the Corvette even though it was minus a top. Wind noise and rattles limited the conversation to directions about where to turn. Moore didn't try to grill him about his day snooping at the track. She seemed willing to have a night off. Leave the shop talk for tomorrow.

Once on the freeway he poked along in the inside lane, free to admire her profile. She'd done something to her hair in the bathroom. It glowed. Tossed by the wind, the unruly waves wedged out from her neck in back, bounced forward to caress her cheekbones. Great cheekbones. Graceful neck. And that full bottom lip. He flicked his eyes forward as he changed lanes. She wasn't so shabby from there down either.

He exited Route 76 onto city streets. Feeling like a high school senior on the way to his prom, he reached for her hand at a light. She let him hold it. Warm, thin fingers with blunt nails. Soft. Hands that didn't feel like a mechanic's. Not that he'd held hands with that many mechanics. The corner of her mouth lifted as she shot him a sidelong glance. He grinned back over the rumbling exhaust until the light changed.

He turned left where Moore pointed, guided the car into the public parking garage next to the Circle Center. She ditched the field coat behind the seat. They rode the elevator down, standing close, feeling self-conscious in evening dress.

She hugged her arms as they exited the garage and crossed the street to St. Elmo. According to the blurb in the tourist's guide the steak house was a fixture in Indianapolis, the must place to eat. It had been around since the early nineteen hundreds, located in the same red brick building on South Illinois Street.

A throng of would-be diners spilled out of the

restaurant and clogged the sidewalk. Some looked irked, like they'd been waiting through the decades. Several turned, nudged one another as they approached. He wondered who the gawkers thought they were. Celebrities for sure. Moore reinforced that image when she greeted a liveried driver having a smoke next to a late-model fern green Rolls-Royce.

Soto voce, she told him that the Silver Spirit belonged to Peyton Madison.

Naturally.

Fifteen

The stares turned hostile when Moore led the way past those who had been waiting in line for hours. Mick reached for her arm as they were escorted inside. Not to protect her. He didn't want to lose her in the crowd. A self-satisfied maitre d' preceded them through the dining room, where Moore got sidelong glances from observant men and their envious dates. She didn't seem to notice. She was taking in the decorations on the wall and listening to the general chatter floating toward the high tin ceilings. She twirled around the bannister and headed downstairs.

The cellar was low, long and narrow, packed with about forty people. Small linen-clad tables had been moved against the outer wall to allow room for milling about. From his vantage on the stairs, Mick absorbed the spectacle and nodded in approval. His most promising suspects had been dressed up and were captive in one room. An investigator's dream. Let them drink liberally and talking to them could be enlightening.

Peyton greeted them as they reached the bottom step. Though they'd met briefly at the track, he waited to be reminded who Mick was. He intended it to be annoying. It was. Like every other guy in the place, Peyton licked his lips as he ogled Moore. He probably regretted letting her bring anyone as her escort.

Or maybe not. The team owner struck him as a man more enthralled by power than swept away by passion. Sex might be an amusing diversion, but it would never overshadow business or replace a sure bet.

Halfway along the narrow room Evans's bulk caused a logjam. His formal wear was shiny in back, snug around the middle. On his arm was a frizzy blonde who, likewise, had packed too much body in too little dress. The halter top showed more cleavage than was desirable given the leathery nature of the skin. The slit in the skirt gave a pretty good indication that the lady sunbathed au natural. The crew chief's color was high, like he'd stopped at a local watering hole on the way over to the restaurant.

Evans didn't acknowledge Moore as they wiggled past. His gaze was locked on Peyton Madison, who was having a cozy conversation with Whitten. It was a toss-up whether Evans was irked at his boss for hobnobbing with the enemy, or worried that Whitten would mention their meeting during the lunch break. The Brabham team owner studiously ignored Evans, though he had to be conscious of the stare. Then again, maybe he was used to it. Whitten dressed as if he expected people to stare and to like what they saw.

A waiter sashayed past. Mick relieved him of two

flutes of champagne. When he turned to hand one to Moore, she was missing.

He spotted her inside the wine cellar, posing with Browning—driver *extraordinaire* and race pole sitter. That made him sound like a mugwump. He looked about as decisive as one. He had pale skin, red hair and refined, symmetrical, features. The gangling kid had developed into a good-looking WASP who would have been irritating even if his arm wasn't encircling Moore's waist. As predicted, the media was salivating over the pair. A chatty photographer urged Moore's arm around Browning's waist as well. *Too cute.* Mick probed the driver's face and posture, trying to find the defeated teen who'd escorted his sister to the party that killed her. He wasn't there.

Mick drained the first flute and deposited it on the closest table.

"Next time, bring me a full one." The sultry voice was pitched low, aimed in his direction.

He ducked down to locate the owner. She was half hidden in the shadows where the glow from the table lamp barely reach. A bit old, but stunning in brilliant blue. "I'm an interloper. You feel like a fifth wheel. We're a natural pair." She flashed him a 100-watt grin.

It took him a second to place her. When it clicked, he returned the grin. *The voyeur from the track.* He signaled to the waiter and slid behind the table to join her. "I didn't recognize you without the field glasses. I'm Michael Hagan."

"Elise Carlson. Did you catch your daughter? She's very quick."

"Too quick."

"Really? And you a police officer. I would think you could keep a small child in your sights."

The waiter off-loaded two flutes. Mick kept his expression neutral as Carlson accepted a glass, smirked at him over the rim. He was surprised that she knew he was a cop. Wondered why she cared. He was even more curious about which of the nomads at the track today had filled her in. Had the news of Moore's cop bodyguard been passed like a relay baton from Browning to his crew chief, from the crew chief to Whitten, from Whitten to the guy in the gray suit and on to this woman? *Why?*

He was tempted to let it drop, to enjoy the evening, be amused by her company. Forget that he was a cop. He just couldn't. "Too bad you didn't stop the kid for me. You seemed to be keeping close tabs on her."

"Not at all. I was bored watching cars, became intrigued by what she found so fascinating in the infield. When you gave chase, my curiosity increased. I should learn to keep it under control."

Mick sipped. It was plausible. He asked if she'd really crashed the party.

"Not really. I've been away from racing for some years now. It was time to come back. As I have money to invest, it was easy to get invited."

She reached for a cigarette, pointed it toward the photo shoot being staged in the wine cellar. "Is that your wife, or girlfriend? Probably not the little girl's mother. Still, you three must make a colorful household. Yes?" Mick shrugged, sipped. She prattled on as if she hadn't expected a response. "I'd prefer it if you were single and moonlighted with an escort service. If so, may I have the agency's number?"

That made him laugh. "Trust me, Mrs. Carlson. That woman is not my wife. And if you're between husbands, you may have all my phone numbers."

Creases of mirth etched her face. She was easy to look at. Sensuous in a worldly European way. Still, his focus kept drifting past her shoulder to where Moore, the race driver and the owner were playing coy for the media.

After several attempts to talk racing, Carlson swatted him lightly on the wrist, shifted her chair to join him in watching Moore. "I met your friend today at Nordstrom's. Did she tell you? It was obvious she was dressing for someone special."

"For this. She knew she'd be in the limelight."

"Nonsense, the fabric's too subtle to photograph well. I suspect she has a more tactile activity in mind. Unless you're really in town for the racing, despite your feigned indifference?"

"Not feigned. No interest."

"Pity. Perhaps you'd care more if you had a small wager on the outcome? I assure you, it makes the race weekend more exciting."

She shifted again. Her knee pressed against his. She mentioned a Calcutta. He asked if he needed his passport. She smiled briefly, unamused. The Calcutta wasn't a side trip to India. It was some kind of betting nonsense taking place in the wine-tasting room.

According to Carlson, Calcuttas were traditional in Indianapolis before a major race. They'd begun with a group of movers and shakers making friendly wagers on the cars entered in the Indy 500. Her late husband had been a devotee. When Formula One came to the town, the idea spread to that venue as well, though the rules had to be modified to accommodate the dominance of certain car manufacturers. Fans banded together to form cartels for the purpose of betting on the outcome. Your driver didn't have to win. In fact, you could put money on a driver to lose.

Many of those betting didn't follow racing and lacked basic knowledge of the series. They just liked being part of the festivities, enjoyed it more thinking they could go home richer. Carlson had missed the rush of gambling since her husband died. She'd been told that Peyton Madison shared her passion. "But, as you can see, he's busy and you're available. Shall we?"

"Inviting, but I can't afford to lose so I don't bet." He pushed back from the table. "If you want to meet Peyton, I'll introduce you."

"You know him well?"

"I know his type."

Carlson reached for her purse as she rose. In heels she matched his height. She waited for him to offer his arm.

It was an irritating, short walk. Even though the photographers' lust had shifted to food and liquor, Browning still had his arm around Moore's waist. Peyton was whispering in her ear, effeminate fingers playing with the softness on the inside of her elbow. The tableau was enough to turn Mick's stomach, but he couldn't take his eyes off them. He stopped a yard away, jaws clenched tight enough to produce an instant headache.

Carlson's introduction was preempted by the entrance of Whitten carrying two glasses that were probably single malt Scotch. It was that kind of restaurant, and Whitten looked to be that kind of imbiber. He raised an eyebrow at Peyton and lifted a glass in challenge. Peyton nodded and reached for the drink.

Before relinquishing his hold on the glass, Whitten turned his chin in Carlson's direction. He stretched his mouth to approximate a smile. "Forgive me for barging past you, lovely lady. It didn't occur to me you would want to speak with Peyton. Unless of course, it's a business matter and that would be a pity. If you have money to invest, call me, please. Peyton's not a safe bet."

Carlson raised one eyebrow. "Really? Why is that?"

Whitten let Peyton take the highball as he insinuated himself between them, still flirting with Carlson. "You haven't heard that the team is jinxed? Or are you so fearless that you'd rush in, while most backers are buying thermal socks for their icy toes?"

Peyton pushed past Whitten, knocking him into the table, sloshing the drinks. Since the move necessitated he drop Moore's arm, Mick smiled. Peyton took it the wrong way, snarled in his direction though his remarks clearly were intended for Carlson. "Whitten is a practical joker with an effete sense of humor. You'll have to forgive and forget him. I'm Peyton Madison and you are . . . ?"

Carlson stood demurely, allowing Mick to do the honors before offering her hand. As Peyton clutched it, his eyes lit with a predatory glow and his drawl got broader. "Mrs. Carlson, I'm honored to meet you at last. But have I erred? I was expecting you tomorrow. You should have contacted my assistant and informed me you were here. I am distraught." He finished the sentence with the hint of a pout.

Carlson waved it away as the nonsense it was. "I'd joined a small party for boar hunting in Argentina. Do you hunt boar? No. Well, having bagged what I went for, I flew back early."

"I am so flattered that you're here. How I wish· though you'd been with me at the track today. My Lotus is on the pole."

She flickered an eyelash in Mick's direction. It could have been an appeal to say nothing. Or a check to make sure Mick was listening. Peyton missed the exchange. He tucked her hand under his arm, reeling her in. "Now that we've met, you must allow me to look after you. I will tend to your every wish."

"How paternalistic. At least, I imagine you speak like a father. I never knew mine."

"Mine I know too well. Boring compared with you—someone I would like to know better."

Mick sipped his drink to keep from snorting. He was willing to bet that Southern charm was bouncing off Carlson's hide and running down to pool on the floor. She had too much savoir faire to swallow that malarkey. Browning, likewise, was having trouble stomaching it. He rolled his eyes and relinquished his hold on Moore. With Peyton distracted, he sidled off to talk shop with another driver.

Moore glided over to his side. "Having fun yet?"

He didn't answer. As long as he pretended the event was part of an investigation, he didn't need to be amused. Unless she was the amusement.

Hand on her arm, he edged her in the direction of the bar. Peyton and Carlson were nose-to-nose in conversation, talking about their fathers and growing up rich. He had; she hadn't. If they wanted a drink, they could send someone else to fetch it. He was getting his own.

Or would have, but a bald man blocked his way. The guy looked familiar, maybe everyone was starting to. He was in his mid-fifties, prosperous with a small paunch, dressed in a simple suit, sky-blue striped tie with a grease spot on the tail. His left thumb rubbed back and forth across his fingers, reminiscent of Bogart as Queeg fretting with his marbles. It was the worried look that placed him at the track, where Mick had seen him in serious conversation with Whitten, just before he met up with Carlson. His eyes were locked on Carlson now, slinking through the crowd toward the tasting room with Peyton salivating close behind, one hand on her bare back.

Moore tapped on his arm, did the social thing and extended a hand along with a smile. The harried man wrenched his gaze away from Carlson. His eyes flicked in Mick's direction and widened in panic. Moore soothed him, gave her name. He nodded quickly a few times, said he was Brian Franks. She asked if he was affiliated with one of the teams? He shook his head so hard a strand of hair combed over the top flopped to one side. "Investment consultant. This is not what was planned. I shouldn't be here."

Moore bit. "At the party or at the race?"

He flapped his pate from side to side. Set down his drink.

"The gambling make you nervous, Franks?" Tired of waiting, Mick slipped by him, sidled up to the bar.

Franks thought about it, blinked a few times then mumbled, "In a manner of speaking. Yes, it does. Excuse me." He pushed past them.

Moore leaned against the bar. "Was it something we said or someone he saw?"

They turned, shoulders touching.

Franks was worming his way past the food tables, ignoring platters of petit filets mignons on toast points and iced dishes of St. Elmo's signature shrimp cocktail with horseradish potent enough to peel paint. A man of willpower, or lacking an appetite. His eyes kept skittering toward the tasting room as he moved away from it in an arc, skirting Carlson like a negatively charged filing being repelled by a magnet. Until, at the apex of the arc, he broke loose, set down his untouched drink and headed up the stairs.

Moore shrugged, pushed a lock of hair back from her face. "Think Carlson is his investment client?"

Mick shrugged. "Logical guess."

"Then he has good reason to be worried. Peyton's eyeing her money like a gator sighting a wounded duck."

Sixteen

The tasting room was only a tad larger than the wine cellar. It bulged with more than a dozen guests who had squeezed in then separated into clusters of three and four. Stepping across the threshold, Rebecca could feel the tension, see the strain on the bettors' faces. The intensity united them into a herd with a common affliction. She was very glad she didn't gamble.

Peyton was hunched over a corner table conferring with Evans and the svelte Elise Carlson. She'd lit a thin European cigarette and was exhaling the smoke through a grin. She was the only one in that group who seemed to be enjoying herself. From the body language it was obvious that she was encouraging the men to do something they were uncomfortable with. Predicably, the male egos were responding to her taunts even though their hands itched to clutch their wallets shut.

Derek Whitten was holding court at the next table.

Jacket unbuttoned, one leg crossed over the other, just the proper amount of gartered stocking showing, he projected confidence and élan. Either he had insider knowledge, could afford to lose more, or was a natural thespian. Maybe all three.

One of his fellow bettors opined that a Brazilian rookie driver was too reckless, crashed too often to be worth a bet. Whitten wagged off the criticism. "Au contraire. It's Darwin at work, eliminating those who are unfit. We bet on him to fail. Put him down as the first DNF."

Elise stubbed out her cigarette as if it had inexplicably turned rancid. Massaging her left wrist, she rose to greet them. "Rebecca, how lovely you look. Explain DNF to me. Then tell me what you think about this South American youngster. Will he finish in the points at ten-to-one?"

"DNF: Did not finish—catchall for engine failures, crashes, blown tires and the like. The Brazilian is a long shot. Unless it rains and his gearbox holds. Then he could be a factor."

"Intriguing. They're predicting rain by afternoon on Sunday. As a mechanic, can you pray for the gearbox?" Not expecting an answer, she rested both hands on the back of Peyton's chair, spoke just above his ear. "So it's a long shot, but not impossible." She winked at Rebecca. "Taking risks adds such spice. Perhaps you can persuade him. He's immune to my charms."

Peyton cut off his conversation with Evans. Raising his head put him eye level with the drape of Carlson's bodice. He looked like a man who sensed the ice was getting thin, but was too macho to backtrack to shore.

He maneuvered the chair sideways and stood. Elise had him dangling where she wanted him.

Whitten, who was blatantly eavesdropping, poked him with his foot. "Go ahead, Peyton, bet. Your abysmal luck is bound to change sometime."

Peyton swatted his leg. "What are you implying? There's nothing wrong with my luck, or my skill."

"Really? Have I been misinformed about the, ah, mishaps plaguing your pit? Rumors fly around the track. Guess they can't all be true."

Splotches of red appeared on Peyton's cheeks. He was about to, what—deny the incidents, explain them away?

Elise forestalled his response. "Don't worry, Peyton. I'm sure this will be a lucky bet. If it isn't?" She shrugged and twisted to face him nose-to-nose, her hipbones skimming his. "You undoubtedly have valuables? Gems or art that would amuse me? I shall buy them, hold them as collateral. That way you will be indebted to me. It could be the beginning of a most interesting collaboration."

She reached past him, tapped her nail at the betting form lying on the table. His eyes flickered, mind whizzed, weighing the promised gain against possible loss. Finally, he uncapped a pen and signed. Carlson wrapped her arm through his. "Come, I'll treat you to a glass of your own champagne. Or something stronger."

Rebecca waited for them to pass and blend with the crowd before sneaking a look. She nearly choked on her wine. Her boss had committed to an obscene amount of money. She whistled softly. "There goes a conflicted man."

Beside her Evans slugged his drink. "Conflicted, yeah, but gutsy. He'll be higher than a kite if he pulls it off. He wins that bet and Carlson will match his winnings, plus come in as a silent team partner. Damn. That's my idea of a perfect woman. Rich and silent."

Hagan butted in. "Think your boss's good fortune will spill over into your lap?"

"What's good for him is good for the team. Me included. He's a prick, but a generous one when he's feeling flush. Can't help spending everything he's got."

They left Evans to his dreams and his scotch. In the outer room the ideal woman was leaning on the bar, elbow-to-elbow with Peyton. As they maneuvered past, Peyton asked something about a jealous husband. Elise assured him she didn't have one, but did have transportation. She'd drive herself. It sounded like the budding partnership might involve more than money.

After another hour of small talk, Rebecca took Hagan by the hand and led him toward the stairs. His patience had to be stretched thin. Twice in the last half hour he'd reminded her about The Oceanaire, a trendy seafood restaurant within walking distance on South Meridian. Claimed Carlson had raved at length about its food.

The idea of a sit-down meal, just the two of them, had appeal. She could use something starchy to sop up the champagne. The party was breaking up anyway. Ian had left earlier with two other drivers. Evans was grazing on the remaining steak tips. Whitten was charming the pants off a couple of potential inventors too drunk to be in a hurry.

Once upstairs she excused herself and found the ladies' room. Washing up, she noticed the borrowed necklace reflected in the mirror. She should find Elise Carlson and return it, thank her.

Elise, however, wasn't on the main floor, nor was she lingering in the dining room or upstairs bar, though Peyton had surfaced and was exchanging words with Hagan near the entrance.

Rebecca turned and headed back down to the cellar in case Elise had forgotten her purse, or was negotiating for a case of wine. The lower rooms were empty except for two busboys whisking linens from the tables.

When she reentered the bar, her quarry was disappearing out the front door. Peyton blocked the entrance. He'd stopped for a last poke at Hagan. Uttered something short and emphatic that she couldn't hear. Evans could and he laughed as he followed his boss out of the restaurant.

She crossed to Hagan. His jaw was tight enough to reverberate. She raised an eyebrow. He shook his head. Not in the mood to discuss it. She persisted. "What? You invited them to join us for dinner and they declined?"

"Just Mrs. Carlson. You can share a meal with your boss if you want, but don't include me."

"Did you really invite her?"

"Jealous? Yes, I did. Figured we would be better company than Peyton. She said she had prior plans but was delighted we were going to try her restaurant suggestion."

Rebecca pushed open the door and stepped outside, hoping Elise would be lingering on the sidewalk. The night air was dense with humidity. Beads of moisture glistened under the street lamps and on the hood of the Silver Spirit. The driver sat inside, head lolling against the headrest as he listen to something mellow on the sound system.

There were a few tourists strolling along on the way to their cars. No sign of either Peyton Madison or Elise Carlson. They'd probably gone to fetch her car from the parking garage. Rebecca wondered where her boss was planning to entertain Elise that demanded transportation. Not leading her straight to the bedroom, presumably; his hotel was next door.

She shrugged, slipped her arm through Hagan's. If Elise intended to form a partnership with Peyton, she'd be hanging around the pits over the weekend. The necklace could be returned to her later.

Seventeen

Rebecca swayed to a halt after exiting the elevator. Hagan continued on, turned when she didn't follow three paces behind. He looked handsome in a rumpled Humphrey Bogart, play-it-Sam kind of way. Rumpled, but still alert. Or maybe not. It was dim in the parking garage. The murky lighting could be coloring her judgment. Or it could be impaired by the champagne consumed at the party, the bottle of Pinot Blanc that accompanied her grilled salmon and the snifter of Remy Martin in lieu of dessert.

Hagan sagged against the side of someone else's car and leered at her. Waiting.

She crossed to the Corvette and pulled out her keys. "I'm driving."

"Toss you for it."

She agreed. Watched as he flicked a quarter into the air and failed to catch it. It slipped through his fingers, rolled into a drain under the front tire of a Mercedes

SUV. Clearly, she'd won the toss. She slid behind the wheel.

Not that she could navigate any better than Hagan, but she felt responsible for the car. Even inebriated, she figured she'd care more about guiding their borrowed steed back to the barn than Hagan would sober. When she was a kid watching television Westerns she never minded if the cowboys shot the Indians, or vice versa, but she panicked over a stray bullet hitting their mounts. No matter that the horses were card-carrying, stunt professionals paid to fall down on cue. She always worried about the horses.

They made it to Patricia Street without incident. Without any conversation either, though Hagan's hand strayed to her thigh more than once, imparting its own form of communication. The message was hard to ignore.

She parked against the curb, handed Hagan the house key. While he fumbled at the front door, she detoured to the side gate. Inside the enclosed yard, she checked the redwood table for a photograph. There was a sliver of white showing beneath the geranium. She eased it out far enough to make sure it was a snapshot, then left it there, content that her friend had come back despite Hagan's interference. She'd deal with it in the morning. Right now she had to deal with Hagan.

She knew he'd entered the house and made his way to the kitchen. She could feel his eyes on her. When she turned from the table, he was standing in the open doorway, backlit by the light over the sink. He beckoned her toward him. She took a small step to the edge of the light.

He motioned again. She stayed put, her eyes locked on his.

Was she ready for this?

Apparently, he was. He moved outside and reached for her, placed a tentative hand on her arm. Slid it upward, wrapped it around her biceps. He repeated the move on her other arm and slowly pulled her close. She could feel his breath.

A shaft of moonlight peeked through the massing clouds and sparkled off his eyes, alive with mischief. A breeze tossed branches overhead, rustled them against the roof. The night was cooling rapidly. Despite her scanty attire, she was warm. It could have been the alcohol or Hagan's touch on her skin. Or it could have been the dress. What was it Oscar Wilde had said? "No woman, secure she is in fashion, has ever caught cold."

He continued tugging gently on her arms, inching her closer. He was humming a tune from the forties. She rose to her toes but remained rooted. *Was she feeling that unsure, or in the mood to tease him? Or did she want the moment of anticipation to last?*

He closed the gap, his feet straddled hers. With a finger he traced her collarbone just below the necklace. His lips were invitingly close but in no hurry.

Was he nagged by doubts, too? What was he waiting for?

A blaze of lightning answered. Followed a second later by a crack of thunder. She laughed at the appropriateness of nature's response. Before she could share the joke, the clouds dumped the rain they'd been collecting all evening.

Hagan grabbed her waist and propelled her into the kitchen. With the slider closed and thunder booming, she tried to justify her mirth, to ease the frown from his face. Then she gave up on words.

Enough anticipation. She slid her arms around his neck and pulled him to her.

The first kiss was deep and long. Tingles went through her body, heating her skin from the inside out. She didn't care if it was the result of months of pent-up desire or a surfeit of vintage bubbly. It felt wonderful, all-consuming. A path to forgetting all horrors. A chance to feel alive.

As his tongue began exploring, her arms moved lower, probing taut back muscles through the damp tuxedo. *Too much fabric.* She insinuated her hands beneath the lapels and eased the jacket up and off his shoulders. Hagan baulked; he didn't want to stop caressing her spine. She didn't want him to, but she wanted equal access.

He held his arms down, the jacket slid free and landed on the linoleum. He back-kicked it across the floor. His lips clung to hers as he reclaimed her body. Then he released her mouth to let his fingers skim the rise of her breasts, tease her nipples through the thin cloth while he hunted madly for the zipper. She could sense his smile when he discovered it sewn into the left seam.

Nibbing at her shoulder, he eased the zipper downward. With his free hand he cupped her backside and pressed her body against the length of his. She sighed, circled his back with her arms, fused the two of them together. The zipper slid lower. Through the opening, the tips of his fingers whispered against her flesh. She moaned. His mouth was back. Tenderly, she bit his lower lip. She wanted—

The front door opened.

She froze, teeth clutching his lip. "Sssh."

Hagan came alert.

Muffled footsteps padded across the living room carpet coming closer. Paused. Keys clanked in the brass bowl on the bookshelf.

Damn it—Ian.

She tried to pull away from Hagan as the kitchen light snapped on.

"Oh, dear. Sorry."

Ian didn't look sorry. He looked mildly amused and disheveled by the downpour. He brushed water from his tux. "Went for a bite. When they dropped me back at the track, I was locked out of the motor home. Damn door's bolted from the inside. Had to phone Evans. He gave me a lift here. Didn't know where else to go. He didn't want me at his place. Guess you don't either. *Tant pis.* I'm not going back out in the rain."

He smiled impishly. "Mind if I fetch a chaser?" He squelched across the room, pushed the fallen jacket aside and reached into the fridge. He came out with a soda. Eyed them naughtily and muttered, "Carry on," on his way through.

Hagan sagged against the counter, raked his fingers through his hair. "What is it with us, Moore? Think the gods are conspiring against us for our own good? Are we just too stupid to know we're a lethal combination?"

"Compelling question. Are you really in the mood for a philosophical debate?"

"Maybe."

She tugged the zipper closed then melted into a chair at the kitchen table. Maybe they should talk. Maybe they had put it off for too long. She assumed that when, if, the physical side was consummated, it would answer most of the questions. Weak-kneed as she was feeling, maybe tonight was as good a—

A burst of thunder jerked her out of her seat.

"The photograph."

She raced for the sliding door, shoved it open, dashed to the table. Pushing the plant pot out of the way, she picked at the corner of the photo with her nail. Rain had wicked under the pot. Nine-tenths of the picture was saturated through. She gently peeled it loose from the redwood surface. Gripping her soggy prize by the corner, she sprinted back into the kitchen.

Hagan held out a square of paper towel to receive the photo. Most of the image had been obliterated by the rain, dissolved into a rainbow-colored blur. She dabbed at it with a second sheet of toweling. That made it worse. She turned it over. There on the back-side, still visible in crayon were two words, "Gun? Jasmine."

She sank onto the chair. *Jasmine.* Her admirer had a name. Hagan hadn't been lying; she was a girl. "Did you notice the photograph before we left for the party?"

He shook his head. Imitating Ian, he rummaged in the refrigerator, came out with the champagne they hadn't opened before the party. "Your admirer must have showed after we left. You may not have a picture, but you've got a name: Jasmine. Sounds like a flowery tea. Girly, like the barrettes."

Rebecca blotted the photograph again. Held it to the light before Hagan's words penetrated. "Barrettes?" She was up and in his face. "The other night it was too dark. You couldn't tell she was female much less wearing hair clips, which means you saw her today, in daylight. I should have realized it sooner. Did you talk to her?"

He sat down with two bubbling glasses and admitted that he'd seen the girl lying in the stands with her camera focused on the historic car pits. He'd spooked her and she'd run, a lot faster than he could. "I would have told you sooner, but you went on your errands without me."

She reclaimed her seat and stared at the indecipherable mess. Had it once been a picture of the shooter? Had the child seen the person taking aim at the team and snapped his photograph? It made her queasy to think of a kid being in proximity to someone wielding a loaded gun. What were her parents thinking? How could they let her hide out at the Speedway with a stalker on the loose?

"This raises the stakes, Hagan. She saw the gun, she could have seen the shooter. And he could have seen her. What if he's afraid she'll talk? Peyton has to report the incident to security now. Alert them to be on the lookout for the gunman."

"Fat chance. He's too concerned about financing his hobby to risk getting bad press. He went green around the gills when Elise forced him into the wager."

"Elise? You're on a first-name basis with her? Or

didn't you two just meet? Did you bump into her earlier at the track as well?"

Hagan pulled back. "Actually, I did." He went on
quickly. "But I didn't know who she was until the
party, honest. She, however, seemed to have done her
homework on the guest list."

"You noticed." She aligned a salt and a pepper
shaker side-by-side, moving them fractionally until
they were centered on the table. "It made me uneasy
that she knew so much. I put it down to my nagging
shadow called paranoia." She bit at her lip, leaned forward, knocking over the shakers. "When I ran into her
at Nordstrom's she already knew I was Peyton's mechanic. Revealed that he likes to gamble before she
met him. She identified you as a cop. I overheard her
discussing art with Ian, something about the current
market for postimpressionists. I work with him, room
with him, but hadn't pegged him for an art collector.
She did."

Hagan scraped the chair closer. "Relax." He lightly
touched her face, ran a finger over her shoulder, con-
tinued down her arm, pushing the sleeve lower.
"Maybe she's an investigative reporter like you were.
You busybodies know everything about everybody.
You should check her out. In the morning."

"An investigator would please me more than a gold
digger after what there is of Peyton's money."

"Are you worried that he's not good for your salary?
Be a shame if you spent a month here for no pay."

She smoothed the soggy bodice into place. "He'd
better be good for my salary, considering what I spent
on this."

Hagan toyed with her hand, slipping between each finger. "For me?"

She hesitated. "For us."

"In that case, let's hang it up before it's ruined."

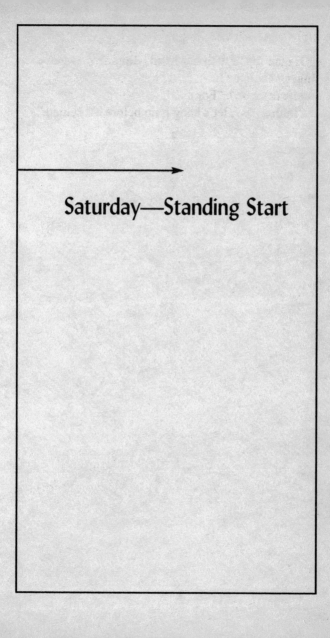

Saturday—Standing Start

Eighteen

Rebecca was conscious before the birds. She listened as they came awake, scratching in the shrubs, chirping in the branches. A squirrel pounded across the roof overhead, claws scraping on the gutter. She forced her eyes open. Light leaked in between drapes sagged into scallops from too many years of hanging.

The shaft of brightness brought back the dream. In it she had been the only living thing afloat in a vast sea. A speck. Then a shadow descended and plucked her out of the water like a crab clutched in a gull's beak. It soared upward in silence. The sea disappeared. She looked down, frantic, searching for land. Water sheeted off her back in layers, each layer a different color, falling downward, growing in intensity until it shattered. The shards blended into a rainbow puddle, muddied like the dissolved photograph. When she twisted her head to ask the gull what it meant, the bird squawked, "You know the answer, Rebecca." The face metamorphosed into that of Jo Delacroix.

She rolled onto her side. Hagan was not lying in bed next to her. She wasn't exactly sure why not. Despite his romantic suggestion, he had not helped her out of the limp designer dress. Granted, Ian's interruption had deflated a passionate moment, but it could have been restoked. Instead, they'd both backed off, slipped into the more comfortable role of colleagues. They'd sat up for another hour, draining the champagne, speculating on questions like who locked Ian out of the mobile home, and whether Jasmine would risk introducing herself after Hagan's attempt to snag her at the track.

"I told Carlson the kid was my daughter."

"You what?"

"It was the first thing that came into my mind. Probably because I've been thinking about my father lately, which is mostly your doing."

Following that announcement, Hagan had become atypically open, which was far more startling than sex would have been. He talked about growing up without a father, rebelling against overbearing grandparents, taking up smoking cigarettes and becoming a cop. He'd given up smoking when his mother remarried, to a man who was asthmatic. His mother's second union edged perilously close to the subject of David Semple—one subject neither wanted to discuss.

Hagan sidestepped it by jumping on Jo's bandwagon, insisting that she had been extremely lucky in her upbringing. By the time she'd acknowledged how blessed she was, and defended her decision to avoid her parents until she'd thought it through, she hadn't felt up to an amorous encounter. He didn't press her.

Perhaps they both wanted the first time to be perfect and knew last night it would have been as lackluster as the rainwater pooling on the patio.

She rolled over, flattened her face into the pillow. Thoughts of Hagan hadn't woken her. Remembering that the original windshield had to be installed on the Lotus for the press photo had. Peyton was a stickler about authenticity. She didn't blame him, particularly since the splintered reproduction glass was being held together with duct tape. She would have to pop over to the track and install the original before the media showed. Hagan could enjoy his beauty sleep for another couple of hours. With luck, she'd be back before he knew she'd left.

Decision made, she shuffled to the bathroom for a brief shower. A clean red turtleneck, team coveralls in white-and-gold-quilted Nomex, a dab of makeup to minimize the circles under her eyes, and she was ready to meet the press.

She tiptoed down the hallway and paused outside the door of the spare bedroom. Cocked her head. *Could she hear light snoring coming from the darkened room?* Even money said Hagan slept on his stomach like an infant, blankets tangled between his legs.

There was one way to find out.

Wrapping her palm around the doorknob, she turned it away from the jam. The tongue clicked as it retracted. Not locked. Her hand grew slick on the knob as she hesitated, not breathing. *Should I?*

She bit at her lip, wagged her head from side to side. *Not now.* The car had to be made ready. They could be alone after her required appearance at the track. Judging from last night, they might be able to sort things out. Hagan was making the effort to open up. She should be willing to do the same.

In the kitchen, she propped a note against the toaster for Ian, telling him she'd see him at the track. Hagan's note she slipped under his bedroom door where he'd be sure to trip on it.

The photographer from *The Indianapolis Star* had agreed to be at the tent by eight A.M. to take publicity shots. Peyton, in turn, had extracted promises from Ian and Rebecca that they would be suited up, looking perky and confident for the camera. He was thrilled to get coverage for his team alongside the Formula One write-ups. He couldn't wait to see his name on the same page as Frank Williams and Ross Braun. The Sunday paper would have an entire twenty-four-page section devoted to race coverage.

Outside, there was just enough light to see the numbers on her watch: six thirty-eight. Plenty of time. The morning air was cool, clouds were breaking up. It promised to be a brighter day than yesterday in lots of ways.

She trotted briskly down Hulman Avenue and crossed the wooden foot bridge at Twenty-second Street, slowed to watch geese pull at the reeds in the gutter. A fat one had definitely gotten up on the wrong side of the bed. He squawked whenever another bird found a tasty blade. Normally, their squabbles would have been drowned out by the distant roar of race cars circling the track. Not this early. The cars were under wraps, waiting for their chance to shine.

She entered the track through Gate 10. One of the senior security guards was just coming on duty. Holding the edge of a foam cup with his front teeth as he zipped up his jacket, he nodded, checked his Timex in mock horror at the early hour and wished her a good day.

"I'm counting on it, Henry."

She followed Shaw Road as it cut through the infield without seeing another person. Drinking in the silence, the inactivity, she felt in control. Early mornings at the newspaper had been her favorite time. Only a few early risers milled about and the phones were blessedly quiet—both were conducive to creativity.

Today she didn't have to be creative, just attach the Plexiglas windshield so the Lotus would be ready for its publicity stills. Tighten a few nuts, say cheese for the cameraman and she could do as she pleased for the remainder of the day. She would have whistled, if she could pucker up and carry a tune.

In the half light, the paddock tents looked dingy. They were limp, coated with heavy dew. The sides had been lowered and lashed together in anticipation of last night's storm, ropes knotted around the pitons hammered into the tarmac. All should have been safe and secure.

But it wasn't. Partway along—near where the Lotus sat—a loose section of canvas luffed in the breeze like a sail at dusk.

She circled the tent to investigate. Tom, or more likely Johnny, must have forgotten to tie off the ropes and they'd worked loose in the wind. An irritating oversight. Mentioning it could wait until after the race. There was no point in relacing; the sides would be removed shortly anyway. She rolled the flap back and tied it out of the way.

Sufficient light drifted in through the opening to guide her to the tool chest. She rooted in the drawer for a rachet and a flashlight. As she closed the drawer a gust of wind kicked up a candy bar wrapper, riffled the sides of the tent on its way in.

It was then that the odor assaulted her nostrils.

The hairs on the back of her neck prickled as if alive with static electricity. She froze. Suspended breathing. Listened.

Nothing. No movement. No noise.

She scanned the periphery of the tent, eyes skimming the shadows beyond each low-slung chassis, between the tool chests. Nothing unusual except the smell.

She twisted in the direction of the race car. Nothing remarkable at all except the smell.

And the shapeless mass filling the cockpit like dough rising in a bread pan. *What the devil*—

Rebecca swallowed. Forcing herself to relinquish her hold on the tool chest, she fumbled with the switch on the flashlight. The beam shook as she played it over the humped shape in the car, trying to make sense of it. Stared through the gloom until it evolved into the bent shoulders of a person.

Oh, God, no.

The flashlight slipped from her hand, smacked the tarmac and rolled, flashing circles of light around the tent. The wrench fell at her feet.

Her hand flew to her mouth as she smothered a

gasp. She should have seen it coming. Two days ago, when the shot exploded out of nowhere, a premonition should have followed it like a contrail.

The shot had been a warning.

Not a prank, not an accident. It had been a prelude to this.

But no frisson had shivered up her neck. The bullet sank into the tarmac and its threat slipped from sight. She was so concerned with the image she presented to the crew that she'd accepted the party line and dismissed it as an act of petty intimidation. After venting to Jo, after Hagan arrived, she'd brushed it aside and gotten on with her work.

Her hands fell in fists to her sides. *How could she have been so blasé? So obsessed in her own problems that she'd ignored the impending danger?*

Breathing deeply through her open mouth, she tried to steady the pounding in her chest, to diffuse the odors of urine, sweat, fear and fried electrical wiring. Reluctant to touch the car, she squatted down, balanced on the balls of her feet, straddled the puddle oozing from under the Lotus. Too frazzled to hunt for the flashlight, she wrapped an arm across her chest and waited for her eyes to adjust enough to separate substance from shadow.

Gradually, the body came into focus.

It had been strapped into the cockpit. The left leg was stretched out, invisible beneath the housing; the right knee banged against the steering wheel. The shoulders were hunched forward, pale hands flopped palms-up in his lap. His head was bowed by the weight of the helmet, in an attitude of defeat or supplication.

There was no blood that she could see. No indication of a wound. Just the reek of burnt flesh.

She closed her eyes, conscious that the water from last night's storm was seeping into her shoes. She should reach out, feel his neck for a pulse. Unsnap the harness pinning his body tight against the seat. Go through the motions. She should tilt the head upright, remove the garish green and orange helmet or at least raise the smoked visor and gaze at his face in death.

She couldn't do it. She didn't want to see one more body up-close. This one would be personal.

It was someone else's turn. Curling her fingers over the damp edge of the cockpit, she shivered, gripped hard and hoisted herself to standing.

Outside the tent she began jogging, cutting through the mist back to Gate 10 to find Henry. He would know what to do. He was a security guard, an impersonal official trained to take charge.

Over the rim of his coffee cup he watched her coming closer, her ragged run telegraphing the message that something was wrong. He listened to her disjointed plea, blanched as he set down the foam cup, then knocked it over reaching for his two-way radio. Taking her word for what she'd found, he connected with the security office, yelled that they should call 911, send the ambulance from the emergency center. And tell the police to hurry.

Rebecca hadn't brought her cell phone; she begged to use his. He freed it from his pocket with shaky fingers and handed it over. She dialed the house.

No one answered.

Henry told her to stay put, wait for the others. "I'll go keep watch."

She ignored him. Arms locked around her ribs, she retraced her route to the tent, to the car with its body. She tried to stay in observer mode, keep her mind switched off. Tried to keep from wishing she'd opened the door to the guest bedroom and seen Hagan sleeping there. Witnessed Ian puttering in the kitchen, amusing her with a limerick. She cursed both of them for not answering her phone call.

Henry plodded along behind her, puffing to keep up. At the tent, they halted. Neither wanted to go inside. They waited, upper arms touching in support.

The paramedics arrived within minutes. They barely listened as Rebecca told her story. They were already moving in under the canvas, barking orders with lowered voices, as much deflated by the weather as in deference to the victim.

She remained outside, staring in, tensed as they lifted the visor of the race helmet. Craned her neck to the side. There were too many technicians bustling around and she was too far away to catch a glimpse of the driver's face.

But she saw the oxygen mask quickly fastened into place. Heard them call for an IV.

She and Henry exchanged stunned glances—the victim was alive.

Henry sighed, braced her arm as she sank down onto the retaining wall. She still didn't know who was strapped into the car, but his synapses were firing, he was capable of breath. She took a deep one of her own, held out her hand for Henry's cell phone. Willing her fingers steady enough to punch the tiny buttons, she tried the house again. "Come on, Hagan, put down your coffee, come in from the patio, answer the damn phone. Tell me Ian's on his way over."

No one picked up.

Patting the guard's arm, she rose, and handed back his phone. "I can't stand it. I have to know." Henry nodded. He understood, but he wasn't moving any closer. He could live with the uncertainty a few minutes longer.

Rebecca entered the tent. After terse negotiations with an unshaven technician, she was permitted inside the circle hovering around the victim. Before she could bend down, someone on the opposite side hollered, asked if she could remove the windshield so they could get the vic free of the chassis.

His sidekick shook his head. "That's not the problem. Damn belt's stuck. Going to have to cut it."

"Stuck? I doubt it." She'd checked the release yesterday; it worked fine. If a fire broke out, she wanted Ian out of there fast. She leaned into the cockpit to demonstrate.

A hand grabbed her arm and tugged her upright, smack against a substantial bulk of a Speedway cop. The black uniform was stretched taut across his stomach. A frown cut across his face. She bent back far enough to read his name badge—*Chief Leonard Patten*. He gripped her other arm. "Hold on, Miss. Can't have you messing with things."

She yanked free. Explained that she was only going to show them how to release the harness.

"Nope." The chief's stomach swelled. "You tell me how it works. You don't touch a thing."

Drawn forward by the figure in the car, she acquiesced, moved along the car weaving between two technicians.

They'd removed the helmet and fastened on a neck brace to stabilize the head. The face was tilted away from her, obscured by the oxygen mask. It was in three-quarter profile: eyes closed, mouth sagging open, a spittle of drool rolled down his chin. She had no trouble recognizing him.

A tear started to swell in one eye. She shook her head in relief, sank to her knees.

It wasn't Hagan. Not that she'd really expected it to be. There was no reason for him to be at the track; no possible explanation why he would crawl into a race car. But in the dark hours sometimes she was irrational, fearing that the fates were sadistic enough to strike when they could inflict the most pain. With her once-secure past breaking up on the rocks, she wanted to look ahead. She didn't want to lose Hagan without knowing if they had a future. He was a friend.

The victim wasn't Ian—the most logical person to be in the cockpit. If he'd woken early he might have come over to commune with the deserted track, or just to sit in his car and meditate on the upcoming race. He'd been unnerved Friday by the gunshot, complained about not being able to practice on Saturday because he didn't want downtime to dull his edge. Thankfully, he was sulking elsewhere.

Nor was the inert body Wayne Evans. The snide crew chief might have remembered that the windshield needed to be changed. He could have come to the track early to do it. It would take only a few minutes to show up the lax mechanic and win points with his boss for efficiency. That would have appealed to Evans. In this case, though, his boss wouldn't have appreciated it.

The victim strapped in the car was Peyton Madison.

Rebecca placed a hand on his shoulder and squeezed, doubting he was aware of her or anything else.

What was he doing unconscious in the race car? Last seen, he'd been chatting up guests at St. Elmo. If she'd overheard correctly, he and Elise Carlson had planned to keep the party alive. If that had fizzled, why wouldn't he have retired to his suite at the Canterbury Hotel? What would have induced him to come to the track before dawn and crawl into the Lotus? Unlike most team owners, he had no interest in driving. Or did he? Was it possible he secretly fantasized about taking it for a spin around the track in the dark, no headlights. So he hopped in and then what—passed out?

No. No way. No how.

Peyton had not sat in the car willingly. His arms were pinned against his ribs by the shoulder straps, hands flattened against his thighs under the lap belt. He was held securely in place, no chance of escape.

And he hadn't just passed out. Someone had helped him lose consciousness. Underlying the stench of body fluids, lingered the smell of singed hair. An assailant had harnessed him into the cockpit and—

The chief tapped her shoulder, pointed in the direction of the car. "Thought you were going to show me how?"

Gesturing, she indicated which way to turn the release and gave him room. The medical personnel grumbled: They'd already tried it. No stinking luck. They were vindicated when it wouldn't turn for the chief either. She wasn't surprised. The other whiff she'd recognized in the cockpit was glue.

She squeezed past Patten and crossed to the far side of the car, stubbing her toe, tripping on a battery charger en route. On the ledge of the double-decker tool chest was a tube of epoxy. It had been pinched in the middle. Cap off, a drop seeped from the tip. Had the assailant brought it with him? If not, and it was the team's tube, how had he known where to find it? And why drag out the battery charger? Had he been planning to start the car?

When she looked up, Chief Patten was watching her. She pointed at the tube without touching it. Said it could explain why the buckle wouldn't unfasten. "Will you let me unbolt the harness from the frame rather than have them cut it?"

He wheezed in disgust. "We'll see. First you explain what else's bothering you. Your eyes are roving all over the ground like that Indian that went west with Lewis and Clark."

"Sacagawea. She looked up, following the flight of birds."

With the toe of her boot, she indicated the battery charger. It was usually stashed next to the tool chest.

Someone had attached jumper cables, plopped it in the middle of the open space inches from the puddle that had settled under the car.

The chief shrugged. "Probably one of your crew left it out."

"I stowed it myself yesterday before leaving." She squatted down and pointed. "If you look closely, you can see scorch marks on the asphalt."

Patten remained erect. "So what."

"So, it's possible that your perp was hiding in the shadows on this side of the car. He heard Peyton approach, waited for him to step into the puddle then zapped it with the jumper cables. The puddle water would have conducted the current under the car and into him."

The chief grabbed at the nearest technician. "That dinky charger be enough to knock a guy unconscious?

The tech bent to look then nodded. "On boost, yeah, enough voltage to shock him. Fifty volts of juice. Would have stunned him long enough to wrestle his weight into the car. For sure."

Patten slapped his foot at the edge of the puddle. Rebecca mouthed *Jaup* as the muddy water splattered his trousers. His frown deepened. "The perp's so sure this guy's coming that he's got the battery charger ready and waiting? Got glue in hand to hogtie him so he can't hop out and run away. Why? Who in his right mind would go to all that trouble? Simpler to just shoot him. Make my life a whole lot easier. I was looking forward to a simple corpse." He pushed closer to Rebecca. "That was what you said, right? A body.

Why the hell didn't you check his pulse first? You look brighter than that, Moore."

Brighter was questionable. She was definitively experienced enough, but she was too weary to explain about the recent spate of dead bodies in her life and her fear of becoming one of them.

She pointed at the inert body. "Why is he still unconscious? The initial shock would have worn off fairly quickly, wouldn't it? But he's still comatose hours later."

Or wasn't it hours later? Could the assailant have left just minutes before she'd arrived? Maybe he heard her approach? Not a comforting thought.

Patten had more immediate problems. Eyeing the young trooper dusting the battery charger for prints, he flapped a hand in her direction. "You get that windshield off, undo the belt, so the medics can help this man."

She was already pulling a socket and rachet from the drawer. Four layers of local police clustered around to watch her work: Speedway Police, Marion County Sheriff's department, Indianapolis City Police and the State Police. The last seemed to be the alpha dogs, which didn't sit well with Patten.

When she finished, she escaped from the bustle under the tent and rejoined Henry. It was seven forty-five. That didn't seem possible. Time had slowed down and sped up simultaneously. Ian and the photographer from the *Star* should arrive any minute. She hoped Hagan would be tagging along and that he'd be allowed to take her home. From past experience, she

knew that was unlikely. Once again, she asked Henry
for his phone, this time to call her lawyer.

She was listening to the unanswered ring when Ian
arrived. Ignored by the police and medics, he gravi-
tated to her side, fidgeted until she finished leaving a
message. "What's going on, Reb? Who's in the
bloody car?"

"Peyton."

"What? Why?" Ian turned sheet white, not a good
color for news photographs. He begged for details.
Hearing them, he fell silent, stared at his car as if it
had come to life like the toys in *The Nutcracker* and
been responsible for the heinous act. Or been violated
by it. She touched his arm, asked where he'd been, he
mumbled, "Out jogging."

"Did you see Hagan?"

"Don't ask."

He was having trouble taking it all in. He started
several sentences then aborted them, letting his
thoughts fade like ripples dissolving on the shore. She
gave him a hug, which he barely returned. It was understandable. She was nearly two hours ahead of him
in assimilating the incident and its impact on the race
tomorrow. Until contradicted, she was proceeding as
if Peyton would recover and want the team to race as
scheduled.

The EMTs lifted his limp body from the cockpit
and onto a stretcher. It was done smoothly, with no
damage to the car. After a good scrubbing, the Lotus
would be ready to run. Assuming Ian felt up to it.
When she asked, he shrugged and walked away.

Nineteen

By ten o'clock, Mick was pacing. Moore hadn't returned from the photo shoot. He'd been disappointed
to find her gone and the house empty when he finally
rolled out of bed, but took heart when he read her
note: *Back by eight-thirty or nine. The rest of the day
is ours.*

Okay.

He'd dressed and was nosing in the refrigerator
when Browning appeared, looking much too well
rested. Obviously he hadn't tossed and turned all
night. His sunny smile rankled. Mick leaned back
against the counter. "So, Browning, how come you
weren't booked on a drug charge when your sister
overdosed? Too young? No prior offenses? Or was
your daddy too well-connected to mess with?"

Browning blanched like someone had gut-punched
him. Orange juice trickled down the corner of his
mouth as he set the carton down. "Occupational haz-
ard, Hagan? Can't keep your nose out of other peo-

ple's business? I thought you were here to protect Rebecca? I'm no threat. I wouldn't hurt her."

He tried to storm from the room. Mick caught him by the elbow. "Why is that? You two have a special relationship I should know about?"

The minute the words were out of his mouth, he bit his cheek. *Idiot.*

A—it was none of his business. He had no claims on Moore; she was an adult and free to chose her own partners. B—he didn't believe it. There was no chemistry between her and the driver. He would know; Moore couldn't act. She was too transparent. Every expression registered on her face.

Besides, he'd tiptoed through the house for a room check in the early morning. Browning was passed out on one of the twins in the third bedroom.

Color returning to normal, Browning waded in for round two. "You know so much about my past, Hagan, you should be able to figure out Rebecca's attraction for me. No? Well, let me show you."

He fled the room, bare feet slapping down the hallway. When he returned, he was holding a dog-eared color photograph of a teenage girl, presumably his sister, Katherine. Mick took it. There was a superficial resemblance to Moore, something about the eyes, slender neck and the tilt of her head. No way identical, but close enough to strike a chord in someone who still blamed himself for his sister's death.

"I know Rebecca isn't Katherine come back to life, but it makes me feel good seeing her around, talking to her openly, the way I imagine I would have talked to Katie. If I thought Rebecca was at risk, I'd force her to leave here. How could I live with myself if something happened to her because I'd ignored the potential danger? Again. I was an immature brat when Katie and I went to that party. I don't have that excuse now."

Mick returned the photograph. "Is that why you race? Keep putting yourself in harms' way waiting for the fatal crash and instant oblivion?"

"I guess." Browning slumped into a chair at the table. "That, and the expense really annoys my father."

Mick leaned over. "Don't count on a quick death, boy. The gods are sadistic sods. They get a kick out of letting you live with your nightmares."

Browning was still staring at the dingy linoleum floor when Mick left the house in search of an all-American, midwestern breakfast. After that he planned to check out area motels. He was ashamed of how hard he'd come down on the race driver, but he wasn't going to let Browning get in the way of time alone with Moore. If the driver was going to camp out in the third bedroom, alternative private lodgings would be desirable. Make that mandatory. Somewhere with locks on the door, room service and a guarantee of anonymity.

A short walk from the diner, he stumbled upon a fifties motel tucked away on a side street. A time-warped relic, it was a place Jack Kerouac would have included in a travelogue. No room service, but it had plenty of ambiance. Only six tiny cabins separated by irregular swatches of grass. A single window box was nailed to the front of each one, festooned with plastic mums stuck in the dirt. The end unit was masked from the houses on the neighboring street by a row of white pines. You could smell them through the open window. He gave the hobbling Dolores a deposit and said he'd need the room for three nights.

He'd been working on rationalizations for Moore. Using the motel tonight would allow Browning to be alone at the house, get a good night's sleep before the race. Tomorrow night, he'd want to celebrate with friends, or drown his sorrows; both better done without them as audience. And Monday, well, that was backup in case the rent on the house ran out once the race was over. There was no reason he and Moore had to scurry back to Maryland. Maybe they'd see something of Indianapolis that didn't smell of gasoline.

His planning presupposed that she wanted to be alone with him. Last night she seemed to.

He was feeling pretty smug until he got to the curb. In the ten minutes he'd chitchatted with Dolores, hoodlums had smashed the driver's side window. The safety glass had shattered into a thousand glass pellets. A brick lay in the gutter next to the tire.

He swept the shards from the seat and drove to Patricia Street, where he called the insurance company. They didn't sound any more broken up about the heap than he was.

At ten fifteen, when a bell sounded, he nearly lunged for the phone, then realized it was the front door. He opened it to the feisty coot he'd met at the shipping store the day before. Forty pounds overweight, cigarette dangling from his lips despite talking through a trach tube in his throat. The guy had agreed to deliver Zimmer's return fax as soon as it came in. He licked his lips as he handed over two pages and took thirty dollars for his trouble.

No surprise that two sets of fingerprints got hits in AFIS. He was betting that both Tom, the yuppie Rastafarian, and Chet Davis would show up in the federal data banks. But Davis was either law-abiding or he'd never been caught. Tom, whose last name turned out to be Benedictine, was less than monk-like. Or maybe closer to it. His offenses were minor and involved purchasing substances that might induce mystical meditation. No wonder Tom was perpetually smiling.

Wayne Evans was a surprise, though maybe he shouldn't have been. He turned out to be a convicted pugilist, printed a decade before for a drunk and disorderly in Connecticut. Bar brawl over a woman who was dating a member of a rival car team. That fit. Evans still liked to drink and preferred flashy women who exuded pheromones. Booze and a temper could make Evans something of a liability around race cars.

Mick made a note to ask Moore about Evans's past work experiences. If he had a history of losing jobs because of the bottle, it could explain his don't-rock-the-boat attitude. Peyton might be his last chance at steady employment. Or, conversely, it could justify his buttering up Whitten as a safety net. The old swinging monkey theory: Don't let go of one branch until you've got a grip on the next.

When the phone finally rang, Mick knocked it off the table grabbing for it. He shouldn't have bothered.

It was Delacroix, sounding as mellifluous as James

Earl Jones's younger brother. Clearly audible, even as a loudspeaker made a garbled announcement in the background.

Yes, Mick muttered, he'd arrived safely. *Yes,* Moore was fine so far. The belle of the track, the queen of pit lane. No one had shot at her in days. The only tension seemed to surround ridiculously heavy wagering on the F1 race. Sure, he would let Jo talk to Moore, only she wasn't there. No, he didn't know precisely where she was, or when she would return.

He could hear a chill like Montreal in January settle in the lawyer's voice. "I thought you were there to protect her, Hagan? Isn't that difficult to do when you can't find her?"

"Don't get testy. She's fine. At the track posing for front-page publicity."

"She'd better not be posing as a corpse. Have her call me." Delacroix hung up.

The phone rang again before Mick could find a house key to lock up. He expected it to be Delacroix annoying him again with more words of sagacity. The term fit the lawyer to a tee—from the Latin, all wise and foreseeing. It even contained the word *saga,* as in a long tale of heroic deeds. Nothing Delacroix liked better than an epic with a moral.

Mick snapped *hello* into the receiver. Heard nothing but empty air, light breathing. Finally there came Moore's voice, barely a whisper. She asked if he would join her at the track, in the historic cars' paddock area. Please. Very formal: clipped tight sentences, emotions being held in check.

He forgot about Delacroix. Forgot about how late it

was, how annoyed he was because she'd slipped out. Kicked himself for planning a sexual interlude while Moore was off somewhere getting into trouble. Hell of a bodyguard.

He whistled softly into the receiver. "You want to tell me what's going on?"

"Just come. Please."

He ran the three-quarters of a mile to the track. It wasn't likely to kill him. Once a year during PT quals, he was pretty good at the timed-mile, which frosted a lot of his coworkers, especially the ones who did five miles a day just to stay limber. Barely panting, he stumbled into the crime scene eight minutes after Moore called.

She was sitting cross-legged on a concrete wall, mesmerized by the length of crime scene tape that had come loose at one end and fluttered straight out from a tent post. A stoop-shouldered security type—about sixty, with Egg McMuffin crumbs on his stomach—guarded her like a pit bull. There were five police officers hanging around: two Staties, a local cop and two very local Speedway uniforms. The head trooper had Browning cornered inside the tent. Evans and Elise Carlson were conferring with an earnest youngster representing the Speedway. Everyone else stared as he entered the pit area.

Moore jumped down from the wall, trotted over, gave him a soulful look before burying her face in his shoulder. His arms went around her; he squeezed gently. When she made no move to pull away, he nuzzled her hair, relishing the feel and smell of it before whispering, "Somebody dead?"

She mumbled into his shirt front. "No. Not yet. Maybe not. It's Peyton."

"Your boss? What happened?"

She led him to the retaining wall and introduced the security guard. She asked Henry if he thought he could find two cups of coffee. He said he could probably find three and went off to fetch them. Mick sat. Moore paced, related the macabre details of discovering Peyton's unconscious body in the race car with the battery charger nearby.

"Mick, he was strapped in, the buckle frozen shut with epoxy. The EMT thinks someone was torturing him, shocking him with the boost voltage from the charger. There are clamp marks from the jumper cables, bruises, singed hair. Who would do that? Why? What was he doing here in the pitch dark?"

He gave up searching pockets for a toothpick. Picked up one of Moore's hands and played with her fingers. "Didn't Browning say he was locked out of the motor home? It's reasonable that Peyton was the one inside. It's his RV, right? Maybe he woke up restless, walked to the pits for exercise. Sat in the race car to see how it felt?"

"Slid into the car and then what? Some demented psychopath happened by? Intrigued by the theory of electrical conductivity, he decides to experiment on Peyton?"

"You have a better explanation?"

She raked her fingers through the hair he'd just nuzzled. She agreed up to a point. Peyton might have fretted over more sabotage to the car, so decided to play it safe by spending the night at the track. "It doesn't look like he planned to sleep. He was dressed, well, half-changed into a crew neck sweater over the tuxedo pants and dress shoes."

"Clothes he could have pulled on in a hurry, whatever was handy? Have the cops checked out the motor home yet?"

She shook her head, set her waves bouncing. "Too busy interrogating us and pacifying Carlson. They know where their paychecks come from, particularly the Speedway cops. Race revenue. That means bowing and scraping to her. She didn't wait for the bet to be decided, she bought into the team last night. Committed two million for next season in exchange for fifty percent ownership. Peyton left a message on Evans's answering machine. He sounded as giddy as a kid at his sixth birthday party. At her insistence, the cops have agreed to release the car in time for us to prep it for Sunday's race. Everything will proceed as normal."

"Minus your boss."

"Replaced by Elise Carlson."

Twenty

With his nose pressed against the scratched window, Jo watched the approach into Logan Airport. It was much like landing on an island. The plane circled over the Atlantic, banked, skimmed along the water of Boston Harbor and hit the runway facing into the strong off-shore winds.

He disembarked, strode through the airport carrying only a briefcase and looking like a successful businessman who didn't realize, or care, that it was an unseasonably warm Saturday morning, tailor-made for planning a pre-game cookout.

Only a handful of tourists lined the curb waiting for cabs. His driver was a gaunt Slav who wore a battered woolen cap pulled low on his forehead despite the sun baking the interior of the car. He nodded at the downtown address and activated the meter. Before he'd pulled away from the curb, he began chatting about the Red Sox and kept it up until they cleared the tunnel. When he tired of Jo's one-word responses, he turned his attention to the pre-game show on the radio. Jo asked him to turn the volume up. He didn't listen, but welcomed the mindless distraction.

The house at 27 State Street was three stories high, built from old rose brick, with tall windows on the bottom floor. It was set back from the sidewalk far enough to permit four pink tea roses to bloom in the full afternoon sun. A low wrought-iron fence abutted the sidewalk and turned the corner invitingly, promising a secret garden out back away from prying eyes. The fence wouldn't keep intruders out, but it clearly separated those who lived inside from the riffraff passing by.

Jo paused at the gate. The briefcase, a near-empty prop for the upcoming scene, dragged at his arm. He was about to meddle in Rebecca's life without her permission. She would not thank him. She might not forgive him. Still, it was something he needed to do, and he was here now. He strode up the steps and rang the brass bell.

The woman who answered the door was squat, wrinkled and dressed totally in black. Flour dusted the front of her skirt. Without doubt, she was the housekeeper who had doted over the young Rebecca and loved to attend funerals.

Jo smiled. "Mrs. Bellotti?"

Her black marble eyes widened then narrowed. "Don't have no rich relatives to die and leave me money. So why's a lawyer's come calling on Saturday?"

"What makes you think I'm a lawyer?"

Mrs. Bellotti snorted as if it were only too obvious.

He set down his briefcase. "Guilty. But I'm not here to see you. I'm here on behalf of Rebecca Moore. I'm expected."

The woman's face sagged and her eyes clouded with concern. She turned and waddled into the house, leaving him framed in the open doorway.

Before Jo could fish out a handkerchief to polish his glasses, Robert Moore emerged from a room at the back of the house. He raised his head and walked briskly toward him. Rebecca's father was slender, perhaps six feet tall, dressed in weekend khakis and a button-down shirt. His shoulders were squared but bowed downward, as if from years of carrying work back and forth to the office, or weighted down by the deception of Rebecca's birth. He had dark hair, which was graying in streaks at the temples. Laugh lines were etched on his face by years of sailing. Under other circumstances, his smile might have been welcoming.

They shook hands. Robert led him into the library to the right of the door, then excused himself to fetch his wife. The room, with its dark green walls and white bookshelves, just missed being comfortable. It was too glossy with the sheen of new money trying to pass for old. The Oriental rug was undoubtedly authentic but not worn enough to bespeak of generations of use. Not yet faded by the intense sunlight slanting through the windows.

Outside, a cluster of children chattered as they drifted down the sidewalk. Inside it was hushed. Enjoying the moment's solitude, Jo traced a finger along the molding of the built-in bookcases, glanced at the titles. Sailing, architecture, history dominated the lower shelves. On the middle shelves, the covers of best-selling fiction were pristine, spines unbroken. Over the summer, he'd promised himself that he would transform the smallest bedroom at the farm into a reading room with bookshelves on all walls and a skylight overhead. Like many of his daydreams, it would have to wait.

Hearing footsteps, he turned. Pauline Moore entered the room ahead of her husband. When she paused to take stock of the lawyer, Robert stepped to her side.

It was easy to see how the couple had passed as Rebecca's parents. From Robert's family Rebecca had inherited the body type, as well as the shape of his eyes. But not the color: Hers were gray-green; his were Atlantic blue. From Pauline came the outward expressions: the erect posture, the tilt of her head, the nervous hand gestures. Unconsciously or intentionally, Rebecca had mimicked Pauline's mannerisms and her style.

Pauline finished crossing the room to Jo and took his hand. She was gracious, cordial because breeding dictated it, but mistrust showed in her eyes.

When she released his hand, he rocked back a half-step and nodded to them both. "Thank you for agreeing to see me on such short notice. I gave you the impression that I'm here in an official capacity. For that I must apologize. It's not the case. Mrs. Wetherly did not send me. Rebecca does not know that I'm here."

Robert faltered. "You said you were her lawyer?"

"I am. I'm also her friend." He opened his hands, palms up. "An interfering one, I'm afraid."

Pauline grinned and slipped out of the room. She returned with coffee and biscotti, off-loaded them onto a pie-edged cherry table. She sat opposite Jo while Robert lingered near the windows, looking out, apart from the civilities. Lost in his own thoughts, he might not have been listening.

Dunking a dried slice into the thin china cup, Pauline asked polite questions. Beneath her Bostonian accent, Jo heard a softer cadence. Occasionally a Southern expression popped through. Rebecca had never mentioned her mother's origins. Obviously not New England. "Natchez?"

Pauline looked startled. "Where I'm from? Nowhere so grand. A four-stop intersection west of New Orleans."

"You've strayed very far north."

"I came to be educated and stayed."

"Even when staying meant raising another couple's child, pretending she was your own?"

"Rebecca is family: Robert's niece. His brother was dead. It was the least we could do." She lowered her voice and cranked up the country charm. "Though believe me, lawyer, I would have suckled gator pups to stay in Robert's world." She pushed her cup aside. "Besides, it was no hardship; Robert and I wanted children."

"Yet hadn't had them, after what, seven years of marriage?"

Pauline shook crumbs from her fingers onto the napkin. "You've done your homework. And you are merciless. I understand why you and Rebecca get along."

Jo smiled. He didn't mind being considered ruthless like Rebecca. Perhaps he was more ruthless, for he'd discovered a chink in the very smooth veneer Pauline wore. One Rebecca would never have noticed. There was a story behind their initial lack of offspring.

Pauline left the room to refill the coffeepot. Jo blotted his lips on the small square of linen. He longed to ask Robert Moore the question taunting him: *Why did you never tell Rebecca the truth?* What would the man say? That at first Rebecca was too young to understand. Then as time passed it grew harder to explain. Everyone apparently accepted her as their daughter. Telling her the truth would have served no purpose, only inflicted hurt. As it was doing now. Hurt doubly painful because Rebecca could not tolerate half-truths. But Rebecca's father faced away from him, waited for his wife's footsteps before turning.

When Pauline sat, Jo linked his fingers like a boy in Sunday school. He'd had enough socializing. "How did you pull off the deception within the family?"

Pauline was not offended by his abruptness. She smiled a wide seductive grin. "It all fell into place so smoothly, Mr. Delacroix. It seemed like fate."

"Please, call me Jo."

She nodded as she continued. "So smoothly, Jo, it was like the gods had choreographed it. The lies simply became truths. Thanks largely to my mother."

She hitched her chair closer, putting her back to her husband. To shield him, or to exclude him? Perhaps to prevent his hearing a variation on the truth she'd fabricated especially for the nosy lawyer? Jo leaned back, ready to listen with the trained ear of a storyteller, with the jaded one of a lawyer.

Like a proper Southerner, Pauline began with her past. She claimed she was the product of the union between a mediocre insurance salesman and a failed Delta queen. Her mother, Suzanne Blanchard, had failed at so many things—marriage, child rearing, life—that she had no choice but to drink her sorrows away. When particularly drunk, which included those few occasions that she was invited to their holiday gatherings, Suzanne liked to remind her daughter that she likewise was a failure.

"No offspring, despite being married to a stud from such a fine, frigid family. Her words. More coffee?"

"No thank you."

She went on as if oblivious to Robert's presence. "When I could no longer tolerate her jibes, I announced I was pregnant. It was just to shut her up. I planned to 'lose' the baby before having to produce it. Then Jamie's sailboat capsized and we found Rebecca."

Her voice softened as conflicting emotions flickered across her face. He wondered how she would describe the event to a close friend: as one of the most overwhelming days of her life, or one of the most joyous? Or a little of both?

Robert walked into her range of vision, ending the confession. He picked up the story. "My mother-in-law's drinking was an asset, as was her distance. She lacked the money to travel and Pauline rarely returned to Louisiana."

At the mention of drinking, he crossed to a built-in cupboard and produced a bottle of Lillet, splashed the pale liquid into three etched glasses. He placed one near his wife's arm and handed another to Jo. It was too early for him, but he said nothing. Robert Moore invited him to stay for lunch. Jo declined, saying he had a twelve o'clock flight. Moore nodded before taking a sip.

"By the time Pauline's mother first held Rebecca, we'd convinced her that she had misremembered the birth date. Lied that our daughter had been born many months earlier. Pretended to be affronted that she couldn't even get her granddaughter's birth date correct. Rebecca was a petite infant and toddler, so the deception was plausible, if not totally convincing. I'm sure Suzanne has always suspected something wasn't quite kosher, but she can't deny the family resemblance. Most likely she assumes Rebecca is my love child, whom Pauline agreed to raise. It doesn't matter."

Except to Rebecca.

"And your own parents?"

Pauline took over the thread of the story so smoothly it seemed rehearsed, or at least pre-arranged, with each of them assigned specific chapters to narrate. She leaned forward, a fingernail trailing along the design in the glass. "As I said, the fates were kind. Thad and Eleanor Moore spent from nineteen sixty-five to seventy-eight in Europe. Thad was a economics professor assigned to a think tank in Geneva. They were totally immersed in his work and the circle of friends they'd made. In all that time, they returned to the States only once. They were dependant on my letters and Robert's occasional phone calls for news of home.

"Jamie was such a disappointment to them. He was their Peter Pan son who left home to sail out of any port that offered him a job on the water. He'd be gone for the better part of year and we'd never hear a word. Rebecca was six months old before we knew she existed. I'd never even held her before the accident. So—"

She pushed back, opening out to include her husband. "So, we agreed to not tell Thad and Eleanor that their youngest son had sired a child out of wedlock. Somehow writing, 'PS your bum-of-a-son has a bastard daughter,' seemed a bit déclassé. We allowed Jamie and Nicole time to decide what they were going to do with their lives."

Jo met her stare, thinking: *Or were you waiting until you also had produced an heir?* Pauline Moore did not impress him as the sort who would settle for princess when the crown was up for grabs.

Robert circled to stand behind her chair. "Mother had a severe case of bronchitis the spring Jamie and Nicole died in the sailing accident. The doctor would not allow her to leave Geneva and fly back for the funeral. She was immensely despondent. So distraught that we added a direct lie to the earlier one of omission. Having never told them about Jamie's child, we decided to pass Rebecca off as our own.

"Over the phone, I confessed to my mother that Pauline had given birth to a girl some months earlier. I took full blame for not telling them sooner, invented complications during the pregnancy and with the birth. Insisted that Rebecca had been so sickly, we feared she would die. We hadn't wanted to burden my parents when they were too far away to do anything.

They were hurt, as you can imagine, but delighted to learn they had a grandchild. It helped get them through losing Jamie. Six months later, when they finally visited, Mother realized that Rebecca was nearer two years old than one. 'Overly precocious,' was how she phrased it. We told her the truth."

"She agreed to say nothing?"

Robert grinned for the first time that afternoon. "Not even to my father, who is oblivious to everything except the economic repercussions caused by political upheavals. Rebecca could have sprouted two heads and he would have patted each one without comment."

So a tragedy had been layered with lies and turned into a blessing. An undersized, perhaps undernourished orphan had been given a home and raised with every advantage. Pauline had produced an heir out of the cold Atlantic, quieting her mother and giving hope to her in-laws. Robert had been able to see glimpses of his dead brother live on in Rebecca. A near-perfect ending.

Not until he'd boarded his return flight did Jo analyze his meeting with Robert and Pauline Moore and term it a personal success. Despite his guilt over going there without Rebecca's knowledge, he felt relieved. He'd given her parents some insight into Rebecca's state of mind. Ammunition that might help them deal with her. He had no right to do that, but he'd known that before he boarded the plane in DC. What he didn't know was how they would react to him. As it turned out, he was going home with a heavier briefcase and a lighter heart.

As Robert was walking him to the door, Pauline had rummaged in the bookshelf. She handed him a photo album and a bound Moore family genealogy with a cracked spine. Both were for Dorothea Wetherly, to provide her concrete evidence of her granddaughter's family. While she would never know Jamie, she could study every phase of his early years. Lower her magnifying glass and pour over snapshots—curled rectangles in black and white, which revealed so much apparent in the grown Rebecca. Dorothea would be pleased.

What pleased him was their acceptance of him as a friend who cared for their daughter.

Though too old to need it, he'd never outgrown the need for parental approval. Pauline's was laced with wry understanding; Robert's was more reserved, but he hadn't dismissed Jo through the back door.

They didn't ask if his relationship with Rebecca extended beyond friendship, which was just as well. What would he have answered? That he cared enough to risk his life to save her from drowning? He would do it again without hesitation if necessary. He would save her over and over and over, like a dream you repeat nightly, hoping that the ending will change.

Or praying it won't.

He would protect Rebecca because he had not saved his first love. There had been no parental approval then, from either family. Yet now Angelica's father, Thomas Levy, was dying and wanted to see him. As the captain announced their final approach into Ronald Reagan National Airport, Jo leaned heavily against the seat and watched the sun blaze vermillion above the Potomac. In three days he would be on another airplane, traveling into his past. With luck, he would meet with Levy and finally have answers.

Twenty-one

After two and a half hours of unrelieved boredom, Mick got his fifteen minutes of Indiana fame giving his statement to the cops. Neither State Trooper Gunn nor Chief Patten of the Speedway Police was impressed with Mick's police credentials. The rookie was skeptical that he'd come all the way to Indy to attend a race he didn't care about. "How could a man not care about open-wheel racing?"

Mick assumed that was a rhetorical question and let it pass.

The officers were irritated that neither Hagan, Ian Browning nor Rebecca Moore could vouch for each other's whereabouts in the hours just before the body was found, despite the fact that they were sharing a house. Which seemed too cozy and a mite peculiar. Particularly to the cop with the dimple. He'd gotten a good look at Moore. Even in a race suit, the package looked prime, for an older woman. The kid snorted. No way she should sleep alone with two men in the house. Mick didn't blame him. Sounded pretty unbelievable to him, too.

Gunn's patience ran out faster than Mick's questions. He ordered him to stop asking, since he wasn't about to answer any more. Professional courtesy aside, the trooper saw no reason to share his findings with Lieutenant Hagan. "I will confirm that, at the moment, we're treating the case as an assault by person or persons unknown, for reasons unknown. As soon as we talk to Mr. Madison we may know more, which I will not be sharing with outsiders." Gunn walked away.

Mick turned to Patten, cajoled him for the name of the hospital where Peyton had been taken, claiming Moore would want to send flowers. Maybe she would. Maybe flowers delivered to her ailing boss would assuage her guilt and they could hibernate for the rest of the day, lick each other's wounds. He'd ask her as soon as she was free.

At present, she was giving her statement to another officer for the official, soon-to-be-typed-and-signed version. Elise Carlson stood a few feet away, waiting for her turn to speak to her mechanic. In contrast to last night's party mood, the lady was somber. No longer soignée, though still elegantly groomed. Her daytime attire consisted of Brooks Brothers' resort wear: navy silk trousers and matching turtleneck, tan tweed blazer, cigarettes in the breast pocket behind a crest. She was the most put-together person milling around on the tarmac.

He sidled over to commiserate with Browning and the security guard. One direct question about where the race teams kept their transportation elicited the information he wanted. There was lust in the security guard's voice as he described the mother of all motor homes belonging to Peyton Madison. "Can't miss it. It's parked right outside the track, lot two. Size of a Greyhound bus and painted in the team's colors of red, white and gold. License plate says *PM003*."

Mick exited at the nearest gate, walked down Sixteenth Street, turned right on Georgetown and crossed at the light. Lot number two, reserved for RV parking, was maybe an eighth-of-a-mile walk from the pit area. If, as Moore suspected, Madison had slept in the bus to keep an eye on the race car, how would he have known that an intruder was messing about in the tent? Was he doing rounds of the track every hour on the hour? Why not just hire a security guard, pay Henry overtime to come on duty early?

The lot was packed full of motor homes like he'd never seen in a roadside campground. These were upscale, country-club cousins of those advertised on the Tom Raper Mobile Homes billboards that flashed by every two miles on Interstate 80. He could hear people stirring in a few as he walked past. The odor of coffee wafted from an open door. Some ambitious nomad had erected a Weber grill outside on the pavement and was frying bacon on a griddle.

Peyton's bus was parked diagonally near the back, taking up at least six spaces while warding off all neighbors. It was impressive, even if you found bus travel less appealing than tandem bicycling. Shiny, freshly painted, smoked-glass windows. In addition to being a block long, both sides of the bus expanded outward a couple of feet, making it look like one of those toads that puffed out its cheeks to attract mates.

He circled the bus, listening. Other than the hum of a compressor, all was quiet, as expected.

When Browning had been dropped off after the party, his key wouldn't open the door to the bus. He'd pounded but no one answered. His timing might have been off. His boss might have been in the bathroom. Or passed out and didn't hear him. Or entertaining company and didn't want to be bothered. Hell, it was possible that he was already fried and unconscious in the race car and the perp was inside searching the bus. Just like he hoped to be.

He scanned the area looking for trash, retrieved a waxed hot dog wrapper from up against the chain-link fence. Used it when he inserted the key he'd borrowed from Browning into the lock, then placed the paper carefully over the chrome door latch and pulled. The latch released and the door swung open with an hydraulic whoosh. *Good.* No need for picks, no breaking and entering.

He hollered out *hello,* not sure what he'd say if someone answered.

No one did. He pulled himself up the two high steps into the bus and whistled in amazement. It wasn't a bus, it was a suite. The driver's and co-pilot's seats were white leather, swiveled at a touch. There was a matching leather banquette along the left side with a teak coffee table in front of it. Another seating arrangement on the right, then Corian counter with cabinets above, dishwasher below. Microwave, sink, bathroom with large glass shower stall, separated off by a sliding mirrored door. At the tail end was the master bedroom with queen-size bed and a wall of closets. All the comforts of home and then some.

For a second, he fantasized about packing in Moore and the cats. Start driving. Go wherever they wanted to go, stop when they felt like it. Eat at roadside diners, wear polyester and take lots of snapshots for the folks back home. Then he laughed, scratched at a stiff hair on his cheek. Moore wouldn't take time for a long weekend at the Jersey shore. She was driven. Just like he used to be.

Burnout, a common affliction among cops, had been lurking just around the corner ever since his step-brother's death. David Semple—product of his mother and her second husband—had been eight years younger. He was a good-looking, glib weasel who demanded instant gratification any way he could get it. A brat he'd given up on when the kid was still in his teens. When David got caught by the Feds with his hand in the SEC's cookie jar, he opted for a quick bullet to the brain rather than a long jail sentence.

Mick had spent the last year trying to work through the guilt of not having been a better brother; burnout had been his constant companion. He pictured it looking like the grim reaper dressed in jailin attire, boom box pressed against one ear, bopping along the sidewalk just ahead, giving him the come-closer finger wave. The invitation must be getting through. Here he was trespassing on a scene, which might be related to a crime, without alerting his fellow law-enforcement officers. Not a cooperative, career-enhancing move.

He started searching in the bedroom. Usual stuff:

alarm clock by the bed, bottle of pills for allergies, wineglass with a splash of champagne going flat. The bedcovers were thrown back on the side nearest the door. One cordovan-colored loafer stuck out from under the spread. The Johnston & Murphy in his hand had a substantial bottom. He wondered what shoes Madison had been wearing at the time of the attack and how thick the soles had been. He squatted down to locate the mate. He spied it near the head, was reaching for it when a voice hissed in his ear, "Go home."

He jerked to attention, whipped around.

He was alone in the motor home.

Again he heard the voice. "You're not needed here. The others will take care of the car. I'll call you tomorrow, once we've had a chance to discuss the situation."

Mick recognized the husky voice of Elise Carlson, but where the hell was it coming from? He dropped to his hands and knees and rummaged under the discarded bedspread. Between the bed and the nightstand he spotted a white plastic speaker box. As he stretched along the floor, Moore's voice emanated from it. "Please, let me help prep the car."

Mick used a dirty sock to slide the box closer. It took him a minute to realize what he was holding. It was one half of a remote baby-monitoring system, the type nervous parents bought at Sears to alert them the second their precious infant woke up. Peyton was using the setup to keep an ear on the paddock from his motor home. He'd cranked up the volume loud enough to disrupt his dreams if someone started pounding on sheet metal. Old PM003 was clever as well as paranoid.

Moore, on the other hand, didn't sound clever. Even through the tinny speaker, her voice was thick with tears of anger or rejection. Carlson didn't want her around. After all she'd gone through, the dismissal hurt.

He left the speaker on the floor and stood. If Moore was being sent home in disgrace, he should be a gentleman and escort her, which meant getting back to the pits. He also wanted to locate the other half of the monitoring system. It had to be near the car. Why hadn't the cops found it? Maybe they had and were keeping it to themselves.

He retraced his steps through the motor home, using his shirt sleeve to wipe prints on anything he might have touched. From the teak table, he picked up a napkin to protect the door latch, then noticed the smudge of lipstick. He dropped it back on the table.

Poking it as if it were a coiled snake, he flipped through a mental list of lipstick wearers. Moore didn't during the day, but had put something shimmery on her lips last night. Carlson had worn a dramatic red, which might have worn down to resemble the smudge on the napkin. He hadn't taken a good look at Evans's date, not from the neck up. Given the rest of the trappings, her lips were undoubtedly well and loudly rouged. Whatever. He wasn't so jaded that he would intentionally carry off what might become evidence. He snapped a half sheet of Bounty from the holder over the sink to use on the way out.

He was on the second step, with his fingers on the interior latch, when the door swung open.

Unbalanced, he tumbled down the high step and careened into Wayne Evans. His arm flung wide, slapped the crew chief on the side of his head. Evans tottered backwards, landed hard on his tailbone. He squeezed his eyes shut and began swearing.

Mick hung on to the pull bar, balanced, then jumped down and offered him a hand. Evans scrambled to his feet on his own, stiff-armed him in the chest. Knocked him into the side of the motor home, cracking his skull against the side extension. Evans slammed into him again. "Nothing but trouble. You and that bitch. What the frig are you doing here?"

It might have been smacking the back of his head, or his old friend burnout giving him the shove, but he figured it was Evans's calling Moore a bitch that made him see red. For the first time in years, he let loose.

The first punch landed in Evans's gut: beefy but not running to flab. Pain flickered in his knuckles as he swung again. The second shot caught Evans on the left cheekbone and snapped his head back. He stumbled, smacked down hard on his ass. Again. Yelped loud enough to bring the bacon cooker running, which was too bad—he was just warming up. The fry cook screamed, "I'm calling the police."

Bouncing like a contender in a title match, Mick searched for a way past him. The chef brandished a long fork, poked at his midsection. Mick stopped prancing and shook his sore hand. Reached into his pocket with the other one and extracted his metro badge. He flashed it at the short order cook. "Shoo. Go on. Your bacon's burning."

Fork at half-mast, the chef backed away, mumbling about NASCAR having classier fans.

Mick stood over Evans, straddling his legs. "Browning gave me a key. I was searching for evidence that someone was inside last night with your boss. What are you after?"

Evans glared, rolled onto his right hip. Reached for a hand up. His heft threatened to unbalance them both as he struggled to standing. Once upright, he poked at his cheek with his fingertips. "What'd you find?"

"Lipstick on a napkin and half of a sound monitoring device. You know anything about that?"

Evans did and admitted it. Claimed he spotted the receiver once the medics cleared out. Dead center under the Lotus, back near the engine. Not easily seen, but it would pick up conversations or activity around the car. "Peyton's more paranoid than he has reason to be."

"You know who's contributing to his paranoia?"

Evans moved his jaw from side to side. "Nope. Why should I?"

"You have access to the pits, and the tools. I saw you getting cosy with Whitten. Your boss is a pain to work for. Maybe you figure a little bad luck for him will translate into good luck for you."

"I wouldn't damage the Lotus. Or the Arrows. Jerk that took the potshot at the team must have stripped those bolts and cut the brake line. Sure as hell wasn't me." He was sufficiently indignant to be believable, more concerned about the car than the driver. Drivers were a dime a dozen. The Lotus 49C was one of a kind.

Mick flexed his knuckles. "What about Whitten? Maybe he wouldn't shed tears over the Lotus, or over

Peyton. Would he be likely to up the pressure that way?"

"Who knows what the rich consider sport? I wouldn't have thought it. Wouldn't be cricket, or some such shit."

Twenty-two

Rebecca walked back to the house with Hagan. They were side by side, not quite touching. He was keeping his hands in his pockets on a day when she could use one to hold. So far his conversation hadn't offered much comfort either. She squeezed her arms around her ribs. "Elise can't seriously think I had anything to do with what happened to Peyton, can she?"

"Not if she's rational. Maybe it's not about you, Moore. Maybe she wants to be the queen bee in the hive. She just shelled out big bucks for the privilege."

"Male drones only?" She looked around for a boulder to kick. Something sizeable that would fight back.

Hagan prodded her to keep moving. "Or maybe the crew isn't keen about an investigative reporter snooping around. One of them could have demanded that you be sent home. They know about your nosy talent?"

"Naturally." She punted a pine cone into the gutter.

During her first week at Indy, Ian had been embarrassingly vocal about her investigative past. Over beers, he'd regaled the crew with an embellished version of her going undercover in a nightclub to stop the senseless killing of young dancers only months after she'd battled a deranged maniac who'd murdered a man in her shop.

"So, if one of the crew was sabotaging the team, he might use the assault as an opportunity to get rid of you—an unwanted outsider, a snoop."

She stopped walking. "But why would one of them torture Peyton?"

"What, he's too nice a guy?"

"Far from it. He's whimsical and controlling."

"Right. Too arrogant to cave in to petty intimidation, which is why the first incidents didn't cause him to pack his Gucci loafers and leave." Hagan snapped off a strand of yellowed grass growing beside the road, stuck it in his mouth. "How will he react to being tortured?"

She harvested a blade for herself, wound it around her finger as she started down the road. "He won't back down. He has a damn-the-torpedoes drive, a recklessness that says he's out to prove something to someone. But he's sly. The type who feigns giving in, then circles around to pounce from an unguarded vantage. Or gets someone else to poke at the fallen hive."

"Manipulative."

"Wouldn't you say so? The only reason he hired me was to goad the guys into working harder so they're not outperformed by a woman."

Hagan reached out and cupped her face. She thought he was going to kiss her. He tipped her chin up and whispered. "Wrong. He hired you for your PR value. Sexy mechanic. You're front-page material. A looker, even in coveralls."

He let go of her to pitch away the soggy stem of grass, but she caught the grin on his face. The first time they'd locked horns, she'd been wearing denim coveralls, steel-toed boots and had grease smeared on her cheek. Maurice, the shop cat, had refereed the match stretched out on the table between them. Obvious Hagan remembered the scene.

She ripped the grass from her finger. "More like a convenient scapegoat for anything that goes wrong."

"It's beginning to look that way. You want the low-down on your pals? I got the fingerprint results back from Zimmer."

Hagan started before she could nod. It was no surprise that Tom had a real last name and a record for minor drug offenses. The sweet smell of marijuana clung to the mats in his hair. Like Hagan, though, she'd expected Chet Davis to have a record. His reserve and monosyllabic conversations reminded her of Frank, who claimed that doing hard-time made a man quiet and wary. Wayne Evans's record for fighting explained something that had bothered her from day one. He was demanding and argumentative, but an excellent crew chief, good enough to be working for a major series. A police record would explain why he wasn't.

Evans was the most obvious person to be behind the car incidents. He had unrestricted access to the pits. He had the mechanical knowledge and the tools. He could have filed the wheel bolts, cut the brake line, and added water to the gas.

He was also the only member of the crew to have

been away from the pit area when the shot was fired. He'd refused to say where he'd been or what he'd been up to. Presumably, he knew which end of a rifle to point since he'd bragged about going skeet shooting with Peyton during a junket in Florida. When Peyton had been tortured, Evans claimed he was with his bouncy blond friend. Maybe not. If she'd passed out, he could have left without her realizing it.

"Why would Evans attack the team?"

"He's not my first choice." Hagan stopped to lean against the bridge embankment to watch something below in the ravine. Over his shoulder, he admitted to exchanging words with Evans in the RV lot. The crew chief had hotly denied damaging the cars. Hagan believed him. "He's up to something, though. He and Whitten were plotting at the track, making eye contact at the party. Would Evans have allowed Whitten to sabotage the team, hoping to rattle Browning so the team would pull out?"

"What would Evans get out of it?"

"Besides money? Ingratiate himself with a more profitable team, hoping to be hired on? Or maybe it's retaliation. Get back at your boss for low pay or a strangling contract."

It was an idea worth contemplating. Ian claimed that Evans was locked into a five-year contract with Peyton. He could want out, especially if Whitten made him a better offer. Peyton was too much of a prick to let him go easily. But if the team went under, Evans could walk away with no ramifications, no fines, lawyers or name-calling. He would be free to join Whitten or anyone else.

Hagan was still gazing at the creek. "What about Browning?"

She bit at her lip to keep from snapping, *What about him?* Ian's laid-back manner and his dry sense of humor were engaging. And he was a damn good driver. She didn't want him to be involved.

Could she swear that he wasn't? "Ian couldn't have fired the gun, Hagan. He wouldn't have filed the wheel bolts or cut the brake line: personally too risky. It's possible that he went to the track with Peyton last night and tortured him before arriving at the house. Maybe he barged in on us to establish an alibi. But is it really likely?"

Hagan didn't respond, which was just as well. If pressed, she would have admitted that Ian had a callous streak. It was easy to imagine him sitting cross-legged, one side of his mouth turned up, listening to Wagner as he calmly pulled the wings off flies. Or jolted Peyton repeatedly with the battery charger on boost.

Squelching that depressing thought she turned the discussion to suspects outside the team: Derek Whitten, the rival; Brian Franks, the agitated investment counselor; Elise Carlson, Peyton's new partner.

Carlson seemed the least likely since she had a financial stake in Peyton's success. It appeared that they'd met for the first time at the party. Before that, she was unknown to the race community. Plus, she'd only arrived in town yesterday from out of the country.

Franks also was a recent arrival and an outsider who wouldn't have had free access to the pits. The only tool he'd be comfortable with was a retractable pencil, and then, only if it had an eraser.

That left Whitten as the most likely candidate. He could have strolled in and out of their pit area without attracting attention, and he had a motive of sorts, even if it was only to best Peyton.

Hagan said he'd nose around. He winced as he shoved his hands back into his pockets. Served him right. She'd noticed the swollen knuckles and assumed that he and Evans had done more than talk. Why wouldn't he admit it? She turned to face him, walking backwards.

"I keep stumbling over motive. Torturing Peyton, leaving him alive and strapped into the race car overnight wouldn't ensure that the team would pull out of the race. He's the money man, a figurehead. With or without him, Ian will race and the crew will work the pits. Particularly now, with a new owner at the helm."

"Carlson know anything about running a race team?"

She shrugged. "Probably as much as Peyton. Maybe more. She knows a lot about everything. Like how to reach his father in South Carolina. She's already phoned with the news of the assault. Who knew he had a father, much less how to get in touch with him?"

Hagan swore. "Hayes did." He raised a protective hand. "Don't scream, Moore, I forgot to tell you he called. It wasn't intentional."

That stopped her. "Hagan, in the past two days, you've neglected to tell me that you'd spotted Jasmine at the track, and that you met Elise Carlson. Now you've forgotten to tell me that Hayes called. Anything else slipped your mind? Like how you damaged your hand."

He flexed his fingers. "Ran into a door?"

"Named Evans?"

He opened his mouth with a comeback then shut it again.

"Fine." She turned and headed back to the house at a jog.

Hagan caught up as they neared Patricia Street, tugged at her arm to make her slow down. He tried to pacify her by recounting the gist of Hayes's phone call. Claimed that most of it had been biographical background on Peyton Madison II, the family patriarch. Not much on Peyton junior. Hayes had e-mailed some business articles and a list of suggested reading directly to her computer. From his back pocket he extracted a sheet of paper, handed it to her still folded. Smoothed open, it was a bad copy of a black-and-white photograph. Peyton Madison II and family, circa mid-seventies.

They entered the house through the patio. She asked Hagan to make coffee before he put ice on his knuckles.

In the bedroom, she fired up the ThinkPad, studied the photograph while she waited for it to load. Peyton Madison II did not look like a fun person to live with. Only the edges of his thin-lipped mouth turned up; his eyes were so cold they were opaque. When the computer completed its ritual, she slid the picture aside and called up Peter's e-mail. As she expected, Hayes had been a busy boy.

She skimmed through the articles. On the father there were excerpts from write-ups spanning three decades that had appeared in *Forbes, Economist, US News and World Report*. The elder Madison had been the kind of success story those magazines craved. Starting out, he'd worked for a chemical manufacturer headquartered in South America. When still a young man, he'd acquired the rights to a handful of patents and moved to the States to begin his own firm. Ten years later, he was on the Fortune 500 list.

By contrast, Peyton the third worked at making a name for himself in racing and a fortune at the betting tables. Per the automotive rags, he hadn't yet succeeded in either venture.

She printed the articles and sent Hayes a reply, thanking him. He'd given her more information than she needed, and leads to follow up, if she felt compelled. At the moment, her main concern was Peyton's health.

Hagan was in the kitchen pouring coffee. She took a cup. "As soon as I drink this and change, I'm going to the hospital. Do you want to come?"

He declined, saying he had errands to run and asked if he could use the car. The insurance company told him not to drive the Dodge until an adjuster looked at the damage, which he would do when he brought him a replacement. She waffled. He pleaded. She was going only one place—the hospital—she could take a taxi there and back. He had multiple stops, wasn't sure exactly where he would be going. It would be much easier if he had the car.

They compromised. They'd both go to the hospital.

If Peyton felt up to having company, she would stay and hold his hand. Hagan could leave and take the car. If Peyton wanted to be left alone, she'd go with Hagan. "After all, aren't you supposed to be protecting me?"

He grunted something unintelligible, which she took for agreement.

While she rummaged for the car keys, Hagan noticed the blinking light on the answering machine in the living room and punched the replay button. She rarely used that phone or checked the messages since most were for Ian.

Most but not all. The hesitant voice on the recording was one she'd recognize anywhere, there was no need for him to identify himself.

"Rebecca, this is your fa—, Robert Moore. Please call us. We've had an intriguing visit from a friend of yours. We'd like to talk to you."

Twenty-three

The Methodist Hospital of Indiana was a stone's throw from Interstate 65 on Senate Boulevard. Rebecca won the toss again, so she was driving. Hagan listed to the left to study the instruments as she wove through neighborhood streets. The gleam in his eye might have meant he was ready to scrap the Jeep and get a car that was fun to drive. After the crash outside the gentlemen's club, it was going to cost more to fix the Cherokee than it could ever be worth.

She welcomed his silence. Her own thoughts were jumping to conclusions, then leapfrogging over themselves to change direction. Someone had given Robert Moore the phone number for the house where she was staying. Only two people had it. Frank—it was posted at the shop. And Jo—he had it in case she wasn't answering her cell phone. Frank hadn't left Maryland in eighteen years. Eliminate him and that made Jo the intriguing visitor her parents had entertained. That would explain why she couldn't reach him in Head Tide. She braked too hard when a Volvo cut her off, punched the poor excuse for a horn. *What gave him the right to visit her parents?*

The question continued to annoy her as she parked the car and entered the hospital. It was Saturday quiet; few people strolling the halls who weren't paid to be there. The volunteer at the information desk found Peyton Madison's room number and pointed them in the direction of the elevators. Exiting on the second floor, they entered a nearly deserted hallway. Three nurses were positioning equipment outside a room at the end. Something routine, they weren't hurrying. According to the sign on the wall, room 232 was down the short hall veering off to the right.

The door to the room was slightly ajar. Hagan hung back, fidgeted with coins in his pocket. She almost asked for one to flip. Heads she'd go in, tails she'd leave unannounced. Yes, she was worried about the state of Peyton's health, but she'd come mostly out of curiosity. Not the best reason for visiting a hospitalized victim. She should turn around, leave him in peace.

But she wouldn't. From the time she could mouth the word "why," she'd hated unanswered questions. She didn't always need the correct answer: Being a reporter had trampled the notion that there was only one right answer to every question, or that the answer was the same for every individual. She just needed an explanation that made sense. Nothing about the attacks on the team or on Peyton did.

She knocked and pushed through the door.

The lights were dim. Peyton was lying with his

head elevated. His dark hair contrasted with the white pillow; his face was the same color. There was an IV in his arm. The neck brace had been removed. He was breathing without oxygen. Those were good signs.

Hearing her footsteps, he rolled his head to the side and opened his eyes. Stared at her while he licked at his lips. "Moore. Help." His voice was a dry croak.

There was a water glass with a bent straw. She held it while he sipped. He swallowed as if his throat hurt, sank back against the pillow. "Help, please. You. No police."

She followed his gaze to the doorway. Hagan was glued to the threshold. His expression said that Peyton's demand was fine by him. No police, no problem. He was ready, willing and eager to leave.

She held out the car keys. Hagan crept into the room, felt his way along the mobile monitors like an octogenarian with bad balance, looking anywhere except at the man in the bed. She reminded him that the car needed gas. He mumbled "Yes, dear" on his way out.

Peyton's eyes had drifted shut again. She lifted a molded plastic chair and slid it quietly next to the bed. The night's ordeal had erased all smugness from his face. The bruising under his eyes made him appear vulnerable, like a puppy who'd been kicked. What did he want her to help with that he didn't want the police to know about? Why did he think she could?

"Ian. Says you investigate?" His eyes were still closed. His tongue flicked around his lips, seeking moisture.

She responded yes. It was simpler than trying to explain that she'd been an investigative reporter, not a detective. And that was in the past.

His eyes fluttered open; they were Basset hound sad. "Trouble."

"Involving the team?" She didn't want to be drawn in. Despite his present weakened state, the man was arrogant and effete and probably deserved what had happened. But the crew didn't. Could she live with herself if someone else was hurt? "Is the team in trouble?"

He wagged his head. "Me. Hoped, they were acci— accidents. Assumed the Lotus wasn't ready. Maybe bolts had rusted. Arrows, hoses were old. You told me. My fault. Then the shot. Gunshot. Thought it was warning. Pay up." He swallowed hard. "No."

She hitched closer as if she had trouble hearing him. It wasn't that. His words were audible, but they weren't making sense. Had Peyton really dismissed the car problems as routine mechanical failures; taken the gunshot as some kind of unrelated warning? Knees pressing into the mattress, she prodded him to recount his last twelve hours. Guided him as she had others she'd interviewed. It was slow going. Mostly, she listened, tried to piece together the fragments. Occasionally she flicked out a question to keep the ball rolling.

After the party, Peyton had decided to stay in the motor home. Earlier, he'd rigged a monitor to listen into the paddock area. Around two A.M., a noise woke him and he went to investigate. Entering the tent, he crossed to check on the car. It was then that he'd been shocked. Fell. Dazed. Someone hoisted him into the Lotus. When his head cleared, he was strapped in, a helmet on his head. He couldn't see anything. Couldn't move.

Peyton paused, his breathing was labored. He looked bewildered.

She patted his arm. "Lubrication grease had been smeared on the visor. Your arms were trapped beneath the harness." His head lolled when he tried to nod. He was tiring fast. "When you woke, were you alone?"

Again his head rolled. "No. Voices."

"Whose?"

He didn't know, or wasn't saying. She melted back in the spindle-legged chair to give him a minute to recover. Tried to imagine the scene and come up with a rational explanation. Torture implied that Peyton knew something worth torturing him for. What?

"Tape." He rotated his index finger in a circle. "Voice tape."

Not a person speaking to him, but a voice on a tape. Odd. As far as she knew, the police hadn't found a tape recorder at the scene. But then, the assailant could have carried a pocket recorder, played it, taken it away again. That implied preplanning. What did he want Peyton to listen to?

He coughed. She offered more water. He nodded thanks, whispered: "Crackled, hissed. Two. Old voice. German."

He thought one voice was a woman's, though she didn't say much. The other was so gravelly it could have been either male or female. He insisted it spouted gibberish in German. The only words he understood were *mutter, vater*; mother, father. *Peufel*, German for evil, and *erbschaft*, meaning inheritance.

The tape droned on for a few minutes, then stopped. He sensed he was supposed to answer or comment, but he didn't understand what was being said. When he protested that he didn't speak German, he was shocked. Then the tape began again. Then paused, waited for an answer. Then the shock. Over and over for hours.

His hand fluttered above the bedclothes. "I offered money. Pleaded. No answer. Just the voice screaming: *Heinrich Kauffman. Heinrich Kauffman.* Who is he, Moore? Find out. The painting. How did the voice know about Coro—" He coughed, choking off the word. A string of mucous dripped from his nose.

Someone had pushed open the door, letting in light from the corridor. She felt the tension level rise, heard ragged breathing behind. When she turned to look over her shoulder, an old man posed in the doorway.

He snapped at her. "Who are you?"

His posture was erect, jacket hung without a wrinkle. Steel-gray hair swept back from a high pale forehead creased with parallel lines. He had the same pinched lips as the man in the hospital bed, the same glint of condescension. She had seen a younger version of his face recently in a grainy magazine photograph. Except for the hint of jowls, he hadn't changed much in thirty years.

Annoyed by her silence, he crossed to within inches of her, leaned on the back of her chair. "I asked your name. I expect a courteous reply."

By standing, she forced him to back away. "You must be Peyton's father. I'm Rebecca Moore, the team mechanic."

She glanced back at Peyton. He'd shrunk, sunk into the mattress. Beads of perspiration clung to the hairline. His eyes were tightly closed as if he didn't want to watch the bedside scene. Or feared being kicked again.

The old man picked at her arm with bony fingers. "I will thank you to leave. My son has a weak heart. Your chattering has tired him."

He shifted to one side to let her pass. Close to, his face showed no trace of sorrow over his son's condition, no concern, no weakness of any kind. He had to be nearly eighty, but Peyton Madison II was still a force that would not be ignored.

Twenty-four

Mick borrowed the yellow pages from the talkative codger at the hospital's information desk. He looked up the phone number for the You-Mail-It Store he'd visited the day before, punched it in on his way out the front door. According to the recorded message, they were open until seven.

He wiped perspiration from the phone case with his sleeve and restowed it in his pocket. Breathed deeply. The air was cool and bright after the storm. Even tainted with exhaust fumes from loitering taxis, it smelled better than the antiseptic odor permeating the hospital corridors. He'd tasted a lifetime's supply while his father took his time dying.

Patrick Hagan had caught a bullet fired by a scared punk holding up a convenience store for candy bars and petty change. The bullet didn't kill him outright; septicemia did. Infection from the wounds had seeped into his bloodstream, which carried the poison throughout his body to infect every organ it could.

Once his fever hit one hundred and four, the doctor sent the blood samples off to the Centers for Disease Control, which accurately typed the bacteria. Too late. Massive quantities of strong antibiotics were administered intravenously for weeks, but the sickness had its hold and wouldn't relinquish it.

With a typical adolescent's ego, Mick first felt responsible for his father's death. Then blamed him for dying, for leaving him alone to take care of his mother and muddle through life. Later, his thoughts turned darker and he wondered if Patrick Hagan had left this world willingly. If he'd been fed up with a frustrating job, overbearing parents, a too saintly wife and a rebellious, unappreciative son. Death had seemed a peaceful alternative. Mick never shook the sorrow attached to that assumption.

He was almost to the car when he spotted Brian Franks hiding behind an arrangement of gaudy flowers. The financial consultant was scurrying toward the entrance to the hospital, peeking around the bouquet to keep from tripping on the steps. Undoubtedly, he was going to visit Peyton. The flowers were a nice gesture. He assumed Franks was just the delivery boy, not a concerned fan, and wondered who'd signed the card.

The Corvette looked diminutive wedged between matching blue minivans. Mick let it warm up as Moore had instructed, grinned each time he gunned the throttle. During his teenage years, when driving meant as much as Saturday sex after the movie, he'd been stuck with cast-off Oldsmobiles belonging to one of his uncles. All his mother's brothers drove Oldsmobiles; all of them got a new one every two years. They took turns giving him the castoff. Once on the job he drove a patrol car, followed by the Jeep, suitable for undercover work. He'd never driven anything sporty.

Back on Patricia Street, he parked in front of the rental. Took his kit from the trunk and went inside to transfer his latest set of prints. Peyton Madison III's came from the solid gold lighter he'd foolishly set down while betting on the Calcutta the night before. Carlson's were wrapped around a sleek Mont Blanc she'd allowed Peyton to use when signing away his fortune on the bet. The prints on the barrel looked smudged, but they might turn up something. His coup had been the glossy black matchbox from St. Elmo. Derek Whitten had used the matches to light the cigar he waved in Peyton's face. Ian Browning's were easy, in plain sight on the bathroom glass. Moore would be up in arms if she realized he was checking up on her boy, but he wouldn't be doing his job if he didn't.

Working methodically under the fluorescent light in the kitchen, he transferred the prints, labeled each with names and dates of collection. Zimmer would have to call in favors with state police to have the work done quickly, but he'd do it for Moore. Much as the sheriff bitched about her, he didn't take kindly to his local citizens being the victims of crime. She'd been cheek-by-jowl with more than her share of criminals lately and proved herself a survivor. Zimmer had a healthy respect for survivors.

Mick drove to the mail store, shipped the package overnight and was back in under an hour. He enclosed a note asking Zimmer to call with the results. Cruising past an ice cream stand, he thought about stopping, then decided to wait and treat Moore. Only Moore wasn't home. Disappointing but not surprising. He should have stayed with her. He was less itchy when she was within touching distance.

He wandered into the kitchen, opened the refrigerator, stared at the white, humming void, debating whether it was too early in the day for a beer. Something about Moore made him want to drink: motivated by equal parts celebration, frustration and depression. Most casual observers could figure out the first two. She was intelligent and could be delightful. She was also sexy as hell, not that this keen observation had produced the desired results.

The depression was more elusive unless you'd witnessed their pasts. Hers contained a brilliant but derailed career as an investigative reporter for the *Post*. His contained the step-brother who'd committed suicide when Moore's investigation into investment fraud threatened to expose his crimes. At the time, David had also been Moore's lover. It was a complicated overlapping that refused to go away entirely. Like a blueberry stain on white shorts. His mother recommended lemon juice and leaving them on the grass in full sun.

He slammed the refrigerator, gazed out the sliding glass door. Maybe fresh air would improve his mood. The sun had slipped behind an elephant-sized puffball cloud. It cast dark shadows over the patio. Shadows that obscured but didn't obliterate a flash of movement near the gate.

He froze. Listed to the side, tried to blend with the vertical blind as he inched his hand forward. His fingers gripped the door handle. Breath suspended, he waited for the figure to come into view. Until he'd glimpsed the wraithlike movement, he had forgotten about Jasmine. Now she was as good as caught.

The tiny girl skipped to the table. Went up on toe point, leaned in, tipped aside the potted geranium.

He burst through the slider.

She bolted before she'd recovered from the shock of seeing him. Was almost back to the gate when he grabbed her wrist. The rest of her body skidded through the opening. She kicked and squealed. He held tightly to her thin forearm, braced his foot against the gate wedged between them like a bundling board. When her squirming started to peter out, he said quietly, "The picture got rained on. What did it show?"

She stopped wriggling.

He waited, sensing her dilemma: Should she escape, or find out what happened to the picture? Curiosity won out. She relaxed her arm and peeked around the gate.

"Did it dissolve?"

"Almost."

That was the only word he could choke out as he came face-to-face with Jasmine for the first time. From their previous encounter he knew she was a Munchkin, under four feet and wiry. He expected a child, an unformed cherub. The face scowling at him was that of an ancient. Not wrinkled and sagging, but wise and doubting enough to have lived two lifetimes, which seemed fitting, for her face belonged to two different people. One half was mostly the color of chocolate cake batter his mother made for his birthday. The other side was a ragged splotch of ivory. A milky white band crossed the bridge of her nose, widened to engulf her left cheek around to the tip of her ear. It clipped the corner of her mouth, dipped under her chin where it stopped. Near the hairline, the edges were rippled, irregular. A smudge of white above her right eye lifted her brow in a perpetual question.

Jasmine rounded the corner and faced him squarely. "You may stare. Everybody does." She marched past him and sat at the far side of the table. "Where's the lady?"

"Rebecca?"

She puffed out a breath. "What a lovely name. Rebecca, Rebecca, Rebecca. Who are you? You're not a racer."

He admitted he wasn't. He told her his name and sat opposite her, fascinated by her half-and-half coloring, but trying not to stare like everybody. He added that he was a policeman, hoping it might reassure her.

Her face lit up. "You've come to protect her. How wonderful."

"Does she need protection?"

She nodded sagely. "I saw the gunman. He's a devil."

For the next fifteen minutes, he listened as Jasmine explained her fears for Moore's safety. The girl was truly disconcerting. Part of it was the contrast between her too-wise expression and the childish patter. She couldn't describe the gunman's face. Instead she prattled on about devils and spells and her mystic connection to Rebecca, rolling the name over her tongue like a sour ball. She was clearly infatuated with

Moore. He couldn't get a handle on why. He tried the direct approach and asked her.

The girl gave a quick shrug. "Racing must be like flying. High in the sky like a pterosaur." Her arms shot out, circled like a pilotless plane caught in a cross-wind. "I want to race."

"Rebecca doesn't."

"She does. I saw her."

He remembered the photographs Moore had shown him the night he arrived. In one she was sitting in the race car; in another, she was just taking off the helmet. She'd admitted to circling the Brickyard at one hundred and fifty miles an hour just for a lark. She made it sound like a one-time thing. He should have known better. She probably took it for a spin every time she put a screwdriver to the carburetors. Why was he wasting his time protecting her? She was suicidal.

Jasmine bobbed her head up and down watching him. "I did so see her. And she's a woman. Like me. And she stands outside the circle. I have adopted her to teach me to race."

Okay, we have a clear case of feminist hero worship viewed from afar through the eyes of the very young. He started to ask Jasmine why the photographs, why not just introduce herself. Then he considered the girl's discoloration. He thought it was cute. She might not. Girls tended to be touchy about being different. She caught him staring.

"It's called vitiligo. It's incurable."

Mick returned her stare. "Never heard of it."

"Most people are ignorant. Show me the photograph, please. That's why I'm here."

He fetched the damaged print from the kitchen counter, flipped it picture side up and presented it on the paper towel. Jasmine sighed loudly. She slipped out of the chair and darted toward the gate. He swiveled, ready to stop her if she ran. No need. She only went as far as the patch of leggy Pachysandra. There she retrieved a small knapsack she must have dropped during her aborted escape. It was black and white, cow print. She squatted in the vegetation and unzipped a side pocket. She found what she was looking for and held it aloft for his inspection. It looked like a wafer of black plastic, maybe an inch square.

She bobbed her head with delight. "We'll take it to Mr. Groen. He'll fix it."

Twenty-five

Rebecca called for a cab from the front desk of the hospital. She half-sat on the rim of a concrete planter, waiting for it to arrive. The soil in the planter was littered with cigarette butts. In the center was one struggling yellow mum that no one had bothered to pinch back. A few limp blossoms on thin stalks above yellowed leaves. She never claimed to have a green thumb, but she hated to see cultivated plants being ignored. Why plant them if you're going to let them die?

It was the same abhorrence she felt about victims in inner city slums. Youths abandoned by city leaders who needed splashier causes to generate funding; ignored by parents with too many troubles of their own. Why did people who couldn't afford to raise children—either financially or emotionally—do so little to prevent having them? In light of the AIDS epidemic it seemed unimaginable that couples continued to have casual sex without using protection. Pregnancy was one of the most benign things that could happen, if you didn't care about the resulting child.

As she plucked off a dead leaf a wave of guilt washed over her. Her parents, the ones she never knew, weren't married when they'd conceived her, yet they stayed together. Given the times, they probably considered themselves free spirits who didn't need a formal ceremony, or society's recognition. The truth might have been that they were two near-strangers trapped by the birth of a child and making the best of it. Had they wanted a child? Had they loved her?

She pushed off from the planter, paced the length of the platform. It had been ten minutes since she phoned. How long could it possibly take to get a cab in Indianapolis? Stupid question. It was the Saturday before a major race; the city was bustling.

As she slowed to a stroll her thoughts drifted to the scene upstairs in the hospital room. Peyton had seemed genuinely perplexed as to who his attacker was, or what he wanted. Not money. What else? Why play a tape that your victim can't understand? Or was Peyton lying about not comprehending German? He admitted to selective words: *mother, father*, the name *Kauffman*. Then there was the word beginning *coro—corroded, coronation, Coronardo, Corona beer*, what? Was it the start of a German word? Did it relate to the preceding mention of a painting? Maybe it wasn't part of a word, but a whole one and he'd been trying to say *Corot*, as in the artist? That was almost too easy.

She leaned against the pillar. And what was the tension between father and son? Madison senior entered the room and his son oozed into the mattress, a spine-less vegetable. Dad seemed more upset by her presence than by his son's physical condition.

Too many questions; no answers. And she was too drained to concentrate.

Cursing Hagan, she pulled out the phone to call the cab company again. It rang as she flipped it open. She and Frank said hello at the same time.

"Frank, is that you? Is everything all right?"

"There a reason it shouldn't be?"

"You don't often call. Where are you?"

"Feeding your cats. What you think I'm doing, stealing laundry detergent?"

Frank Lewes had been the head mechanic at Vintage & Classics for two decades, starting a week after he was released from prison. For almost the entire time he pretended to dislike whatever stray cat Uncle Walt had taken in, and there had been a string of them. It was a bogus act that fooled no one. When Billy Lee joined the staff with his Doberman, Maurice was moved from the shop to the house. Frank missed the darned cat so much he often snuck up the hill during lunch hour to play with him and the rambunctious kitten.

She swore she could hear Mo purring in the background. "Why isn't Jo taking care of the cats?"

"You'd know if you ever returned phone calls like folks expect. You do that, I wouldn't have to track you down."

"What phone calls?"

Apparently, Jo had called all over that morning hunting for her. He claimed to have left a message with Hagan. Chalk up another one he hadn't given her. Hagan could have forgotten—he was doing that a lot lately. Or he could have done it intentionally, a petty attempt to thwart her relationship with Jo.

Frank ended his harangue by saying she could reach her lawyer on his new cell phone, which she would know about if she had bothered to check in earlier. He recited the number. She started to thank him, but he wasn't finished with her.

"In case you're interested, Val and Juanita have set a date for the wedding. You remember them? Val works for you, short blond kid, drives a motorcycle. Juanita's the slip of a girl used to live in the house with you, the runaway your uncle took in. Collects New Age music. For some peculiar reason, they'd like you to be at the church service. You might want to call and congratulate them, if you have the time. And you got a new customer arriving next week, who expects to meet you in person."

Her cheeks were burning when she hung up. It was a toss-up as to whether Frank or Jo was more annoyed with her for leaving town. Neither one was about to overlook the infraction.

She leaned against the cooling concrete, stared at the scribbled phone number as if it were in code. Jo had said nothing about buying a cell phone. If possible, he'd communicate via letters sealed with wax and sent by carrier pigeon. What was going on? She bit at her lip. *I'm losing touch with Jo when I don't mean to.*

As opposed to not communicating with her family, which was intentional. She folded Jo's number and put it away. She would call him later when there would be time for a long talk. Right now, she needed to speak with her grandmother.

When Peyton Madison had begged her to help, she hadn't promised. She wasn't sure he deserved it. Nor did she want to become more embroiled with his stalker. But the clues he'd revealed were tantalizing—a tape in German, a man named Heinrich Kauffman, and maybe a painting by Corot. Dorothea Wetherly knew more about art than most gallery owners. If there was a link connecting the German with the French painting, she would know. Or find someone who did. And, she'd be thrilled to do it.

Twenty-six

Jo slammed the door of his car and leaned against it, easing the muscles in his neck. He'd driven to Dorothea Wetherly's home on Maryland's eastern shore directly from landing at National. The trip to Bryantown had involved jousting through erratic traffic on Route 50, then merging with hordes of day-trippers clogging the bridge leaving Annapolis. If he could afford it, and rationalize the extravagance, he'd sell his car and use a livery service. The highways were increasingly jammed with SUVs, pickup trucks and minivans. The bullies of the world were winning. There was little respect anymore for finesse and style. That made Rebecca, zipping along in a battered MG, all the more remarkable. He was thankful that she was nimble and quick enough to get out of the way.

The destination, however, was worth the trip. The early-nineteenth-century home was as stately as the old woman's bearing. Ancient magnolias, with branches so heavy they had to be supported by braces, stood between the house and the lapping waters of the Wye River. Late-blooming roses surrounded a brass sundial set on a pedestal beside the front walk. The lawns bordering the right wing of the house were tiered; the lowest level displayed herbs arranged symmetrically in a cloverleaf pattern of green and gold sprigs amid silver artemisia.

Dorothea Wetherly opened the thick door herself, smiled as he crossed the porch to greet her. She seemed younger than when they'd first met. Having found her granddaughter she was letting go of her self-hatred, one memory at a time. He was pleased for her. He'd be more pleased once Rebecca accepted the situation.

They were sipping sherry in the day room when the phone rang. Without inquiring, Talmadge handed the receiver over to his employer. The lines of her face turned upward with pleasure. She mouthed, *It's Rebecca.*

Jo shook his head frantically. He did not want Rebecca to know he was there, meddling in her affairs for the second time that day. Still, he tried to eavesdrop. What he could hear sounded like ordinary chitchat.

When Dorothea hung up, she was frowning. "Counselor, did I ever confess that I don't much like women? In my day they were either dyspeptically weak and simpering, or nasty and underhanded. Rebecca is neither. She's very direct and inquisitive." She tapped a fingernail against the thin bowl of a stemmed glass to get Talmadge's attention. He went to the sideboard.

Jo leaned forward. "Are you going to expound on that comment?

"She asked about my day."

"And?"

"My day included lunch and a dreadful art exhibit with Marlene Kauffman. Before I could describe the wretched cubist landscapes, Rebecca blurted out, 'Any chance she's related to Heinrich Kauffman?' What a queer thing to say."

Dorothea took a sip from the replenished glass, held it tilted at the same angle as her head, lost in her thoughts.

Jo stood the silence as long as he could. "Is she? Related to Heinrich Kauffman?"

"Who'd want to be related to Marlene? Though, as I told Rebecca, I do know of a Heinrich Kauffman from a long time ago. Not likely it's the same person."

She picked at a strand of white hair, yanking it back from her cheek. "The Heinrich Kauffman I recall was a prosperous German scientist who had disappeared after the end of the Second World War. He wasn't the only one. At the time, scads of missing Germans were wanted for questioning about missing works of art. Leon served on several committees or commissions, or whatever they called themselves, trying to locate valuables that had been stolen from Jewish families. You know, of course, about the ERR?"

Jo admitted his ignorance, settled back in his chair, ready to be enlightened. Leon Wetherly had been an art dealer of international fame from the nineteen-forties through the seventies. Dorothea had traveled with him, shared his love of quality paintings and had herself become an art authority. She clearly knew more about misplaced German art than Jo would ever care to know. This was his chance to learn.

ERR, the *Einsatzstab Reichsleiter Rosenberg*, was an operation headed by and named for Alfred Rosenberg. It was the brainchild of Adolf Hitler. A frustrated painter, Hitler planned to make his home town of Linz, Germany, the artistic centerpiece of the world. To achieve that, he tasked Rosenberg with acquiring Old Masters from Jews in the Netherlands, France and Austria. Hitler preferred Dutch or Italian and certain prized German paintings. *Modern* art, which he considered degenerate, was also to be confiscated, to be traded for better pieces.

"Rosenberg was given full license, you understand. Some pieces he acquired by forced purchase. Some he simply took when they were abandoned by families fleeing their homes. Others were, what was that silly term? Oh, yes: *Aryanized*. Sounds like it should come in an aerosol can for use in the bathroom, doesn't it? Only it wasn't anything sanitary." Her foot bounced, the pace increasing with her agitation. Like Rebecca, even seated, she couldn't stay still.

Aryanization was the practice of Jews being forced to sell their valuables to approved Gentile families. It began around 1939, when the Nazis were first exerting their power. Jews, denounced as inferior, were not permitted to own fine works of art. Some families agreed to sell their treasures in the hopes that later they could retrieve the property. Those families were as naive as they were optimistic. For most of them, there would be no later.

"Heinrich Kauffman was known to have Aryanized art for several families in the area south of Stuttgart. Though it seems to me it was sometime later, maybe in the mid-fifties, that he made the newspapers."

"Why?"

"The usual reason. He and the artwork he'd acquired had vanished."

"Interesting." Joe stretched as he stood. "But what possible connection could Rebecca have with that man."

It was then that Dorothea told him about the attack on Rebecca's boss, his torture and the scratchy tape in German. She was surprised that Jo didn't know about it, until she remembered that he'd been traveling. She nodded toward his briefcase. "Did you bring me a present from Boston?"

He smiled. "We'll share it over dinner. Right now I want to know what Rebecca is up to." He crossed behind her. "So, I repeat: Is there any reason to suspect that her boss was referring to that Heinrich Kauffman?"

Dorothea shrugged. "Rebecca's mind seems to work like mine. She strings things together with the flimsiest of threads, which often hold. Peyton described the tape as old. The speakers on it were German and repeatedly mentioned Heinrich Kauffman. I know of a World War Two scoundrel from Stuttgart named the same. So the idea that they are connected is not impossible—to Rebecca. Plus, there could be an art angle. Where are you?"

She craned her neck backwards to find him. "Rebecca overheard a guest at the party last evening tease

Peyton about a wager, saying that if he lost he could always sell his art. And, if I let my imagination run amok—which Talmadge cautions me against doing—I can throw something else in the pot. What does *Corot* mean to you?"

He bent close to her ear. "Jean Baptiste Camille Corot—that Corot?"

Dorothea laughed. "You've been very well educated."

The sentence ended with an upward lilt. He assumed it was a subtle probe, an invitation to disclose more of his past. Or, she could have been expressing her disbelief that a mixed-race refugee from the islands had been educated in the gentler arts. Would it matter to her if he came from nothing and had worked his way up? Or would she prefer her granddaughter's lawyer to have sterling-silver place settings in his past?

She waved away his nonresponse. "Rebecca's not certain what Peyton was trying to say. He bit off their conversation abruptly when his father appeared. The last word, or partial word, sounded like *coro*. After forty years of listening to Leon, my mind leapt effortlessly to the French painter. That, and of course, I own one."

"You own a Corot?"

"A tiny thing, an anniversary gift from my husband. A sketch of frolicking nymphs for the *Idylle*. He did not steal it from a doomed Jewish family. I promised Rebecca I would quiz my friends, ask a few questions. It could be fun tracking down an odious felon after all these years. Care to help?"

Twenty-seven

The black square, Jasmine explained with much eye rolling, was an xD card from her digital camera. It contained all of her recent photographs. It had a billion, gazillion gigabytes. Mr. Groen, Sammy to his friends, would make a print to replace the ruined one. Then Mickey could see the gunman.

Mick cringed at the epithet, but agreed that developing another copy of the lost photograph was a good idea. They flipped an acorn to see whether they would go by bike—Jasmine riding hers; Mickey walking behind—or by car. Having never flipped an acorn before, it was difficult to discern whether it landed heads or tails. He took her word for it that it came up tails when she announced that he could drive her. Before they left, Jasmine asked if there were any peanuts for Fred. Mick had no idea who Fred was, but he knew there was no edible junk food of any variety in the house. He promised they would buy peanuts on the way back.

Jasmine's eyes widened when he pointed to the Corvette. "Cool." She yanked a black-and-white-checked baseball cap from her knapsack and hopped up onto the door, slid her skinny butt over the edge. She hunkered down in the seat, fastened the lap belt when he refused to start the car until she did. He was skeptical of her ability to direct him to the photographer's since she couldn't see out of the car. With a dramatic sigh, she asked if he could find Georgetown Road at Thirty-fifth Street.

Before they reached the intersection, Jasmine tugged on his arm, pointed at an alley, saying there was a parking lot around back. She squirmed out of the seat and vaulted over the door before he got the shifter into reverse and the engine shut down. He heard a screen door slam and a deep voice call out, "Leibchen, all that Jaz, where have you been?"

The sign next to the door said PARKING FOR SAMUEL J. GROËN, PHOTOGRAPHER, which helped Mick redraw his mental image of the proprietor. His expectations had been colored by Jasmine's pronunciation of the photographer's name—*Sammy Groan*, she chanted, *Sammy Groan*. He'd pictured a skinny electronics wiz with numerous chains and an attitude. He figured "groan" was his handle. The umlaut over the *e* made Samuel Groën a horse of a different color, though in person, he was almost deplete of color. He was an elderly Jew, dressed entirely in black, riding in a black wheelchair. The monochromatic deadness was relieved by chrome wheel spokes and the gray in his black beard.

And by the grin on his face aimed at Jasmine. "I have been worried. You do not come all day."

Jasmine shrugged like it was no big deal, but her smile said differently. She dug the xD card from the pocket of her slacks. "My picture melted. Can you make me another?"

"Melted? Like ice cream? Chocolate or vanilla—"

"Or both!" Jasmine squealed and darted toward an opening in the wall masked by a black curtain.

Groën watched her go. "Such a delight, that child. You are a friend?"

Mick said yes, hoping that the one-word answer would suffice and save a lot of explaining. He told the photographer about the picture being left out in the rain.

"Ach, she uses the machine at the drugstore again. How many times do I tell her? There is no fixative to protect the pictures over time. Or from the weather. She should let me do them, always. You know which number the photograph is?"

Mick didn't. He was saved from admitting it by Jasmine's return. Most of her face was hidden behind an ice cream sandwich. She'd bitten off all four corners and was licking the vanilla around the edge of the chocolate wafer. She mumbled what sounded like "fiftootle," which turned out to be number fifty-two. Groen made a note of it on a paper bag that had once contained a Hallmark greeting card. He wheeled around Jasmine, shifting his shoulder to avoid the dripping ice cream confection she held out to him.

"No, I do not want to lick. Wash your hands before

you leave." He slipped the disk into a bin containing other orders. "I will have this for you at four o'clock. Mrs. Swenson's vacation photographs come first. You will return, yes?"

Jasmine looked up at Mick. He said, "Fine." He definitely wanted to be the one to come back for the photograph. It would be worth the wait to see the expression on Moore's face when he presented her with a picture of the shooter.

Groën spun his chair around at the sound of the door opening. A hefty woman in a turquoise pants suit entered, lugging two albums decorated with daisies. She was followed by a couple of lovebirds still in their teens, cooing as if they were secluded in the dovecote. Groën introduced him to Mrs. Swenson. Jasmine wasn't around to be introduced. She'd evaporated faster than a witness at a gang shooting. He could see her through the back-door screen, slouched down in the car, only the crown of her checkered cap showing.

A hand clutched at his wrist. Groën peered up at him. "You are friends with her race driver, yes?" Mick nodded, a tad miffed that everyone liked the idea of Moore squealing tires at breakneck speeds.

The photographer bobbed his head in response. "Good. You will marry, maybe? Give Jasmine a proper home. You could not have a better child. Think about it." Still nodding, he wheeled off the deal with his customer.

What the blazes was he talking about?

Moore was definitely not mother material, married or not. Old Groën's imagination was as wild as the kid's. They made an odd couple: an elderly Orthodox

Jew and a precocious kid with a skin disorder. She should be playing tag with friends her own age. Not hanging on his wheelchair. Didn't she have a family? Didn't he?

Twenty-eight

Rebecca felt like walking. She asked the cabby to leave her at the corner of Thirtieth and Falcon, a few blocks from the house. Two deciduous trees had been planted in front of nearly every house on the street. Beech, or something with oval yellow leaves, alternated with maples in crimson and gold. The leaves were drifting down, dancing on the breeze, layering on the concrete sidewalk. The colors were intense, as was the sky. It made her smile. Or maybe she was smiling over the conversation with her grandmother. Dorothea didn't think she was crazy to ask about Heinrich Kauffman. Didn't scold her to be careful. She was eager to join in, promised to contact a volunteer with a Nazi-hunting group and pick his brains.

"Rebecca, I promise you'll hear the moment I learn anything."

The quest was a long shot. The connection, if there was one, would be moldy with age. What were the odds that Dorothea's Heinrich Kauffman was same man mentioned on the tape, or connected with him in any way? Still, the search would amuse her grandmother and it might not be futile. To borrow Hagan's expression, the German connection was an itch worth scratching, particularly as it pertained to the elder Peyton Madison.

She stooped to pick up a red leaf, fed the stem through a hole near the center and rolled it into a sheath for her index finger. She wrapped it tightly and began picking off the edges. Ruminating, as she shed tiny leaf fragments like breadcrumbs marking her path.

One magazine article said that Madison II got his start working for a German chemical company in South America. Argentina was a favorite relocation spot for Nazis after WWII. None of the magazines said where he'd come from prior to that, but the photo caption in *Life* magazine gave his first wife's name as Ingrid Thierman, the son's name as Karl. Very Germanic-sounding. Not much of a leap to penciling in Germany as the family's country of origin. Granted, Madison didn't sound German, but his father wouldn't have been the first to change the surname when fleeing the homeland.

She dropped the tattered leaf into the gutter and forced her hands into her pockets to still them. Her thoughts kept moving.

Now, after more than fifty years, the son of his second marriage is inexplicitly tortured by an unknown assailant playing a tape of a German voice yelling *Heinrich Kauffman* over and over. At the back of her brain, the overture from *Cabaret* began to swell. Humming along, she shuffled through leaves, trying to quell the beat enticing her to join in, life was a cabaret.

It wasn't much fun for Peyton at the moment. What did he know, or what had he done, to deserve being tortured? Could he be descended from a hated Nazi collaborator? Would that explain his current troubles? There were days at the track when he acted like he'd trained with the Gestapo. It didn't take much imagination to see him with a bristling mustache, barking out orders, goose-stepping in shiny boots. *Achtung.*

When she rounded the corner, her humor faded, the soundtrack stilled. A black and gold police cruiser was parked in front of the house, doors open. The Gestapo were there in the flesh—Speedway cops in their black uniforms—hauling Hagan onto the lawn. She recognized two of them from the track that morning: Chief Patten and the rookie with the dimple.

She sprinted down the sidewalk. The chief looked up, waited for her beside the cruiser. Hagan was arguing, refusing to get in until they let him lock up the house. Patten wagged his chin in her direction. "She can lock up. You're coming with us now."

Rebecca demanded to know what was going on.

Hagan cut her off. He spoke very distinctly, as if English was not her native tongue. "I had a run-in with Evans. He's pressing charges for assault. It's nothing to worry about. Go inside. I'll call you when I need a ride. Oh, and Moore, don't upset my Jasmine tea. I left it cooling outside."

She hugged her arms to her body as he was bundled into the cruiser. She knew Evans had been on the receiving end of the bruised knuckles. Hagan was younger and more physically fit, so Evans probably was sore and in foul humor. But he didn't seem the type to go whining to the police.

Had someone with more clout encouraged Evans to do it? Someone like Elise Carlson or Peyton Madison II, who might find it convenient to point the cops in Hagan's direction. Blame the outsider. The police would buy it in the blip of a siren. Assume that if Hagan would pick a fight with Evans, he might have attacked the team owner as well. Evans's gripe would put Hagan behind bars, as least temporarily. Everyone else could get back to racing.

Or was she jumping to conclusions? Patten's officiousness could be posturing. The State Police had pulled rank on him this morning, stolen his limelight. Frustrated, he might have decided to take out his hostilities on a visiting police officer with an attitude.

When the cruiser turned the corner, she hurried inside.

No translator had been necessary for Hagan's parting comment. He didn't drink tea. If he did, he certainly wouldn't have drunk anything flowery like Jasmine. Lipton, strong to the point of bitterness, maybe.

She sprinted through the living room, into the kitchen, crossed to the sliding glass door. The patio appeared empty except for a squirrel brazenly sitting on the redwood table, shelling a peanut. He cocked his head at her, chattered, decided she was no threat and resumed gnawing at the crack in the shell. She slid the door open and stepped outside. The squirrel leapt from the table. His movement was followed by a rustle near the corner of the fence. The shadow of the azalea bush expanded and moved.

"Jasmine?"

The shadow stilled. Twigs snapped as the girl wiggled her way clear of the branches. She stood close to the bush, tugged unevenly on the hem of her sweatshirt. She raised her face to Rebecca and waited.

Rebecca could not overlook the facial discoloration. It reminded her of a Sycamore tree: strong dark trunk, peeling away as it rises up, leaving irregular patches of ash white. She was particularly drawn to the pale arc that raised the child's right eyebrow in a perpetual question. How appropriate, given the intelligence and curiosity in the imp's expression.

Jasmine scrutinized her in return, judging, tension in the set of her thin shoulders, the twist of her mouth.

Hoping she wasn't disappointed, Rebecca stepped forward and opened her arms. "Jasmine, I'm so delighted to meet you at last."

Her hand flew to her white cheek. She blinked, pursed her mouth into a perfect "O" and exhaled. Then raced forward and wrapped herself around Rebecca's legs.

Together they rooted through kitchen cupboards and found powered lemonade mix. While Jasmine slurped the diluted yellow liquid, Rebecca reassured her that the cops wouldn't hurt Hagan and he would soon be back. The girl was more interested in shelling peanuts for the squirrel named Fred. She insisted that he visited every day when she snuck in to leave the pictures. He waited for her. He knew she'd come. She was very dependable, Fred counted on that. Jasmine made that last statement with such sincerity that Rebecca had no doubt of it.

For an hour Jasmine amused Rebecca as she replayed the events of the shooting, acting them out on the patio. Standing on the table, she pretended she was spying on the pit area. She swore she had snapped a million pictures so she could ask a zillion questions later. She would have taken more, but the birds suddenly flew away squawking.

"What birds?"

"The birds that snack with me."

Jasmine's routine was to dot the bleachers at the track with shelled peanuts or crusts from her hot dog roll. Thursday afternoon she'd covered a distance of about thirty yards between her perch and the VIP suites. When the birds suddenly took off, she turned and saw a reflection, like sunlight off metal, poking out from the shadow of the building. She thought it was another camera until she looked through the lens. It was the barrel of a gun. As it inched forward, she started snapping pictures. Then she heard the explosion.

She leapt down from the table. "It was awful. I was afraid you had been killed by the demon. But you turned your head in my direction. Looked up. Everything was right as rain." She clapped her hands over the miracle.

"Did you see the shooter?"

She frowned. "He ran down the stands, very fast. All in black like the devil. Or a vampire." She made a cross with her two index fingers and bared her upper teeth.

Rebecca had to laugh. The child's personality, like

her skin, seemed to have two distinct sides. Close-up, she was confident to the point of being defiant. But she said she kept out of the way of crowds, like at the races. People stared. Sometimes they made fun of her.

"They can't help being ignorant. They don't understand about the disease. Lots of people have it, it just shows up best on us with black skin."

She hopped from the table and took her glass to the kitchen sink. When she turned, sunlight through the slider spotlighted her face. The dark/light coloring was exotic and slightly whimsical, the way a pinto horse appears playful. Rebecca wondered what Jasmine's parents looked like, her siblings. Were they all similarly marked, or was Jasmine unique? With large bright black eyes and a wide grin, the petite girl was truly beautiful, even in a society that puts too much emphasis on conformity.

At four o'clock, they drove to Samuel H. Groën's photography shop. Hagan hadn't filled the tank so they stopped at an Exxon station on the way. Jasmine borrowed money and slipped into the minimart to buy another bag of peanuts for Fred. That was the most productive part of the trip. Groën wasn't at his shop. He had asked his assistant to apologize. There was an important errand he had to run. Could Jasmine please return at six o'clock? The shop would be closed and he would have time to devote to her little puzzle.

Jasmine sighed and let her shoulders sag. Until Rebecca said yes, of course they would return.

Twenty-nine

Once back on Patricia Street, they had to search for a parking space. A shiny black Lexus had claimed the spot in front of the house. An early indication that the serious race fans were starting to arrive.

Jasmine snatched up the peanuts and ran to the gate. She disappeared through the gap. Then reappeared almost as quickly, backing up, tripping in reverse. Elise Carlson followed in her wake. A galleon in parade splendor: subdued plaid suit by Jones of New York Sport set off by a lemon turtleneck.

Her expression was too somber for the outfit. She held the gate open for Jasmine, waited for the tot to scoot around her. Then she crossed the lawn, indicated that she would follow Rebecca into the house. They were both still standing when Elise delivered the news. "Peyton is dead. I've just come from the hospital."

Rebecca sank onto the sofa. "What happened?"

He'd been exhausted when she'd seen him just a

few hours ago, but appeared in no immediate danger. His burns had been bandaged and he was being administered fluid intravenously. There had been no indication that more acute care was needed. No hint that he was hanging on by a thread. She assumed that he was going to be fine.

Elise sat next to her, rummaged in her purse for cigarettes and a lighter. "According to his father, Peyton had heart complications that were not apparent. Who would have guessed? He looked so superiorly healthy. The doctors refused to comment on whether the electrical shocks weakened his heart, or if there was a drug reaction. They fear a lawsuit, no doubt." She flipped the lighter in her lap end for end. "Either way, he's dead."

The room went silent. Everyday noises took over. A pipe clanged in the hallway, the clock on the kitchen stove hummed.

Elise lit up, inhaled. Expelled a lopsided ring, then looked around for an ashtray. Finally cupped her hand under the ash. "Madison senior is being stoic. He wishes the race to proceed tomorrow as scheduled, which is good news. As a tribute to his son." Her voice was flat and techy.

Arriving at the hospital just after Peyton died, she'd spent two hours holding the older man's hand. He was angry, in denial. He'd rambled on about his son's profligate lifestyle, his reluctance to grow up and settle down.

"Then, abruptly, he mellowed. He said that if racing was so important to Peyton, he would honor that. Try to understand his lost son through his passion for mo-

tor sports. He tasked me to handle the arrangements—
black armbands, a public announcement of the team's
loss. There'll be a memorial service on Monday so the
crew can mourn together. Afterwards Madison senior
will take the body back to South Carolina for a family
burial."

She coughed discreetly, turned it into a sigh. Rebecca rose to find a saucer. Elise stood, but didn't follow. "Rebecca, don't be insulted, but it would be better
if you did not come to the pits tomorrow. The car is
nicely prepared. The crew can handle the adjustments
during the race. Please understand, it's a bad time for
them, and like little boys, they pout. They need someone to blame. You're the most obvious candidate."

"Elise, I had—"

"Of course, I know you're not responsible. But,
still. Enjoy the race with your attractive friend, I'll
arrange good seats for you in turn two. You'll be paid
through the weekend, so don't worry about the—"

"It's not about money."

"No. Of course, it isn't. You're right." She started
to say more, then reached for the plate Rebecca was
holding. Steadied it as she ground out the cigarette.
"Forgive me that you are the last to receive the news.
I tried phoning earlier, but there was no answer. Perhaps such news is better in person. You were out with
the child?"

Rebecca nodded, wondering where Jasmine was
hiding. Elise waited, obviously expecting her to say
where she'd been.

There was no reason not to mention the destroyed
picture. As the team's new owner, she had a right to

know about the earlier trouble. She listened and was mildly amused at Jasmine's photographic exploits, but was no more concerned about the shooter than Peyton or Evans had been.

Rebecca dropped the plate on the coffee table. *Why am I the only one worrying?* "I'm not doing this for my amusement, Elise. If the photograph can be salvaged, it may give the police a lead in the shooting."

"Police?" She poked through her purse for another cigarette. "Isn't that a bit extreme? He died from natural causes. There's no need to involve the authorities."

"But there is. Lawyers for the hospital will insist that Peyton's heart attack was caused by the injuries he sustained at the track, not by anything the hospital did. That claim will make it manslaughter, a police matter. Negative publicity or not, we'll have to tell them about Thursday's shooting. It's too coincidental to think that one mystery sniper took a potshot at the team, and a second assailant tortured the team's owner."

Elise's considered the unlit cigarette. "I see your point. How fortunate that you have access to the original. Are you taking it to a professional photographer? I know someone excellent in the city."

Rebecca assured her that the photographer was well-recommended. She didn't say that the recommendation came from a seven-year old.

Elise shrugged. "I'm sure he'll do. You'll provide me with a copy of the photographs?"

Without waiting for Rebecca to agree, she retrieved her purse and crossed to the front door. She stood for a moment, holding it ajar, and looked across the lawn. Her eyes were unfocused, clearly not seeing the parked cars, the stingy overgrown lots or the single-story houses in need of siding. "Poor Peyton. It's still inconceivable that he died like that. Last evening, he assured me that being half-owner of a race team would be glamorous fun. Apparently, the sport has a darker side."

Thirty

In May, Rebecca had considered adopting a dog. That was right after two brutal murders and the ransacking of her house. Billy Lee, an aging mechanic for a rival restoration shop, had attempted to rescue his employer's widow from her burning house. When he was carted off to the hospital suffering from smoke inhalation, Rebecca had taken custody of his Doberman, Wonder. The dog had remained at her side all night, licking her nose when she needed support, snuggling against her until Jo arrived.

Prior to that, she'd maintained that both dogs and children should be well-behaved and belong to strangers living out of state. Jasmine, like the Doberman, might be an exception. Plopped at the dining table, the girl amused herself with pen and paper, alternately humming or giggling without need to explain her mirth. Occasionally, she'd jump up and run outside to chat with Fred, with whom she did seem to have special rapport. Rebecca always thought she'd been independent as a child. Nearly as happy as Jasmine, though not as outgoing. She didn't remember being on a first-name basis with squirrels.

Jasmine's self-absorption allowed Rebecca to go through Hayes's articles one more time. It was busy-work, something to do. The news of Peyton's death, coupled with her anger at being thrown off the crew, was nearly debilitating. Elise thought delivering the messages in person would soften their sting. It hadn't. Her sympathy over Peyton bordered on perfunctory. She hadn't even pretended to be sorry that Rebecca was leaving. Perhaps Hagan was right and Carlson was one of those successful women who are comfortable only when surrounded by fawning men. By dismissing her, Elise would have the team to herself.

Nothing new leapt out as she scanned the pages from the computer. Madison senior was still a successful businessman. Peyton was still something of a wastrel. No mention of his having an ex-spouse or children, so she assumed that Peyton had died without heirs. Unless his seventy-nine-year-old father had saved up some sperm, the family line was about to go extinct.

Why did she think that progeny would matter to him? She'd faced Madison senior for fewer than five minutes. Yet without hesitation she would have described him as dynastically driven. A patriarch to whom family was everything, while individual family members counted only as his assurance of immortality. She leaned back, stretched out a kink in her shoulders. The irony of that attitude was that often those most obsessed with carrying on their genetic line liked their children least.

According to the alarm clock it was five-thirty. Ian had been moved to the Canterbury Hotel, into the room vacated by Peyton. By calling now, she might be able to reach him before he left for dinner.

He was there, but she barely recognized his voice. It was high-pitched, tense, whining. A combination of pre-race jitters and too many questions from the police. "They're swarming all over the hotel, Rebecca. They don't believe that I went to the motor home, knocked and left again immediately. You've got to vouch for me. They're hounding me. I don't need this now."

Rebecca promised to back up his story, silently hoping that Hagan would remember what time Ian had interrupted them the previous night. She didn't.

Ian ranted on. "They've barely talked to Evans. He could have snuck back to the track after dropping me off. His ditzy date was so drunk she wouldn't have known. And Whitten. He's boasting that he doesn't have an alibi. Says he doesn't need one. Claims Peyton had been threatening him, not the other way around. I'm not involved, Rebecca. I can't deal with all this crap. I have to race tomorrow."

He paused for breath. She jumped in. "Ian, I'm so sorry about Peyton. I know you didn't do anything to bring on the heart attack."

Ian screamed into the phone. "And that's another thing. Who knew the smarmy bastard had a heart? It wasn't weak from overuse. No more than his father's. He's not bothered by his son's death, not one bit. Believe me. I grew up swimming in a sea of sangfroid. That man's got dry ice in his veins." He blew out a breath, sucked in. "He and Carlson have bonded like flipping Siamese twins. They plan to stop by the pits tomorrow to strap me in, then go off to watch the race together. She'll try to wow him with the thrill of historic Grand Prix racing. Encourage him to remain a partner. One cold-blooded vulture cooing at another."

Rebecca slid her knees to her chest and hugged them. She shared Ian's outrage. Elise's obsession with business was tolerable only because she was a stranger who barely knew Peyton. How could Madison calmly enjoy the race with his son lying in the morgue? "Oh hell, maybe he's in shock."

Ian snorted. "It's like Peyton's already forgotten. Oh, there'll be a memorial service so we can pay respects before we pack up and head off to the next race. Then he'll cremate him and FedEx the ashes south. Stash him in the mausoleum. Team be damned, Rebecca, Peyton was his only child. A pretentious little shit maybe, but still he was his son."

The anguish in Ian's voice made her wonder if Madison's paternal indifference was hitting too close to home. She asked him to call her with the time and place of the service if they didn't connect at the track. He sounded genuinely sorry that she wouldn't be in the pits keeping an eye on him.

"Don't worry, I'll be with you in spirit on every turn."

"Right. You and that cop of yours." Ian punched off.

She dropped the phone on the bed. Just thinking about the race tomorrow deepened her depression. Going to the track would be like walking back into the *Post* building after she'd been fired. Face red, eyes downcast, sure that everyone from the mail room clerk to the president considered her unfit to walk through the door.

In the bathroom, she splashed water on her face, stared in the mirror, tried on an effete smile for the sake of the bubbly kid in the other room. She'd collect Jasmine and go pick up the photograph. Chances were it would reveal nothing definitive, but it was important that the girl see it for herself. Maybe they'd go to McDonald's. Hot French fries coated with salt would lift her spirits.

Jasmine wasn't in the living room. Rebecca called her name as she headed for the patio.

She wasn't chatting with the squirrel on the redwood table.

Nor was she playing in the backyard, or sprawled in the grass out front encouraging a rabbit as it scissored the heads off fading mums.

Not in the kitchen, bathroom, or any of the bedrooms.

Rebecca rushed outside. "Jasmine? Jasmine, where are you?"

Her bike was gone.

Grabbing up the keys, she tore to the car. The tires spit gravel as she accelerated away from the curb. She spun the car around one-eighty in the middle of the road. *Screw the one-way streets.*

She wasn't sure why her adrenaline had kicked in, but she didn't like the idea that Jasmine was missing, that she'd left without telling her. Probably, the girl had snuck out to retrieve the picture. Or, maybe she realized it was late and had gone home to dinner. Rebecca prayed she hadn't left the house for an unknown destination. Or with some unknown character.

She dropped down to Thirtieth Street and turned north onto Georgetown, barely clearing the intersection. Just past the Thirty-fourth Street intersection, traffic gridlocked, clogging too far back from the intersection to blame the red light.

She swerved the car toward the center lane as the cars ahead of her inched forward, leaned out of the window trying to see what was causing the traffic snarl. No construction equipment. No blue lights signaling an accident or a speeder pulled over to the side of the road. No signs of a parade, just the black-and-white-checkered banners advertising Budweiser and welcoming race fans.

What was the holdup? Too many visitors all heading for the same location? Maybe Steak 'n Shake was giving away free burgers. Or better yet, Auto Zone was matching every case of oil with a case of beer. Lots of things could cause a Saturday night tie-up on a major highway during a race weekend. Things she couldn't imagine.

Things like a fire.

Like the billowing black clouds of smoke rising up above the buildings about three blocks down on the right. In the same block as the photography shop.

Cars already at the intersection were shoving through to get past the fire before traffic froze. Those in front of her didn't have a chance; they slowed down to gawk. She hoped one of them was calling it in. She didn't hear sirens.

Traffic crept forward. She spotted an alley a hundred yards before the burning block. She cut the wheel hard to the right, clung to the gutter, gunned the engine, drove up the wheelchair access and onto the sidewalk. She shut it down twenty feet from a hydrant, left the keys in the ignition in case it had to be moved. Slammed the door and began jogging.

The thickest column of smoke curled out of the alley on the right. She ran down it, dodging trash cans, puddles and a discarded quart of St. Ives. A block from the photographer's, the smoke was blinding. It stank of something pungent, metallic. Heat like a wall sprang up in front of her. It addled her brain as she tried to remember what chemicals were used to develop film and whether or not they were likely to explode.

Half a block later, her question was answered.

The south wall of the camera shop burst outward, tumbling concrete blocks and sending shards of shrapnel flying seconds before she heard the explosion. The blast knocked her sideways. She went down on one knee and her elbow. A child's black bike flew over her, landed on a trash can and fell to earth, front wheel spinning.

She was choking, scrabbling frantically to get to her feet, panicking, certain the bike was Jasmine's. People were screaming, fleeing from the stalled cars, weaving through lanes of traffic to get to the far side of the road. To safety.

The sudden rush of oxygen fanned the fire. Fumes and smoke escaped through the gaping hole. Her eyes were tearing, blinding her. She stumbled forward, calling Jasmine's name. She doused the tail of her blouse in a puddle. Held it over her mouth as she staggered into the crumbled building.

She nearly tripped over the girl before she heard her. "Help me. It's heavy."

She dropped her shirttail and felt for the child, wanting to clutch her and run. Jasmine gripped her hands, directed them forward until her fingers bumped into something solid.

"Hurry."

She fumbled for purchase, smacked into metal, painfully hot.

Jasmine squealed in her ear. "The chair's stuck. He mustn't die."

Chair? "Wheelchair?"

"Yes. Help me."

Rebecca went down on her knees, felt for the wheels. She found the spokes of the left one and stretched across for the right, reaching the rim. The rubber was melting under her grip, fusing with her palm. She struggled to her feet, grasped the highest point of the wheels, yelled at Jasmine to stand back. She yanked at the chair. It bounced against something immovable and fell back a few inches. She heaved again. The chair barely budged.

A man's voice materialized out of the smoke. "Leave me. Save the girl." It was a command, not a plea.

Rebecca felt tears of anger wash her eyes as she flexed her thighs, lowered her grip on the chair. And pulled. This time, the chair would move.

The paramedics found the three of them huddled in an alley, watching Samuel Groën's photography business turn to ash. The hair salon next door was a total loss as well. A clerk from the minimart across the street had brought them water and damp paper towels. She'd tried to wash soot from Jasmine's face, but the girl skittered away to hide behind Rebecca.

Groën had inhaled too much smoke and was coughing up black phlegm. Other than raw skin on her palms and bruises from wrestling with the wheelchair, Rebecca was whole. The medics strongly advised that they both go to the hospital. They refused.

Jasmine had a burn on her arm that needed to be treated and bandaged. She'd run back into the building to hunt for the xD card that contained her pictures. She was devastated to think that she would never be able to show Rebecca the photograph of the shooter. Jasmine pouted as if she would burst into tears. Mr. Groën told her not to worry.

As the medic applied gauze squares over the burn, Rebecca promised she would urge Jasmine's mother to take the girl to a doctor to have the burn looked at and the dressing changed. She would—if she ever met Jasmine's mother. If Jasmine had a mother, a father, sisters, brothers, somebody. The child seemed to have imprinted to her like an orphan duckling. Rebecca refused to believe that such a loving child had no one at home nurturing her.

But here she was, clinging to her waist and moaning over and over that Sammy had no business and nowhere to live. Finally the message penetrated—the ell of the building that extended into the parking lot had been the photographer's home.

"Less than a home," Groën said. "Merely a place to rest. Don't fret, I belong to a nomadic tribe."

The medic agreed to give Groën a ride in the ambulance as far as the house where Rebecca was staying. With Hagan in jail and Ian at the Canterbury, there was plenty of room. Jasmine approved of the arrangement and announced she would go with them, too. Rebecca didn't have the heart to send the tyke away, even if she knew where to send her. She would have to wring that information out of her later. Or maybe Groën knew. The girl gripped her hand as they walked to the nearest cop and told him where they could be found when he was ready to take their statements.

Thirty-one

Rebecca agreed to call Groën by his given name. Samuel suited his dignity. Sammy didn't. The summer she was six, she'd had a pet salamander named Sammy that had lost its tail to a determined cat.

Groën thanked her. "I wish I could convince the child to drop the diminutive. Easier to change the path of a tornado." He laughed so hard his belly wobbled. It was obvious that whatever Jasmine wanted to call him was fine.

Jasmine insisted the girls bathe at the same time. She splashed in the tub with her arm encased in a plastic bag. Rebecca kept an eye on her through the transparent vinyl shower curtain. The first day at the house, she'd removed the floral outer curtain to let in the light. She didn't expect anyone to sneak up on her in the shower. But she was having trouble with closed-in spaces, which made no sense. Her last scare involved the wide-open river.

They emerged from their ablutions smelling of

every toiletry in her kit. Jasmine was shrouded in one of Hagan's T-shirts. It hung down past her knees and was wide enough to have fit two of her. She christened it her transformation robe and flew into the kitchen for crayon and paper to illustrate a tale worthy of her raiments.

Samuel requested Rebecca's help getting into the bathroom, then out of the chair. He had little strength in his legs, no mobility. On a good day, he could stand without help. Today was not such a good day. "It could be a worse ailment. My sister insists I enjoy being lazy. Maybe. And the chair, well, it isn't so bad for business. Few people take advantage of someone they perceive as being worse off than themselves."

She smiled at the rascal and got him settled for a sponge bath. Trespassing in Ian's room, she flicked through the coat hangers of clothes he'd left behind, looking for a robe. A striped velour wraparound had fallen to the floor of the closet. It was dusty, but smelled clean. She passed it around the edge of the door, asking for Samuel's sooty clothes in return.

When he called her, she resettled him in the chair. He coughed, wheezing as he told her to close the bathroom door. "Sit, please. I am a cranky old man right now, so I ask that you do not judge me harshly." He tugged at the robe of many colors not quite covering his legs. "I demand to hear what puts Jasmine in danger. I have lost my business. That is an ample price to pay for the knowledge, don't you think? I do not blame you for endangering the girl, I simply want to know what evil we face."

Rebecca sank to the edge of the tub. "I wish I knew."

"Ach." Groën slapped his hands on his thighs. "Then together we must figure it out. First, you talk. After, I tell you Jasmine's story."

While Groën made phone calls—to his sister, the insurance company and to Jasmine's family—Rebecca and Jasmine discussed pizza. The girl insisted on picking the toppings, which proved a lengthy process. Their soot-smeared clothes were washed and dried before they'd placed the call to Domino's. In the end she compromised: one with pepperoni for the purists and one with everything. Picky eaters could remove what they didn't like. By the time the pizza arrived, all three were so hungry they would have eaten the cardboard boxes.

With tomato sauce oozing from the corner of her mouth, Jasmine announced she was pleased with her selections. Groën patted his stomach in agreement and eased his chair back from the table. He plucked a crumb out of his beard, tossed it at Jasmine. "I think you will be even more pleased with my surprise. Though, it is not to be eaten."

He wheeled to the sofa to retrieve the borrowed robe. From a pocket he fished out something small enough to be secreted in his hand then propelled himself over to Jasmine. He held out the fist.

She knocked on his knuckles. "Open, sesame." As commanded, he turned his hand over and unfurled his fingers. A small black square fell onto the table.

She squealed. "You saved it. My pictures."

"Liebschen, it was in the cuff of my pants. I forget

putting it there for safekeeping. It is so small. I didn't want yours mixed in with the palm trees and luaus."

The girl pulled on his arm. "We'll develop it right now."

He patted her hand. "I have seen it, Jaz."

His mouth drooped to a frown. Rebecca eased the girl away from Groën. "What did it show?"

"Not so much. A rifle rising up next to a building and the arm holding it."

"Not the shooter?" He shook his head. Rebecca caught his eye. "Then what? Did you recognize the gun, the clothing, the arm? Something about it?"

He shrugged. "It was an arm. White skin. Dark sleeve pushed up. Taut muscles hold the rifle, like so. And, just a small scar."

He picked up his empty glass and asked Jasmine if she would bring him another soda. They would toast to life. The girl hopped down and ran to the kitchen to oblige him.

"Such a well-behaved child."

When she was out of earshot, Rebecca asked him to explain about the scar. Groën responded by saying he had visited an old friend this afternoon, Hermann Friedlander, who also has such a scar. He picked at a loose button thread on his sweater.

Rebecca waited. "And?"

Groën sighed. "I wonder how much dark history is a good thing for an ebullient child to know?"

An excellent question. Would Rebecca have traded her contented childhood to have known the truth about being an orphan? She didn't suppose so. Once something was known, it could not be unknown. As Jo was fond of pointing out, that was the lesson of the Garden of Eden. Knowledge extracts its own price in innocence lost.

Before she could persuade Groën to expound, the doorbell rang. The young Marion County cop from the fire scene looked disheveled, but energized. He introduced his partner, Ellison, who couldn't have been over five feet, five inches tall. He was nearly as wide, so bowlegged Jasmine could have darted between his legs without touching either knee. He asked most of the questions, aimed most of them at the photographer. His partner took notes.

When prompted, Groën relived the hour before the fire. Five-thirty was normal closing. He was expecting Jasmine to return at six o'clock. He finished locking up at twenty till, then wheeled into his living quarters to freshen himself. Ten, fifteen minutes later he heard the window in the darkroom break. He was annoyed, but not alarmed. The window is barred. He assumed it was kids throwing beer bottles. "There's not enough entertainment for the neighborhood hooligans."

Then he smelled the chemicals. The acrid stench.

"Not smoke?"

"That, too. First I remember smelling heat, if such a thing is possible. Then I smell fixative, paper burning. Crinkling. Perhaps I am sensitive because I know fire and my photos mix with very bad results." Groën rocked on his toes, moving the chair back and forth. "How was the fire started?"

"Professionally." Ellison stilled the chair with his hand on the arm. "Someone fired an incendiary round through the window. It produced enough of a flash to ignite your stuff. Paper or chemicals, didn't matter. Kaboom. The shooter could have been half a block away. Don't suppose you saw anyone suspicious hanging around?"

Groën shook his head.

Jasmine, pressed close to Rebecca's thigh, raised her eyes to Ellison. "The devil."

"Yeah. You can say that again."

Jasmine complied. "The devil, devil, devil. The very same devil. Shall I draw him?"

Rebecca pinched her shoulder to silence the chanting. "What devil, Jasmine? The one in the photograph?" The girl bobbed her head.

With Rebecca's arm around her shoulders, Jasmine gave her statement.

At almost six o'clock she'd tiptoed into the bedroom. Rebecca was on the bed, talking on the phone, so she decided to take her bike and ride to Sammy's. He would give her the new photograph, she would show him what Fred had found. Then she would bring the picture to Rebecca and surprise her. It was a good plan.

As she rode down the dirty alley, she heard glass break. Louder than a bottle. She straddled her bike, looked around. There was no one. "Then, in the alley, the devil was walking away. Whistling."

Her description was disappointingly vague, even when embellished. The person was tall, but to her, everyone was. It was also forty yards away in a dim passageway between buildings, obscured by shadows. She wasn't sure if it was a man or a woman, but it carried a duffle bag—a bag of tricks. And it was dressed all in black: black boots, black pants, billowing black jacket, black cap. Of that, Jasmine was sure. When Ellison raised an eyebrow, she admitted that she hadn't really heard him whistle. "But it's what the devil would do."

Ellison hunkered down to her level and thanked her very formally for her statement. She beamed. Then he asked her about the photograph she wanted from the camera shop.

That explanation did not go as smoothly. He was justifiably annoyed that the shooting incident at the racetrack had not been reported to the police. He stressed that if it had, Mr. Madison's assault and the fire at Mr. Groën's shop might have been prevented. The fact that her boss refused to go to the police did not exonerate Rebecca or the other crew members.

She didn't argue. It had been a bad decision at the time and was looking worse daily.

He reminded them that they would have to go to the station house to sign statements on Monday. Rebecca nodded, then asked how? Short of tethering Groën's wheelchair to the back of the Corvette, she had no way to get him there. The young cop said to call; they'd help her work out transportation tomorrow.

Tomorrow sounded good. Tonight was running out of steam. When she suggested that they turn in and save their discussion for the morning, Samuel agreed. His face was sagging, eyes glazing over. He bid them good night and wheeled himself down the hall.

Jasmine wasn't so easy. She held out until Rebecca agreed that they could share the double bed. Rebecca turned back a corner of the blanket, waited while the girl said prayers and slipped under the covers. Once Jasmine stopped squirming, she promised that she would come to bed soon and keep her safe. First she had to make a phone call.

Rebecca wasn't across the threshold before the girl leapt from bed and began digging through the pockets of her jeans. With a toothy grin she skipped over and held out her hand. In the palm was a battered hunk of gray plastic and metal bits. It looked chewed.

"Fred found it. Is it a treasure?"

Rebecca turned it over in Jasmine's palm. It looked neither sophisticated nor dangerous, but it made her nerve endings tingle. *Could it be?* She picked it up and pulled at a small wire soldered in place. Her brain cells screamed *Yes it is* and raced toward a nasty conclusion. Admittedly, most of what she knew about electronic surveillance devices came from watching spy movies. Still she was convinced that the mess in her hand was a bug. She would have dropped it in disgust, but Jasmine was watching.

Rebecca squatted down to her level. "Where did Fred find this, do you know?"

"Come, I'll show you."

The girl scooted down the hall into the kitchen. Rebecca followed, got there in time to help her with the catch for the slider. Jasmine slipped outside, bent down and pointed to the crack where the two doors overlapped.

Rebecca fetched a flashlight from a kitchen drawer and knelt to look. About a foot above the ground was a wad of what looked like chewing gum but smelled like putty. Judging from the indentation, it had once held the bug, or whatever it was, until Fred decided it might be good to eat.

Jasmine was grinning, waiting for approval. Rebecca told her that Fred's treasure was very important. She would explain in the morning, if the girl went to sleep right now. Reluctantly, Jasmine allowed herself to be tucked into bed, a second time.

Squeezing the hunk of plastic in her hand, Rebecca walked out to the patio. If it was a listening device, who put it there? When? How far could it transmit? Was someone waiting in the neighbor's yard right now to overhear—what? The babble of a seven-year-old and an old man?

But they'd just arrived. Before that, she and Hagan were in the house alone. Before that she and Ian. Why would anyone eavesdrop on their conversations?

It was possible that Hagan planted it to listen for the intruder with the photographs, who turned out to be Jasmine. If he'd installed it earlier in the day, he might not have had the chance to tell her. Did detectives carry such contraptions in their overnight kits alongside shaving cream?

Was it still working despite the squirrel's sharp little teeth?

She sat at the table and opened her hand. Maybe she was wrong and it was a sensor for a defunct security system, or a temperature monitor, or something equally mundane. But the metal was shiny and the putty unsoiled. She was willing to bet that it had been installed recently. Why and by whom? What the hell should she do about it? She dropped it into the plant pot beside the dead geranium.

The clouds that had hung around most of the day were drifting apart. A smattering of stars peeked through. She took out her cell phone and opened it, waited while it came to life. Staring into the darkness brought back Jasmine's description of the devil. Cap, shirt, jacket, pants, boots: seen from the back it was unadorned, solid black. From the front it might have been a uniform. Like those worn by the Speedway Police.

That was a depressing, unsubstantiated thought, which led like an arrow to Hagan. Why hadn't he called for a ride home? She assumed the cops would keep him a few hours, just long enough for a testy interview and to satisfy Evans's complaint. A quick check of his credentials and he'd be released. She was itching to ask him about the surveillance device, but should she call him? What could she say, knowing that their conversation might be overheard by the stranger who'd planted it? Or by a cop who had a vendetta against the Lotus team. Paranoid, but conceivable.

It would make more sense to call her lawyer, if she could reach him. Jo might be able to find out what was happening with Hagan, maybe even find out why. Groveling would be necessary. And postponing any confrontation over his visit to her parents. She could do that. She could forget about it entirely, just to hear his calm, reassuring voice. The one she was used to hearing.

She forced the bug deep into the dirt before pressing the connect button. The message window flashed, *Calling Jo.*

Pulling her knees to her chest, she wrapped the

jacket around them. It was a navy L. L. Bean wind-breaker belonging to Hagan, which he'd worn the first time she'd seen him in Head Tide. So much had happened so fast since then that she could scarcely recall what it had been like before knowing him. Or Jo. A cop and a lawyer. The two men in her life inexorably entwined by murder and mayhem.

Thirty-two

The phone rang twenty-one times before Jo freed it from his jacket pocket. Melodious notes he wasn't used to hearing. The caller ID number said it was Rebecca who was being so persistent. He'd guessed as much. He should be pleased.

He was sitting at the edge of the dried-up brook on Ryders' Mill Road. The last of the light had faded an hour ago. A chorus of crickets had begun their evening performance. Staring out over the shallow stream, he'd been reliving a picnic he'd shared with Rebecca the day he learned she couldn't swim, that she was afraid of becoming entangled in vegetation and drowning. He leaned back against a fallen trunk, fumbled for the right button and said hello.

Her voice through the phone line was abnormally soft. She said she had house guests—a seven-year-old named Jasmine and a bluff old Jewish photographer. They were trying to sleep. She couldn't. As explanation for her insomnia, she pieced together the story of finding Peyton Madison unconscious in the race car, his subsequent death, the fire at the photography shop and the little girl's heroism in pulling the wheelchair-bound Groën from the burning building.

Jo kept his mouth firmly shut, but his mind whirled as he listened to Rebecca. Dorothea Wetherly had told him about the attack on Peyton, but not that the man had died. Now his death had been compounded by a fire that somehow involved a disfigured child who might have come too close to the gunman who had fired on the team.

He pushed off from the trunk, paced to the water. What was there about Rebecca that attracted people in extreme need? If he still believed in a god, he'd accept that a divine hand led the downtrodden to her, knowing she would help. Or die trying.

Or maybe it was just Rebecca. She had tenacity programmed into her genes. Maybe others sensed it, latched on to it, used it to their advantage.

One July day Jo had sat on the patio while she weeded wild grape vine from the perennial border. More than methodical, she was compulsive. Holding the broad leaves in one hand, she followed the thin, brittle stalks into the ground, felt in the damp earth, gently loosened the tendrils. Then went on to the next spot where it had sent down feelers. Inch by inch, she teased the vine from the leaf mulch, circled with it through the lilies and iris. As the strand in her grip grew longer, her smile grew broader—until, pulling out the root, she had laughed with glee.

She was fully aware that in another month the vines would be back, smaller but just as insidious. Weeds cannot be stamped out any more than evil can be. But she kept trying. Jo wished she would stop. He wanted her safe, particularly now, when he couldn't be there.

When he tuned back in, Rebecca was describing the child's optimism, her zeal for what must be a hard life, being different from the sea of people around her. From there it was a short sidestep to her conversation with her grandmother touching on the persecution of Jews by the Nazis. "Differences give life its color and complexity. Can you imagine a mind so small that it envisions a world populated by clones all looking, thinking, acting alike?"

He could imagine it; he didn't want to go there.

He sat on a boulder and stretched out his legs. The sky was starless; he was alone with night sounds and unfinished business for company. Lots of it. His impromptu visit to her parents, his dinner with her grandmother, the airplane ticket in his pocket. He pushed them aside, wolves temporarily barred from the door. "Rebecca, yesterday I met with the Borden boys regarding their father's will."

"Is Elton still the loser?"

"They all are. Less than a month ago Cyrus sold his land to a developer."

"Land? I thought he rented a shack and buried spare change in coffee cans."

"He must have dug up the money. Last year he started buying up nonproducing farm lands, quietly. He didn't consult me. No one in town discovered what he was doing."

"If you didn't hear about it at Flo's, no one knew. What land? Where?"

"One forty-acre plot. It abuts your back fields." Jo let it sink in.

He heard a gate slam. Rebecca's voice was louder, harsh. "What developer?"

"One out of Richmond. My contact there tells me he's notorious for land-banking."

"Are you going to explain that?"

"Naturally. I'm your lawyer. It's what you pay me for." He hoisted himself up to standing. "In two instances this developer has purchased farmland at less than market value then leased it for a mobile home park. His strategy was flexible. He'd either drive away the adjoining landowners and buy their properties cheaply. Or attract such obnoxious renters that the town fathers would purchase the land from him at a premium. Third option was to wait until the land was in demand for a commercial project. Not original, but effective, especially since he has sufficient cash flow to bide his time." Silence. "Rebecca?"

"I'm counting to ten. Shit. How did that happen, Jo. The fields are my breathing space. I can't lose them to a trailer park. He has to be stopped."

"Then come home." *Please.*

Her voice was brittle to the point of breaking. "I can't. If I do, who'll protect Jasmine? And look out for the team? Hagan is lolling in jail."

Jail? Damn that man. "What the hell did Hagan do?"

Not really caring, Jo grabbed up his jacket, scrabbled up the bank, crunching dry leaves. He caught enough of Rebecca's explanation to deduce that Hagan had gotten into a fistfight with the crew chief. She rationalized it as a power play, politics. She was fretting because he hadn't returned, hadn't called for a ride. Jo sincerely hoped the police would keep Hagan permanently. It would solve one of his problems. Trumped-up charges would work just fine.

Rebecca's next sentence began with, "Could you—"

He cut her off. "Don't you dare suggest that I come there to bail him out. Hagan is adept at getting into trouble. No doubt, he can weasel his own way out."

"But—"

"But nothing, Rebecca. You have a business to manage. Property to defend. Family issues to resolve. Stop running away after distractions dangled in front of you like candy for children. I don't have time for Hagan's nonsense and neither do you."

He heard the sharp intake of breath. He should have been ready for her attack, for the chill in her voice.

"But you have time to interfere in my life? Time to fly to Boston and hassle my parents. Go barging in where you have no business, no right. What did you think you were doing?"

He didn't answer. He had no defense. Mostly he had done it for her, to smooth the way to a reconciliation with her parents. But he'd also done it for himself. He needed to meet them, to be accepted by them. Before he left Head Tide, he had to know if there was a future to come back to—one with Rebecca in it as more than a client and close friend. This time around, he was getting the parental approval first.

Her voice rose higher. "Do you think I'm incapable of talking to the people who raised me? I will. When I'm ready. I don't need your help. In that or anything else."

Jo whispered a prayer that it wasn't true. He needed her too much. Possibly for ignoble reasons. He hoped that someday soon he could explain it.

Not tonight.

Without looking at the keypad, he punched the end button with his thumb, held it until the phone went dark, then slipped it into his pocket. The moon seemed brighter without the mechanical competition. It was nearly full; the old man might have been smiling. Jo hoped the moon was smiling in Indianapolis.

"Good night, Rebecca. Take care of yourself."

Thirty-three

Rebecca sagged against the gate and stared at the phone. She couldn't believe it. Jo had hung up on her.

Okay, she'd given him reason when she'd yelled at him for meddling in her affairs, but his condescending attitude toward Hagan had sent her over the edge. Not wanting him to worry, she hadn't whined about being ousted from the track, cut off from the rest of the crew. Or carped about Elise's demoralizing attitude. She'd kept those petty hurts to herself. Standing in the dark, outside the fence, she hadn't revealed how alone she felt: solely responsible for Jasmine's safety, guilty about Peyton's death and worried about the bug and what it meant. She'd mentioned Hagan's incarceration only because that was one thing her attorney could help with.

Could Jo be that sensitive about Hagan? *Damn it.* He sent Hagan out here. Some pair they were. Hagan, the controlling, who kept everything to himself, championed by Delacroix, the sanctimonious who dictated how she should relate to her own family. She was better off without either of them. She stomped inside the patio, threw the phone on the redwood table and slipped into the kitchen.

The house was peaceful in sharp contrast to her thoughts. She should sleep, but knew it was beyond her; still she went through the motions of getting ready for bed and eased open the door to her room. Light from the hallway filtered in. Jasmine was on the far side of the bed near the wall, curled under the blanket, the top of her head a dark sliver against the yellow binding. She looked smaller than the pillow, as shapeless as one losing its stuffing. Yet there was nothing limp about her. She had a tough inner core.

She needed it. The story of Jasmine's natural family began as a common urban tale. In Groën's version, a spunky woman, barely out of her teens, got pregnant by an older man, Reginald Quick. He was a decent hard-worker who welcomed the chance for a family. They married and had the child: a girl born with a strange skin disease. The mother tried to cope for a few years, but found it too difficult. Said she was too young for motherhood. She viewed Jasmine's disease as her personal failure. One day she packed and left her family, town, the state.

Reginald hadn't condemned her. He set about to raise Jasmine the best he could. He infused her with his passions, took her to car races and history museums. When she was big enough to hold a camera, he showed her how to compose a picture that told a story. For a couple of years, they were happy.

Then Reginald was diagnosed with early-onset

Alzheimer's. The doctor told him what to expect. There were drugs that might slow it, drugs he couldn't afford. He thanked the doctor, then did the hardest thing a man could do, put the daughter he loved into foster care. Two weeks later, Reginald Quick disappeared.

Rebecca leaned against the doorframe watching Jasmine breathe. A lump was forming in her throat, moisture building in her eyes. She remained outside the room, for fear her sniffling would wake the girl. *Let her dream.* Her daylight reality was too harsh. Far better for her to live in a fantasy world: fight imaginary demons, pine to become a damsel who drove race cars, spend afternoons shelling peanuts and conversing with a squirrel called Fred.

At first, Groën confessed, he'd been tempted to pity the girl. "But how could I? There is nothing pathetic about Jasmine. She is all spirit, a child capable of bouncing back. A survivor."

Rebecca agreed. She ached for Reginald Quick, for what he was facing alone and for the joy he'd abandoned. She wiped the back of her hand across her eyes. *Life is so damn perverse.*

So was she.

Why was she making such a big deal about Robert and Pauline not being her biological parents? Would she have had a better childhood if she had been raised by Nicole and Jamie? From what she'd been told, Jamie had been an irresponsible dreamer. Nicole was so bitter toward her parents that hatred would have poisoned her love for her own daughter. Neither one had a pursued a career, so money would have become an issue. Most likely, they would have separated. She would have had to cope with being the product of a broken home.

She tiptoed into the bedroom, pulled the door to behind her. As it was, she had been raised by a couple who'd given her every advantage and done their best to love her. As had her brothers and both sets of grandparents. *Had her grandparents known the truth? Had her brothers suspected?* She smoothed the sheet next to Jasmine's face.

If she'd call her parents, she'd find out. If she called her parents, she might find out that nothing had changed. She hadn't lost her mooring. One intelligent, spirited elderly woman was petitioning to become a part of her life. How bad was that?

A tear slid down the side of her nose as she promised the sleeping form she would call her parents tomorrow. *Honest.*

Sunday—Final Lap

Thirty-four

Rebecca opened the drapes a crack. The pale gray sky was dotted with layers of fluffy clouds. A few optimistic birds chirped to herald a sunrise still an hour away. It promised to be a bright day, but that didn't make up for the wasted night.

Hagan had not called. Nor returned.

Jo hadn't called back to apologize.

She hadn't slept more than an hour.

Sometime around three, she'd given up and slipped from the bed, causing Jasmine to whimper and turn over. She'd retrieved her cell phone from outside, heated milk in a warped saucepan and sipped it sitting cross-legged on the sofa, going over the team's mishaps and Peyton's torture. She was convinced that all parts were interconnected, but she couldn't see how. Taken together they made a vast canvas, like *The Last Stand* by Remington, where the subjects were too spread out to grasp as a whole. Too much open space to judge which side was winning.

At four A.M., after an hour of staring at striped wallpaper with tiny six-pedaled flowers, she'd fetched her laptop. Once connected to the Internet, she scrolled through a frightening list of electronic surveillance devices used to eavesdrop on the unsuspecting. Name the range you wanted, the size you needed and the price you were willing to pay. All major credit cards accepted. Even mauled by the squirrels' teeth, the unit was recognizable as a bug. If the publicity was to be believed, it could transmit to a tape recorder a half-mile away.

Letting the drape fall shut, she wondered if there was a car parked against the curb, radio turned to a ranting evangelist, driver hunched down drinking tepid coffee, waiting to hear something. Inside, all was Sunday-morning quiet.

Sunday. Race day. She ached to be at the track, prepping the car. Carlson didn't want her: "Rebecca, don't be insulted, but it would be better if you did not come to the pits."

Once the police released Hagan, there was nothing to keep her in Indianapolis. She could run home as Jo demanded and take up her normal life. Leave behind a mystery she couldn't solve and the people embroiled in it whom she couldn't help.

Before shutting down the computer, she'd pulled up flights from Dayton, Ohio, to Boston, Massachusetts, for Monday. Hagan would give her a ride as far as the Dayton Airport. US Airways would get her to Boston in time for dinner. She'd call her parents later to confirm the plans. If they couldn't be reached, well, they'd all survive the surprise.

Discarding the computer Rebecca went in search of a steno pad and a gel pen. It was time to organize the known information into workable chunks. As a senior *Post* editor used to remind her, "When your imagination fails, you can always rely on the facts. Of course, your story won't be as interesting."

Right now, it didn't have to be interesting, just a recognizable story line. The mess reminded her of a favorite childhood toy—a block puzzle of Peter Pan. It was a foot square, divided into sixteen equal cubes. There were four different illustrated scenes, each a different action shot. All sixteen pieces had to be the right side up before you could see the whole picture. During the night she'd decided that not all her pieces were right side up.

She ripped out four sheets of paper. On the first one she listed the sabotage aimed at the team: cut brake lines, watered gas, stripped lug nuts, the gunshot. On a second, she jotted details of Peyton's torture and his subsequent death: the taped voice speaking German, the smeared visor, the name Heinrich Kauffman, *coro*—. The third was devoted to Jasmine's photographs: innocuous pictures of the pits, the race car and one arm of the shooter. The fourth page contained notes on the destruction of Samuel Groën's photography store: the incendiary rifle shot, Jasmine's camera card, the timing of the incident.

She added *bug* to the last sheet.

It was possible, but improbable, that Groën had his own band of enemies, people he'd annoyed to the point of wanting to destroy his business and him with it. But what was the chance they'd do it at that precise moment—while the camera card was there to be developed? Much more likely that destruction of the shop was related to the photograph.

If so, then the eavesdropper was likely to be the shooter.

Throughout the afternoon, Jasmine had repeatedly asked the time, whined that she didn't want to be late picking up her picture at six o'clock. Earlier in the day, she'd told Hagan all about what was on the film. She insisted she'd seen the devil. Groën said the photograph did not show the shooter, but you wouldn't have known that from overhearing Jasmine. To destroy the photograph, all the eavesdropper had to do was follow Jasmine to Groën's shop.

Holding on to that premise, she tore off another sheet; labeled *who, what, where, when* and *why* across the top. Three of the questions were easy—*what,* was a listening device; *where,* was attached to the kitchen door off the patio; *why,* was to listen in and determine what the occupants of the house knew.

Listen to whom? Jasmine and Groën had just moved in. Spying on Ian at the house would have been unproductive: Mostly, he read automotive magazines or listened to heavy operas through earphones. Like Ian, she rarely discussed anything other than racing until Hagan arrived. Hagan, a cop who had shown up unannounced right after someone had shot at the pits. His presence might make a stalker curious.

Who and *when* were even more elusive. The entire crew knew where she and Ian lived, consequently where Hagan was staying. If a stranger had asked for the address, it wouldn't have raised any suspicions. The house on Patricia Street was not a state secret.

Likewise, the bug could have been planted anytime. The house was empty during the day. There was no neighbor's guard dog to scare off an intruder at night. Even after Hagan showed up, the patio gate had been left unlocked to allow Jasmine—and apparently, the eavesdropper—easy access.

Hearing the squelch of rubber on the wood floor, she turned and smiled at Groën. He raked fingers through his beard. "While I sleep, you have solved the mystery, yes?"

"Hardly. You take my notes. I'll make coffee."

She slid her chair back from the table, allowing Samuel to take her place. Nose bent down to the surface, he read each clue, pushed the page aside as he reached for another. He formed the four sheets into a cross, shuffled them to suit his thoughts. Then he took a pen from his shirt pocket and popped off the cap. He scratched tiny lines of notes on the bottom of one page, circled a few words, then swiveled to include her. "Are we certain that there is just one person behind all this?"

She slid cups on the table. "I hope so: one complicated, driven, vengeful loner. Torture by committee just doesn't feel right."

"We start with one." He waved a finger over the papers. "But, loner or not, he was known to your Mr. Peyton. Pains were always taken so he would not be seen. The mischief to the cars was done at night. The shooting from a distance. During the interrogation, vision through the helmet was obscured. Our villain can shoot, yet he doesn't kill Peyton. He missed on Thursday. He could have shot him Friday night at the deserted track, but didn't. We know much and yet too little about his goal."

Rebecca found a hard corn muffin and two slices of cold pizza. She arranged them on a plate and dropped it on the table as she sat. "Killing Peyton was never the object."

"I agree. Or he prefers killing him by degrees: torment, sabotage, little distractions to unnerve his prey. He is Jewish."

She stopped, her hand midway to the pizza. "Jews are the only race capable of such atrocities?"

Samuel bobbed his head, then wagged it sideways. "Of course not. But we are good at it. It makes the most sense. You have not seen Jasmine's photograph. I have."

"You said there was nothing to see."

"Not for you, maybe, but for me. We Jews do not forget." He rolled up the sleeve of his shirt. "You remember I tell you the shooter's sleeve was pushed up so, perhaps to better steady the rifle? Jasmine photographed the arm just after the recoil, as it eased away from the barrel. The flesh was exposed, so the scar just above the wrist was visible. Not really a scar, scar tissue. Not recent and red, but faded like a snapshot from my childhood. I enlarged it. No stitch marks, no burns. Faint ink marks, numbers. An indelible reminder of something removed long ago."

"A tattoo?"

"Not a drawing, Rebecca. Numbers, six of them.

So hateful they had to be grafted over." He nodded at her, willing her to make the connection.

She dropped the slice onto the plate and snatched up the pad of paper. On a clean sheet she wrote *German Connections*.

Thirty-five

The phone rang just before seven. Groën was calculating the current age range for Holocaust survivors. If he was correct and the scar had once been a concentration camp identification number, then the gunman had to have been a Nazi prisoner of war.

"Was the skin on the forearm dry, aged?"

Groën shrugged. "Who noticed? I focused on the scar, not skin."

Rebecca homed in on the ringing; it was her cell phone. She rescued it from beneath a sofa pillow, kept walking to stretch.

Her grandmother was so keyed up she sounded asthmatic. "Did you say that the owner of the race team's name is Peyton Madison? Oh, how is he by the way?"

Rebecca didn't remember mentioning Madison's full name in their earlier conversation, but perhaps she had. "He didn't make it. Died of heart complications. Presumably a result of his ordeal at the track."

Dorothea paused. "He was an elderly man?"

"Fifties. Why?"

"Ah. The younger Madison. Not made of the same stern stuff as the father. They say he's going strong. Of course he may not know yet."

"About Peyton? He—"

Dorothea took a deep breath. "Oh, dear me. Let me begin closer to the beginning. I'd better sit."

Rebecca waited for her grandmother to come back on the line.

"There. Much better. Now, on your behalf, I spent last evening on the phone with acquaintances who track down Old Masters belonging to Jewish war survivors. Do you realize that as of the nineteen-nineties, an estimated thirty billion dollars worth of art was still unaccounted for? Some is surfacing now as the survivors die off because those inheriting are feeling complacent. Sad stories. Many were reluctant to speak with me until I mentioned Heinrich Kauffman. His name was like breaking a dam, got everyone talking. Mainly because he's something of a mystery. At least one of them was. You'll want to take this down."

Rebecca grabbed the steno pad from the table, found a pen on the floor. She scribbled as Dorothea spoke, amazed at the details she'd uncovered overnight.

Heinrich Josef Kauffman, the first of the name, had been a successful chemist in Stuttgart in the decade leading up to WWII. He was remembered as tolerant, kinder than his wife, less shrewd, far less political. When Hitler started making speeches, it was Hilde Kauffman who embraced the cause with fervor. She passed out leaflets to friends, dragged Heinrich, Jr. to rallies, that sort of thing. Her husband went along with her, out of indifference at first. Later because survival and his fortune depended on it. When it became obvious that no Jewish family, however prominent, was going to be allowed to prosper, the gentile Kauffman stepped in to help his Jewish neighbors.

"Opinions are divided, Rebecca, between those who believe Kauffman initially wanted to help his friends, and the other camp, who suspect Hilde was behind the planned acquisitions. Greed was her motive. Or retribution."

"What were they acquiring?"

"Art, of course. Didn't I mentioned the Aryanization of art collections? Well, that was Heinrich Kauffman's game from about nineteen-forty-one until nineteen-forty-five. Just before the war ended in Europe, Kauffman and his eldest son, also Heinrich, vanished. As did the art collections of four prominent Jewish families, collections conservatively valued in the millions.

"Nazi hunters have batted rumors around for years. Some think the family was liquidated when they refused to turn over the paintings to Rosenberg, who was acquiring art for the Reich. If so, the paintings may be in Russia, like so many others. My friend, however, clings to the belief that he—Kauffman, not Rosenberg—smuggled the art out of the country and used it to start a new life. Talmadge has some more checking to do on the computer. First, though, you must congratulate him. He found the new owner of your Corot. At least, I think it's yours."

Rebecca plopped onto the sofa. She hadn't expected that piece of news.

Her grandmother sounded tickled as she explained that a painting entitled, *Une Masion de Paysan aux Environs de Tours* had surfaced half a year ago, quite unexpectedly. Corot had done a series of farmyards in the late 1860s. That particular painting had shown up on the list of missing art. Before Jewish art hunters could confirm the rumor, however, it disappeared again. Off the market. It had been purchased sub rosa by a trading company.

"A holding company really. Only one principal was listed, L. Frankel with an address in Delaware. Naturally, everyone incorporates in Delaware if they can. Such lovely tax advantages." Dorothea tittered.

"At first, we weren't sure it was a real name. Talmadge's only hit was an *L. Frank L.* Or was it *Ell Frank Ell,* spelled out, no initials? Either way, the creature was a sulphurous flash in the art scene a decade ago, not a corporate trader. Signed the canvases with swooping 'Ls.' All the rage for a few weeks."

"I remember."

"You do? How remarkable."

How bizarre. Rebecca leaned against the pillow, closed her eyes. It had to be the same artist. She'd gone to the showing in Alexandria not long after she'd started at the *Post*. Went as a guest of another reporter. Not the art critic, but a social commentator. The opening was in a glass-walled gallery on the second floor of a converted home. There were only a dozen paintings on exhibit.

That was more than enough. They were over-whelming, too large for the intimate space, the oil paint too thick, too intense in contrast to the white walls. They depicted concentration camp atrocities in primary colors. Lime green babies screaming as they were bludgeoned, purple blood spewing from their mouths. Crimson skeletons with canary eyes staring up from a pit of rotting flesh. The paintings were un-skilled, primitive and totally unforgettable. Not art you'd hang in your hallway. Thankfully the artist had not attended.

"Anyway, Rebecca, Talmadge found a tentative link between that painter and a Lisa Frankel who was something of a financial hotshot in the Northeast. There was an interview with her in a woman's maga-zine in the mid-nineties. When the reporter asked her about her hobbies, she admitted she'd tried her hand at painting once. Described the oils as outré and laughed about one dismal showing. Not conclusive, but tanta-lizingly close."

L Frank L. Lisa Frankel. Amalgams of two recent acquaintances? Elise Carlson, Brian Franks? *Elise Franks. Lisa Frankel.* Hagan would call it a stretch: a hodgepodge of similar syllables, nothing more. She made a note to learn Elise Carlson's maiden name.

"Any siblings, other relatives?"

"Give me a chance, Rebecca. How about a mother? The name Sophie Frankel appears on the roles of sur-vivors from Mauthausen. She and an infant daughter were liberated when the allied troops arrived. They came to the United States in late 1947, via England, I believe."

The hairs on the back of Rebecca's neck tingled. She swung her feet to the floor, began pacing.

A child born near the end of WWII would be about sixty years old. Roughly Elise Carlson's age. Was it possible that she was the daughter born to Sophie Frankel in a concentration camp? Had she changed Lisa to Elise and married someone named Carlson? Could it have been her arm holding the rifle that shot at the Lotus team? Her scar that Groën had noticed in the photograph? Why? Who or what was she aiming at? What was her connection?

She bumped the table. Groën looked up. She turned away. It was too far-fetched. Or was it? Had she ever seen Elise Carlson's arms not covered?

She interrupted her grandmother. "Did the Nazis brand numbers on infants?"

"In the camps? I believe so. As soon as they were born they became property of the Reich and added to the roster of those condemned to die. The Nazis were so considerate they even waited for failed suicides to recover before sending them to their state-controlled deaths."

Thirty-six

"Rebecca?"

The phone was still warm in her hand. Her cheeks were flushed. Groën wheeled toward her. "Rebecca, something is wrong?"

She shook her head—something was right. She faced Groën. "Franks. Frankel. Could they be the same name?"

"Why not? My cousin spells ours with a *u* instead of the *o*. Who is Franks?"

"Brian Franks is a harried financial accountant. Lisa Frankel was a successful Wall Street type who may have painted holocaust scenes in technicolor. She and her mother were camp survivors."

"Ach. And where is she today?"

"Possibly passing as Elise Carlson. If I'm right, Franks would know."

"But will he tell?"

"We'll find out."

She punched in the number for the Canterbury Hotel, asked to be connected with Elise Carlson. Franks could be with her. Rebecca wanted him alone and cornered.

Carlson didn't answer. That was good news. Presumably she was either at breakfast or on her way to the track with Madison, senior. Rebecca asked the operator to try Brian Franks. He picked up on the first ring. When she told him who she was, he sputtered that he was in hurry, he couldn't talk.

"Leaving town before the race?"

"I have a business. A family."

"Does it include Elise Carlson?"

Silence. Then, a whisper. "What do you want?"

"One question, just answer one question: Did you know Elise planned to kill Peyton Madison?"

A chair creaked as Franks collapsed. He sucked in a gasp, moaned. The moan turned into the wail of a wounded animal.

She raised her voice over it. "Franks, was it intentional?"

His voice caught, he was struggling for breath, close to sobbing. "God, no. She was obsessed to ruin him financially, that's all. I swear. Nothing we did was illegal. A misleading tip to his broker. A hint about his gambling addiction to the press. He was a man self-destructing. We nudged a little."

"You didn't cut the brake line on the race car, file threads off the wheel bolts?"

"I wouldn't know how to do such a thing. I thought we were turning the screws to make him sell more paintings. That's all."

"Elise?"

He sighed. "She knows how to do everything."

"She shot at the pits, didn't she? Was she trying to hit Peyton?"

"No. The car. It was about damaging the car to cost him money. Don't you understand? It was all about monetary retribution."

She understood that it might have begun that way. She sat. "When did it change for Elise?"

"Oh, God. Oh, God." Rhythmic creaks from the chair as he sobbed. "I tried to warn her—the instant I learned your friend was a cop. Give it up. Leave. Find another way. She wouldn't listen, exhilarated by the danger of getting caught. She bugged your house to keep tabs on him." He let out air like a balloon deflating. "What's going to happen now?"

Rebecca didn't have a clue. She had no official standing of any kind. If she were a nicer person she would recommend that he deny this conversation and call a lawyer ASAP. But she was a former reporter. Instincts persist. She sensed that Franks couldn't take the tension any longer. He was primed, seeping gas, ready to talk. She let him, asked every question that occurred to her and took down notes in shorthand.

Franks and Elise were first cousins. His father, Josef, was Sophie's younger brother. As a child, Josef had suffered from tuberculosis and spent the war years in England. After he married, he came to America, changed the family name to Franks to sound less Germanic.

"My father never criticized Aunt Sophie. He felt her rancor against her Nazi captors had kept her alive in the camp. Once freed, once the Nazi regime was finished, she didn't know what to do with that venom."

"She transferred it to the family of Heinrich Kauffman?"

"Kauffman." He sighed. "In my mind, that name clangs like noises in a ghost story. As children in New Jersey, Heinrich Kauffman was our bogeyman. In Germany, he had lived next door to Aunt Sophie's. Heinrich junior and Sophie were pledged to each other when they were infants. Their fathers worked together. They wanted to build their own empire by joining the families. All I knew of Kauffman was that he was supposed to help my father and aunt, who had survived. But, of course, he didn't. He betrayed them.

"When they couldn't locate him, my father begged Sophie to let it be, forget and go on. For a time, we thought she did." He blew his nose. "Then she started to go a little crazy. More than a little. At an investors' conference in Midtown, Lisa came to me for help."

Franks's voice faded in and out. He was stumbling now, mumbling about how hard it was to speak of it after all this time. Rebecca was afraid she was losing him. She debated about offering to drive to the hotel and pick him up. They could talk it through, face-to-face.

Before she could make the offer, he began again. "In forty-one, before the family was separated, Sophie's parents made her memorize a list of their valuable artwork. She was the youngest, had the best memory, best chance to survive. Dutifully, she learned each artist's name, title of the work, dimensions, medium, its provenance. We all knew bits of it; it was the family legend. Sophie never forgot a single word. In the months leading up to her death she would recite the list a hundred times a day like a nursery rhyme. If she stumbled, she would start again from the beginning. It was so eerie. You have no idea. She listed all previous owners. It sounded like the begats from the Bible going back to the beginning of time. She scared me senseless when she rambled on. Lisa couldn't stop her. After a while she didn't try." He halted, panting.

"When did Sophie die?"

Franks thought for a moment. "Nineteen-ninety one, I think."

That jelled. It was easy to imagine Elise taking up painting following her mother's death. Therapy to expunge the ordeal she'd listened to over and over and could do nothing about. Two years of throwing paint at canvases, resurrecting her mother's demons, and L. Frank L. would have been ready for a showing. Not to sell the works, but to shock the world. Or maybe just flaunt her pain. Rebecca wondered what had happened to those vivid oversized oils.

Franks sniffed. "Aunt Sophie was just too shattered to go on. She wasted away. Maybe once she transferred her hatred to Lisa, there was nothing left to sustain her."

Rebecca thanked him before hanging up. She didn't offer reassurances that all would be well. He wouldn't have believed her. He seemed convinced that his cousin had killed Peyton. It could have been a product of his own guilt. He was too close to the action to be objective. There was no proof Elise Carlson had done anything, just a lot of suggestive coincidences.

The anguish in Brian Franks's voice was enough to

make Rebecca want to exonerate Elise/Lisa for whatever she might have done. It could have been justified.
She dropped the phone on the table. "Samuel, we've
been assuming that whoever damaged the car also tortured Peyton."

He looked up. "What, now you like a conspiracy
theory?"

"No. But we may have one. Elise Carlson was Lisa
Franks, a Holocaust survivor. She claimed she was
boar hunting in Argentina before arriving in Indy on
Friday."

"If that's true, then she has an accomplice?"

"I don't buy it. Who? Not Franks. He wouldn't
know a Phillips from a torx-tipped screwdriver. Whitten? Evans?"

"Too fast, Rebecca."

She took a deep breath. *Right.* She was getting
ahead of the facts. First, find out if Elise had been in
South America. Or, more to the point, find out when
she arrived in Indianapolis.

She pawed through the drawer in the kitchen for the
phone numbers Evans had left when he moved out.
One was his cell phone. With luck, he'd have it with
him at the track, and on.

She paced the kitchen as she punched in the number. Three rings and he answered, yelled over the
sound of engines warming up. "Moore? What the hell
do you want? I'm busy here."

"Elise Carlson, when did she pick up her credentials?"

"How the blazes would I know? Call her yourself.
Or try the administration building." He cut her off.

She checked the clock. It was after eight, the offices should be open, busily handing out parking decals and credentials for one-day attendees. Not bothering to look it up, she dialed 411 and asked a pleasant-sounding operator for the number, let the phone company connect her to save time.

The man on the other end was not pleasant. He refused to stop what he was doing to pull up the inventory of credentials they'd dispensed for the pre-race activities.

Rebecca dropped her voice an octave, spaced her words and lied. She baldly announced that she was a reporter for *The Washington Post* and implied that he would not like what she'd write about the administration offices at the Speedway. He put her on hold. She crossed her fingers that he was searching records, flipping through computer data bases or checking 3" × 5" cards. Not trotting off to complain to his supervisor. Or worse yet, calling the *Post* to confirm her employment status. So what if he discovered she was lying? What could he do? There's no law against impersonating a reporter. Some of her fellow journalists did it daily.

The Muzak stopped abruptly. The administrator growled into the phone. He was somewhat mollified because the record had been easy to locate. Elise F. Carlson had picked up her Lotus Team Credentials and pass for the VIP Suites on Friday.

"The day before yesterday?"

"No. A week ago. She was one of the first."

Rebecca hung up without thanking him.

Elise Carlson had not been in Argentina as she

claimed. That had been a taunt. She'd been in town for over a week, hunting closer to home. With a pass to the track, she could have wandered into the pits anytime in the past nine days. No one would have questioned it. She was just one more person affiliated with some team. Her laminated ID clearly said she belonged.

Thirty-seven

Mick took the phone call at the deputy's desk.

They'd given him a cell for the night, unlocked it in the morning so he could join them for bitter coffee and a round of liars dice. They were betting on beers for after the race and teasing him about his lack of sex life with Moore. They roared over his booking a cabin at Dolores's motel in the hope of getting lucky. A cabin that had gone unused the previous night. Ted wanted to roll for bunking privileges after the race; he figured Mick wouldn't need it.

He'd lost six rounds in a row before they confessed they would have let him go the previous evening, if Trooper Gunn of the State Police hadn't suggested they hang on to him. Something about an unreported shooting at the track that Moore was mixed up in.

The sergeant winked as he handed him the phone. "Speak of the devil."

With no preamble, Moore said, "I know who was harassing Peyton." She didn't sound pleased.

"Someone other than me? That's fantastic. The chief has gone to town to buy rope for my noose. I'll have him call you when he—"

"Listen, Hagan. Peyton was being stalked by a woman bent on revenge. Not against him, but against his family. For her family. For a decades-old crime. If I'm right, his father is now in danger."

Mick leaned against the graffiti-stained wall, stretching his spine to scratch it. "What's the motive and who has it?"

He heard Jasmine chatting in the background, probably to the squirrel, before Moore closed the slider. Wanting it quiet while she decided how much to tell him and what kind of a spin to put on it. When she resumed, it was in a story-telling voice, a good indication that she was spending too much time around Delacroix. "Mick, you're Irish. Do you sympathize with the IRA murdering Protestants, including women and children, and the Protestants retaliating over a treachery that happened hundreds of years ago?"

"You're kidding, right? I won't bet a beer with an Irishman on the outcome of a soccer match. Guys know how to hold a grudge."

"Right. You accept that the mentality for harboring long-term vengeance exists. So, how hard is it to imagine a child of a concentration camp survivor, who decades later sets out to destroy the family that prospered while hers was eliminated? Former neighbors, whose children were once engaged, to whom a fortune in Old Masters had been entrusted. Gentiles, exempt from Nazi atrocities, able to relocate taking the family's wealth with them. A child so twisted by—"

"Moore, relax. Take a breath." He demonstrated. "Have you been drinking Manischewitz with that Jewish photographer? Man's Orthodox. Probably's got the second coming marked on his calendar, he's—"

"He's staying at the house, Hagan. Yesterday when Jasmine returned for the photograph, his shop and the rooms where he lived were destroyed. The police said an incendiary round was fired into the dark room. From a rifle. The photographer's alive because Jasmine and I pulled him out."

Mick dropped his legs over the edge of the bunk. "You okay?"

"Sooty. The shooter knew when to be there, because the house is bugged."

"Bugged? What are you talking about?"

Using short words, she explained that a squirrel had dislodged a listening device from between the sliding glass doors. "It's real, Hagan. I matched it to one on the Internet. It gave me the creeps last night, wondering if a stalker was right outside, listening."

"Hell, he didn't have to be outside. With a recorder he could be as far away as the track. Damn, I should have tossed Peyton's RV more thoroughly."

"Peyton? He might have been naturally sneaky, but he didn't bug the house."

"You know who did?" He sucked the inside of his cheek, wished he had a toothpick. "Who? Tell me Groën saved the photograph and you identified the sniper."

She told him that the photo had been destroyed in the fire, though Groën had the disk. "Mick, he studied the photo when it was enlarged. The shooter's face was obscured by shadows. But he noticed a scar on the forearm where a concentration camp tattoo might have been."

He sagged against the bars. "Moore, listen to yourself. Concentration camps, tattoos, sixty-year-old vendettas." He turned his back on the desk sergeant, lowered his voice. "Is that why you're getting so riled? You think this is a Nazi conspiracy? We're in Indianapolis, for God's sake. Heartland of America. How many Jewish camp survivors are still alive and hanging around the racetrack?"

He heard a drawer slam, the scrape of keys in the brass bowl.

She said, "At least one—Elise Carlson."

Mick paced the cell, flexing the fingers of his non-phone hand while Moore laid it out. She began with Carlson's birth name and circumstances, drawing a path to the present. Threw in Brian Franks's admissions as hearsay evidence. It was tantalizing, convoluted and mostly circumstantial. He didn't want to believe it. And he sure as hell didn't want Moore believing it and acting on it. She was clearly on a tear and he was stuck in the mock jail, which, thanks to this phone call, was starting to rile him.

At first, he'd tried to bond with Chief Leonard Patten. Found him amusing even though the guy had watched too many late-night movies glorifying General Patton. The chief agreed that Evans was a schoolyard bully, mostly bluster. He was inclined to believe Hagan's version of the incident at the RV. He'd nod-

ded in an understanding way when Mick had rationalized why neither Moore nor anyone else on the team
had reported the sniper incident.

This morning, though, Patten was testy. According
to the deputy he'd spent the night building a case to
charge Hagan on the assault of Peyton Madison. In his
book, Hagan was the most logical suspect, maybe the
only understandable one. Mick interpreted that to
mean he was an outsider whose arrest wouldn't annoy
the locals. "Chief, I wasn't in town when the race cars
were sabotaged or the shot fired. I was six hundred
miles east, giving out speeding tickets to pre-teens
dragging farm tractors."

"Did I say you messed with the cars? Nope. I Figure Moore did that. Easy as pie for her. *If* the incidents
occurred. No one on the team complained to track security. Maybe you're lying about them, muddying the
waters. Or maybe Moore lied to you to get you out
here. Damsel-in-distress routine. Set you up. You
wouldn't be the first sap to do the dirty work for some
female. Come to think of it, nobody was hurt until after you showed up." He leaned his face against the
cell, the bars pressing ruts into the flesh of his jowls.
"What I said was: I think you assaulted Madison."

"Why? I didn't know the man."

Patten straightened and ticked off his suspicions.
"First, you were antagonistic toward the vic. People
noticed you two having words at the restaurant party.
Second, you were caught breaking into Peyton's RV
and assaulting his crew chief. Third, Peyton Madison
was seen in public pawing at your girlfriend. Enough
to get a red-blooded boy's dander up, especially since

you're not getting any of what you came to Indianapolis to get." At that, the younger cop sniggered.

At the moment, what he was getting from Moore was an earful of fantasy and intrigue involving Elise Carlson. He tried to calm her—something he'd never been good at. Telling her that it was all her imagination did not go over well. Nor did recommending that she not do anything stupid. She rejoined by telling him to do something anatomically impossible, and hung up.

Mick held the phone tight against his cheek to keep from throwing it at Patten when he stormed into the station. Lacking such restraint, Patten pitched his hat at the desk and faced Mick, hands on hips.

"Hagan, we got ourselves a problem. Peyton Madison did not die of a heart failure brought on by the attack, or through hospital negligence. He was murdered. Snuffed out while all helpless in a hospital bed. That kind of shit's not supposed to happen. So let's hear it. Go over your story again, every step, especially the part when you and Moore decided to visit Madison in the hospital. 'Cause boy, your fingerprints were all over his room."

Thirty-eight

Jo skipped his Sunday-morning ritual of ham and eggs at Flo's Café. For two weeks, Flo had hovered over his table, stewing nonstop about the bagel shop that was moving into a vacant building on North Main Street. The owners had put up flyers all over town. There was an ad in last week's paper. Same page as the obituaries, where everyone would read it.

"You hear me, lawyer? I'll lose my customers, the restaurant. Have to sell my mother's home. And what about Priscilla? She's too sulky to hold down a real job. If she don't work for me, who'll hire her?" Flo was one hundred percent positive that Jo could unearth some legal reason to stop the bagel shop. He couldn't, even if he'd wanted to. Flo, like everyone else in town, needed to adjust to the changes coming to Head Tide. The local politicians called it progress.

He waited in line at the deli for take-out coffee. Drank it standing up, watching Sunday traffic mosey up and down Main Street. Then he crossed the street to Vintage & Classics. Letting himself in the front door, he walked through the office and into the car shop, stood just inside the door while his eyes adjusted to the diffuse light drifting in through windows at the far end. Sunday was the one day when none of Rebecca's workers was likely to be there. Only the magnificent vehicles waiting patiently to be resurrected. He wasn't mechanical, but he appreciated the cars. Their classic lines had endured decades of change, outlived hundreds of fads. They still turned heads as they traveled along back roads. Old men smiled with remembrance, young men drooled.

Mainly, though, Jo liked them because they were used. That was the simple explanation. What he liked about classic cars was the same thing that attracted him to antiques: Generations had used and enjoyed them before him. People he'd never known had sat at his pedestal dining table. When the boards warped, someone had added catches in an attempt to close the center gap. A woman distracted from her chores had rested an iron too long on the surface and left a permanent imprint on one of the leaves. A child doing his lessons had dribbled blue ink, which his mother had tried to get out with bleach.

One evening Jo had sprinkled a benediction of Cabernet from his glass onto the bleached area surrounding the ink spots. Smeared the red liquid in with the blue, adding a touch of his generation to the reminders from the past. Red wine, like blood, ingrained in the cracks for the next owner to ponder over.

He picked up a rag from the workbench. With a light hand, he wiped a film of dust from the headlamp

of a new arrival. Frank had called it a 20/25, a Rolls-
Royce named for the engine displacement or taxation
value or something. Not really listening, Jo had
walked around the elegant open touring car, admiring
it from every angle. Cherry red, brown leather seats, a
low windshield trimmed in chrome. And those over-
sized headlamps.

Alone in the shop, he did something he'd never
done—unlatched the driver's side door and slid onto
the seat. Gripping the steering wheel with both hands,
he played it back and forth. The car fitted him, far better than Rebecca's dainty MG, though both cars exuded the same feeling of freedom. He wondered if he
could drive it adeptly? Would it steer well, brake on
command, corner without slowing to a crawl? He
could easily imagine Rebecca beside him, trying to
capture her hair grown long again as it whipped in the
wind. He saw her face tanned and laughing in the island sun. He should ask Frank who owned the car and
if there was a chance it was for sale.

His cell phone rang, shattering the daydream.

Before he looked, he guessed the number on the
readout display would be Rebecca's. It was. He felt a
twinge of guilt. Silly. She didn't know he was trespassing in one of her customer's cars. He should feel
guilty for cutting her off last night and be thankful she
was still speaking to him. Or feel guilty over his re-
fusal to help Hagan. If the cop had been taking better
care of Rebecca, he might feel obligated. Or maybe
not. He was finished with obligations.

Over the past few weeks, Jo had done little else except tie up loose ends for the absent Rebecca. Friday,

he'd bullied the local magistrate to issue a restraining order against Sergio Dohlmani, the nightclub owner Rebecca had sparred with. No formal charges had been filed; nothing could be proved. Dohlmani was too well-connected to be charged without sufficient evidence to go to trial. The restraining order was a Band-Aid to make Rebecca rest easier. Dohlmani was no more likely to come to Head Tide than she was to revisit his strip club.

Next, he'd filed papers on her behalf to stall the developer from gutting the fields behind her house. He couldn't stop him, but the delay would make construction more costly.

All Rebecca was losing was the view of open acreage; still Jo empathized. His family's tiny plot and house in Jamaica had been forfeited following his mother's death. It had compounded his sense of loss. Every weekend after relocating to Maryland, he'd searched for new land, first stumbling across twelve unimproved acres being sold for back taxes. Then taking out a loan to buy the farmhouse next to it. He was driven to establish new roots in a new country. It would not be the same as the home he'd lost, but he needed a place to belong.

Jo leaned back, molded his spine against the worn leather. The phone continue to chime. She wasn't going to give up. How like Rebecca.

Beyond that, he'd visited her parents, her grandmother, made arrangements with Frank to feed the cats and look after her house. Paulie promised to tend the gardens. The asters were profuse and iridescent in the afternoon sun. It was a pity Rebecca was missing them.

He couldn't bring himself to still the ringing by answering the phone. He was too distracted to talk to her again. The letter from his cousin had stirred up too many conflicting emotions. From the first reading, he'd known he would have to return to Jamaica to confront Thomas Levy. What he hadn't realized was the impact that decision would have on his feelings for Rebecca. One irrational part of him was angry with her for being away. For not communicating with her parents. For being with Hagan, which was ludicrous since he was the one who sent Hagan to protect her.

His other irrational self was angry with her for bringing him back to life. For making him want her and a future with her. He had no right to pursue that until he settled the past.

The phone stopped ringing. Jo pocketed it and slid out of the car. It was time to go.

Leaning over the door edge, he tucked an envelope between the seat and the back. It was addressed to Rebecca.

Thirty-nine

Rebecca slammed on the brakes inches from the bumper of an orange Mustang. Taking the car had been a huge mistake, more frustrating even than trying to reach Jo. She'd made good time gunning it down Hulman Boulevard to Cagle Lane, only to lose it all after merging with traffic on Georgetown. Everyone within a hundred-mile radius was heading to the track, but no one seemed to be in a hurry. Most were scouting out parking spots, slowing while they mulled over which was most important: the cost, the walking distance to their seats, or ease of escape after the race. Those going south wanted to park in lots on the left side of the road. Those going north preferred the right side. Both moves necessitated cutting across lanes of creeping traffic that refused to give way. Only Jasmine's worried face peering over the dashboard kept her from issuing four-letter instructions to drivers blocking the road.

Poking through traffic provided her with plenty of

time to fume over Hagan's patronizing attitude. He was infuriating, possibly more condescending than her crew members when she first joined the team. At least they were willing to accept she knew something. Hagan wouldn't. If it wasn't his idea, if he hadn't thought of it first, it couldn't be right. She thumped the steering wheel. *Damn it, she knew she was right.* As a reporter, her instincts had been correct ninety-five times out of a hundred. She'd learned to trust her intuition, to cut through the web of lies to get at the truth. Her gut was telling her that Elise Carlson was a woman driven to murder. She would stake her reputation on it, if she still had a reputation to stake.

When she finally reached Sixteenth Street, she bumped the Corvette onto the lawn in front of the administration building. She threatened Jasmine within an inch of her life to stay in the car. If anyone official came to yell at her, explain that there was an emergency inside the track. Cry if she had to. Have them send a cop or security guards to the historic car area, Team Lotus.

She yanked out her track credentials, discarded her purse on the seat next to Jasmine and ran. She sprinted east around the southwest vista of the track, heading for the main gate and the underpass into the infield.

During the maddening drive over, her mind had whipped from one improbable scenario to an equally impossible one. In all of them Peyton Madison was in dire trouble, being stalked by the same assailant who had attacked his son. Carlson had only today to get him alone. Tomorrow, after the memorial service, he would return to South Carolina, be back among his friends, cosseted by private security. Following him there would be riskier, require involved planning. Her best shot was today.

Over the din of stalled traffic, Rebecca had replayed her grandmother's cultured voice exposing Heinrich Kauffman's infamy one fact at a time. It began when Kauffman had betrayed his Jewish neighbors and profited from their misfortune under the Nazis. He'd fled Germany with his son, Heinrich junior, and his family. In Argentina, both adult males had gone to work for I. G. Farben, the German pharmaceutical giant that had flourished by producing Zyklon B—the hydrogen cyanide poison used in gas chambers at Auschwitz.

"It was already on hand to fumigate the barracks, Rebecca. Very efficient of the Nazis to use it to annihilate the occupants as well."

Once in Argentina, Kauffman had attracted little attention, until his daughter-in-law and grandson died while vacationing at a mountain resort. After that, he'd become a recluse. The son disappeared.

Some years later, one thousand miles north, Peyton Madison II, a chemist in his thirties, appeared on the business scene in New Jersey. He was married to a Latin beauty. According to the rumors of the day, he had a fortune in fabulous art, which he'd used as collateral. "It could not be confirmed that the art had once belonged to German Jews. Still, gossip between bankers over martinis hinted at the rare quality and value of the paintings."

It had taken Mrs. Wetherly's contacts years to pick up the son's trail once he slipped into America. Heinrich Kauffman, Jr., had bought a new identity to go with the new business. By the time PLM Chemicals was established and he was making a name for himself, the name was Peyton Madison II. After relocating the company in South Carolina, he invented the role of a gracious, though nouveau, Southern gentleman. On paper, he touted the requisite credentials. For nearly five decades the deception had held. Kauffman had lived an assumed life as Madison and made a success of it.

Now, his past was catching up. The sole descendant of a family his father had robbed was tracking him down to claim their pound of flesh.

According to Franks, Elise Carlson had absorbed her mother's hatred, turned it into her personal vendetta. She wouldn't be content with wiping out just the son. Much more satisfying to eliminate the patriarch, too. Carlson had known about the elder Madison before he arrived: where he lived, how to reach him. She knew of his antagonism toward his son's gambling and race habits and the location of the family burial plot. All of which said she'd been tracking him for months. The father, not the son. Peyton had been the tethered goat used to lure his father within striking range.

Rebecca slid on loose gravel turning the corner into the tunnel, grabbed the railing, straightened. The sound of her feet slapping the concrete walkway was drowned out by the roar of engines as cars thundered by on the track overhead. The Historic Grand Prix had started.

Exiting the tunnel, she pushed past an indecisive cluster of teens blocking the walkway and headed for the paddock area. Under the tents, chaos had given way to momentary calm. The Lotus crew had done their job. Ian was on the track in the early laps of the race. He was running third behind Whitten's Brabham and the Ferrari 312 T-2 formerly driven by Niki Lauda. No one wanted to pay attention to her, they were too intent on the video monitors. The race was only twenty laps long; they wanted to savor each one.

She squeezed her way next to Evans, gripped his upper arm and pulled. He swung around. His eyes lit with anger when he recognized her. He opened his mouth. She stepped on his foot. Stretched up to yell in his ear. "Elise Carlson. Madison. Where are they?"

"Why the fu—. Jesus, you were ordered away from here. Don't you listen?"

She punched his arm. "Where are they?"

Johnny sidled over, drawn by the explosive exchange. He grinned lopsidedly at Rebecca. "Crow's nest. Mr. Madison was in the way. He knows squat about racing. Mrs. Carlson took him up high to show him what's going on."

Rebecca faced the kid, hoping he could read her lips over the noise. "Which stand? Where?"

Johnny flapped his head back and forth like a bobble-head doll. He finally twisted one-eighty, pointed in the direction of the southeast vista.

"But—"

One of the crew screamed. Evans's fist pumped high in the air. Johnny swung back to the monitor. Ian had passed Whitten under braking in the hairpin at the end of the front straight. He'd moved into second.

Forty

Mick blinked a few times as Patten's new accusation settled in. Was he surprised that Peyton had been murdered? *No.* Once or twice he was tempted to wipe the smirk off himself. But the brazenness of it, to walk into a hospital, kill a patient and leave without anyone noticing. That didn't mesh with a sniper mentality. Unless the shooter had tired of playing cat-and-mouse and decided it was time to finish off the rodent, comatose or not.

Or, as Moore surmised, Peyton was only an ancillary target. Now that dear old dad had entered the arena, sonny boy was expendable. Her theory about Elise Carlson was starting to sound plausible. Time to run it past Patten.

Patten wasn't in the mood. Red streaks flushed his neck, creeping up like mercury in an old-fashioned thermometer. He sucked a few breaths in through his nostrils, reminded Hagan that he was supposed to answer questions, not ask them.

"I am not in good humor. I counted on being in Section J by one o'clock to see the start of the F1 race. It's my favorite part. Of course, that was before Peyton decided to get himself tortured in a race car. Before he died unexpectedly at the hospital. Before the coroner made me attend the autopsy. Before you started pissing me off.

"It seems the attending physician didn't like Peyton's coloring. The bruising looked suspicious. A hint of petechia hemorrhaging. Gave the coroner impetus for a speedy autopsy. Turns out our boy died of asphyxiation. Something like a pillow was placed over his face and pressed against it, cutting off his air. Not hard, just enough to stop him breathing. Given that he was weak, it wouldn't have taken much strength. The alarm in his room had been turned low, the duty nurse doing rounds couldn't hear it go off. By the time she popped in to check on him he was gone. Dead."

The chief banged the desk for effect. The phone rang. The call was for Mick. Patten threw it at him.

When Mick said hello, Zimmer's chortle came through the line. "Boy, you can't stay out of trouble, can you? You're supposed to be protecting Moore, not lounging in lockup. She doesn't sound pleased."

"Tell me about it."

Instead, he told him about the second batch of fingerprints Mick had overnighted. He'd conned a friend in the State Police to run them ASAP. No hits on the matchbox: Derek Whitten was clean, at least in this country. On the lighter, the thumbprint belonged to Peyton Madison III. No crimes, but he'd done a token two-year stint with the National Guard. Got printed for that.

"The right index finger on the pen belongs to a Lisa Frankel, fifty-nine, formerly from Edison, New Jersey. Prints were on file because she marched at a Vietnam protest rally in her teens, got arrested for disturbing the peace. They stayed on file because she enlisted in the Israeli army. Queer thing for an American to do. Trained with them for four years, then come back to the States to study some more."

The Israeli Army. Intense training that would last a lifetime, give you all the skills you'd need to stalk, shoot, bug, terrorize, murder your enemies, real or imagined. Lisa Frankel had trained with the Israelis. Lisa Frankel was now called Elise Carlson. Elise Carlson was somewhere in the stands with an old man she held responsible for her family's misfortunes. Moore wasn't so crazy after all.

Carlson could have arranged to meet Peyton at his motor home after the party, pretending she wanted to talk about their partnership. Unsuspecting, he would have invited her to linger for a drink or two. That would explain the lipstick on the cocktail napkin.

Then what? She decides to kill him, lures him to the pit area and into the car? Why?

Better question, how? Did she dare him to take the Lotus out for a midnight spin? Could Madison have been so soused he contemplated impressing his date by hurtling a million-dollar race car through the dark on an empty track?

Easier to believe he drank too much and passed out.

Carlson tiptoed out, drove to the pits to disable or de-stroy the car, like she'd tried several times before. Madison might have woken up and wondered where she'd gone. Maybe he heard her through the baby monitor. He rushed down to the pits to protect the car and gets zapped by the lady in waiting.

The scenario worked for him.

Worked him into a panic. Moore was playing bloodhound, running after an Israeli-trained com-mando intent on revenge. Not a smart move. Carlson would not worry about collateral damage.

He handed the phone to the deputy, turned to the chief. "Patten, there's something you should hear."

"A confession? Goody. You want to admit doing Peyton, I'm eager to listen." He sat, hand resting on his firearm. "Hell, if you're going to rat out Moore that's okay, too. No woman's worth serious jail time. You give me provocation and I'll drag her in."

"That a fact, chief?" Mick counted to three, ex-haled. "I hope you know where she is."

Patten flicked his fingers at a deputy to come for-ward with the information. In return he got a shrug, followed by the admission that Moore wasn't at the house.

"Didn't think she'd stay at home, Chief. A ball and chain couldn't stop her from heading full speed into the fray." Mick leaned forward on the bunk. "Do you really think she's involved?"

"Damn straight."

"Then I can understand why you'd want to talk to her. Now. Before she slips out of your jurisdiction."

"Is that what she's planning? Leaving town?" Patten kicked the cell door wider, advanced on Mick. "You know where she is, you better tell me quick."

"I'll do better than that. I'll take you to her. But if you want to see that race start, we'd better hurry."

Forty-one

Rebecca glanced left as she trotted for the mouth of the tunnel. For either the Indy 500 or the Brickyard 400 the southeast vista would have been sold out; it was choice seating overlooking turn two. The Formula One race, however, used the road course cutting through the interior of the oval. The seats in the southeast vista were too far removed. Tickets for that section hadn't been offered for the race. The stands would be empty.

Was Carlson counting on that—being alone with Madison, no witnesses?

If she were intent on killing him, she must be planning a plausible accident. Today security would be too tight to smuggle in a rifle. Not that she'd want a long-distance shot. Payback for her family's ruin would demand a murder up close and personal. She'd waited a lifetime to see the fear of death in his eyes.

What then—an unexpected heart attack like his son? The elderly man climbs to the upper stands to watch the race. Depressed by the death of his only child, the exertion proves too much. His heart gives way, he overbalances and plummets to his death?

It was conceivable and easy to arrange.

Rebecca curled her fingers into fists. Part of her wanted to believe that Elise Carlson was what she seemed: an intelligent, urbane businesswoman; a widow in search of an amusing pastime. It was possible that she was simply being gracious by removing the grieving father from the pit area where he was distracting the crew. It just wasn't likely.

She sprinted under the track for the second time in ten minutes. Her footsteps echoed. No cars were entering or exiting the tunnel. Only one other person: a Ferrari crew member returning with a case of oil. She pushed herself up the incline.

Emerging into the sunlight, she turned left and picked up speed. Stand G was just yards ahead. Beyond that curved the southeast vista. Sweat ran down her spine, her breathing grew labored. She tried to find a rhythm, but her mind was too conflicted to concentrate on pumping her legs.

It was impossible for her not to feel sympathy for Elise Carlson. As Lisa Frankel she'd been an infant when her mother was liberated from the concentration camp; she couldn't have remembered the ordeal. Sophie Frankel, however, had never forgotten the horror she'd endured. Her rage had poisoned her daughter against the Kauffman family, whom she held responsible. Lisa Frankel may have changed her name and obliterated the camp tattoo, but she had never had a prayer of escaping.

As she approached the southeast vista, Rebecca slowed, shielded her eyes, peered up at the section high above. The corner bank was twice as deep as stand G, higher by more than thirty feet. Higher still was the crow's nest—twelve feet above the last row of the stands, suspended over empty air. On this part of the track, it wasn't a tree-house platform on a pole. It was a distinct section spanning the vista, containing two additional rows of bleachers used by team spotters and the media. Each section was accessed by a short stairway. There were metal railings along the back side, one at waist height, a second midback. Chain-link mesh covered the railings and extended above. It would prevent someone from going over backwards. At the end of the rows, however, there were only two bars, the top one hip height. On poles high above flew the flags of racing: yellow, white, red, black, blue, green and the black-and-white checkered.

Two dark figures were visible, huddled close together on the uppermost row. They could have been good friends shielding each other from the wind. Business partners assessing their investment on the track. Carlson stood as tall as the elder Madison, the man who might have been her father had Hitler not set out to annihilate the Jews. What was the comment she'd made to Peyton at the party? "How paternalistic. At least, I imagine you speak like a father. I never knew mine." Had that thought consumed her over the years? Had she wondered what life would have been like if she'd been born into a respected German family, instead of to a bitter, scarred prisoner of war? She leaned into Madison, spoke into his ear, trying to be heard over the drone of the race cars. One hand cupped his elbow. Madison nodded, his face intent on the race.

Rebecca ran to the center aisle, up the access stairs. She began climbing the metal steps between the stands two at a time. Stumbled when a knot of spectators off to the west jumped to their feet, waving their fists, yelling. She was missing the last laps of what must had been an exciting race. She hoped Ian was doing well.

She sprinted to the base of the stairs accessing the highest section, where Carlson and Madison stood. Carlson was urging the old man nearer the edge, pointing to the blur of cars as they swept down the straight toward the final turn heading for the finish line. His eyes followed her outstretched hand, his feet shuffled sideways, closer to the action. Closer to empty air.

Rebecca clamored up the final set of stairs, pounded toward them. Without stopping, unsure if they could hear, she yelled, "Heinrich. Lisa."

The couple froze.

Precariously close to the open end of the platform, they turned as one unit in her direction. Their faces were blank, astonishment yet to register.

She yelled again, repeated their names. "Heinrich. Lisa."

She ran along a bleacher, shrinking the distance to them, unsure what she was going to do other than try to stop—

A roar went up from the crowd. A wave of vivid living color moved in the background. Distracted,

Madison glanced at the giant video screen, to see the winning car.

Gripping his arm, Carlson locked eyes with Rebecca. She shrugged. "You've ruined my surprise."

A flicker of sorrow registered before she transferred her grip to the railing and slammed her body into the old man, propelling him over the edge.

Forty-two

Mick tugged on his seatbelt and sat back, hoping to survive the ride to the track. Patten had absorbed the story; now he was a man on a mission, talking to himself in short bursts. When forced to stop for a red light, he turned to include Mick. "Hagan, you could be a few bricks shy of a load, same as your girlfriend. Then again, you may be on to something. If you are, I get to outshine the State boys, which has been my constant dream for twenty years. Pass me the red light. We're taking the back roads."

They approached the track from the west, through an industrial neighborhood cordoned off to allow only pedestrian traffic. Slowing the cruiser at the intersection with Georgetown Road, Patten blipped the siren to get the attention of the officer monitoring foot traffic. One bark and the youngster snapped into action, moved the barricades aside. Patten nodded thanks and let the siren blare in earnest.

As they negotiated the corner, Mick spotted a white

Corvette on a grassy rise near the visitors' center. A yellow-shirted security guard was bent over talking to the top of a black head with corn rows and barrettes. A tiny arm gesticulated wildly in the direction of the main gate.

Jasmine. What was she doing—

Of course. Now that she'd met her hero, the kid was sticking like chewing gum to the bottom of her sneaker. Moore may have charged to the track in search of a killer, but even in the sports car she couldn't have accelerated fast enough to leave Jasmine behind. He wondered how she'd convinced the tyke to remain in the car. And how long she'd stay put. He said a silent prayer that the worst would be over before she could locate Moore. Assuming he could locate Moore before she did.

The cruiser bucked ahead a few inches. Ignoring the siren, fans clogged the road and sidewalks, carrying banners, buying food, sunglasses and ear plugs, trying to get to their seats before the F1 cars took to the track.

Mick turned sideways, eyes glued on the girl. He wished the security guard would strap her in; he'd provide the Super Glue. Already she was squirming up the back, frantic to get away, head swiveling around in search of someone more understanding.

When she spotted his face gawking out of the police car window, she screamed, sticky fingers pointing in his direction. He glowered, motioned for her to stay there. Like most dogs he'd tried to train, she nodded bright-eyed, but clearly had no intention of obeying once his back was turned.

Patten jerked the wheel to avoid a drunk singing something in Spanish, then gunned the car maybe twenty feet. Mick swiveled around to get his bearings. He grabbed at Patten's arm, gestured in the opposite direction. "The old car pits are off Sixteenth."

The only place Mick could think to start was with the crew. He assumed that Moore would have gone there first. One of them would know where she'd run off to after that. Where Carlson and Madison supposedly were watching the race.

The chief shook his head. He mumbled something as a roar went up from the crowd, signaling the end of the historic car race. The loudspeaker droned out the finishing order as the winners were heading to victory lane. Mick wasn't listening. He waited impatiently for the chief to repeat what he'd said.

Patten didn't waste his breath yelling, he pointed up.

Mick followed his finger. It was aimed at the Pagoda, one of the most famous symbols of the Brickyard. The first tower had been torn down in 1956, the newest pagoda completed in 2000. It was fabricated from metal and glass instead of wood, thirteen stories, 153 feet high. Every few floors, an open-air platform extended out to both sides. From the front, the widest spans were on the bottom. Each subsequent one was less wide. No fancy upward tips decorating the ends, but it gave you the feel of the traditional Japanese structure. According to Moore, pagodas usually had an odd number of floors and were built over a sacred relic. In this case, the sacred object was the strip of bricks from the original race track marking the start/finish line.

Patten's strategy made sense. On race day, the Pagoda was given over to media types and special guests. From the highest levels they would get a bird's-eye view of the stands. If Moore and Carlson were out in the open, they'd be able to see them.

On the flip side, if they weren't exposed, valuable time would be lost. Carlson and her new partner could be snug in the VIP suites, watching the race on the video screens, champagne fizzing over the edge of flutes as they toasted to future victories. Very civilized. Very private.

Patten tromped on the accelerator as they entered the tunnel under stand C. The siren blasted off the concrete walls. Pedestrians covered their ears, stared as the patrol car sped past. Patten hooked a right behind the Tower Suites, pulled up as close to the Pagoda as he could get, abandoned the cruiser at the curb.

Mick was out and running. Patten was a scant yard behind him when they reached the security checkpoint for the media center. The plump redheaded guard wasn't about to let them in without credentials. Patten waved his badge and swore he'd be responsible for Hagan while inside, it was an emergency.

Duty-bound, the guard continued to argue.

Mick studied the flow of camera-toting journalists and groupies entering and exiting. To get in, they scanned a plastic-coated ID across the face of an electronic reader then pushed through the turnstile. When one skinny kid paused, calling out to his friend on the inside to hand over a pass, Mick snatched it. Still attached by a chain to the guy's neck, he swiped it across the reader, pushed at the metal bar and was in.

He dropped the pass, patted the bug-eyed stranger's chest and took off sprinting.

Pounding up the emergency stairs, he reached the second level and kept going.

Moore had said the platforms were on odd-numbered levels, some mystical significance. He pumped his legs, clutched at the railing to propel himself faster.

He bypassed the third floor without slowing—wasn't high enough.

At level seven, he pushed through the stairwell door, paused, hunting for an access to outside. He spotted it. A couple in matching linen blazers blocked his way. He shoved between them and opened the door.

Cool air, the smell of exhaust and the roar of engines blasted in his face. He fished for his police badge, scanned the bodies leaning on the railings. In the south corner a burly, bearded guy was fiddling with one of three cameras slung around his neck, all with long lenses. Mick slammed his police badge against the photographer's nose, pointed at his equipment while mouthing, "Telephoto."

Maybe the guy heard him, maybe not. He backed away, clutching his equipment. Torn, debating maybe he should snap a picture in case he was facing a terrorist. He had a point, but there wasn't time to discuss it.

Mick grabbed the cameraman's right arm, bent it behind him, used it to turn him away from the start/finish line. Reaching around his shoulder, he took hold of one of the cameras. He raised it to eye level, fiddled with buttons until he could see through the lens. Starting with the VIP suites, he slowly panned the vacant stands moving west.

He located them in the closest corner of the southeast vista: two women standing, one old man falling off the edge.

Mick released the camera and the photographer. He pointed where he'd been looking. "There's your story, pal. An exclusive."

Forty-three

Carlson had underestimated her strength, or the senior's fitness program. Or maybe her hatred wasn't as strong as his will to live. Madison didn't fall to his death. The body blow knocked his torso backwards over the railing, his weight carried him into empty air, flipped his legs over the side. But his left hand seized an upright stanchion and held on.

For the moment.

Rebecca watched in horror as the gnarled hand with its age spots began inching down the pole, the weight of his dangling body pulling him lower and lower. A piercing yowl, like a cat in heat, escaped from his throat.

She leapt forward onto a bench, headed for Madison before his grip released. She was within grabbing distance when Carlson reached into a leg pocket on her cargo pants, straightened and spun. In her hand was a padded handle. One snap of her wrist and thin metal bars flew outward, locking into a rod. With barely a flick, she lashed out.

The rod sang as it whizzed through the air. It struck Rebecca across her thighs, knocking her to her knees then off the edge of the bleacher. She bounced into the catch fence, rebounded. Her upper body banged onto the seat, flopped forward, draped like a rag doll as the burning tore through the fronts of her legs.

Carlson glared, a demented instructor of the damned. The rod twitched in her hands. "You shouldn't be here. This is personal."

Rebecca sank onto her knees. "It's not worth your life, Elise."

"What life. Haven't you done your homework? I'm a bastard spawned by an Aryan guard. A by-product, a regrettable reminder."

Stepping off the bleacher, she turned toward Madison. "Did you know that your teenage girlfriend, Sophie Franks, had survived the war and reproduced, Herr Kauffman? Or did you never think about the Jewish families your parents betrayed?"

Rebecca yelled at her back. "Your mother did what it took to survive."

Carlson glanced over her shoulder; a lazy smile twisted her mouth. "My mother let men defile her to stay alive. Let herself get pregnant to make them stop. She survived because she was lovely and a *mischlinge,* a half-Jew. The guards could fornicate with her and pretend she wasn't filth like the others." Carlson hunched down to make sure Rebecca was paying attention. "Mother couldn't pretend. When it was rumored that the Allies were coming to free the camp, she tried to commit suicide. She was too weak to succeed. Unbelievable. Sophie had survived four years in a concentration camp, but wanted to kill herself rather than live with her shame in the real world." Her voice dropped to a whisper. "Would you say she survived?"

Rebecca searched the eyes sunk deep in the face above her. Dark smudges set off the white surrounding amber irises. Crystal clear except for a tiny mote in the one. Intelligent and once perceptive, they'd lost focus on this world, real or not. They could see only the past.

Twenty feet away Madison still dangled off the edge.

Rebecca pulled back from Carlson. She had to distract her long enough for Madison to regain his footing. Together they'd have a chance to overpower her. Their only chance.

They wouldn't be rescued. There were no spectators wandering the empty stands. Once racing resumed, all eyes would be focused on the track. Unless a security guard or nosy fan noticed Madison hanging over the edge, no one would suspect anything was amiss—until the bodies were discovered.

Rebecca harbored no illusions about her own safety. Carlson had walked a lonely, twisted road through the past to get to this point. She'd already come to the crossroads and made her decision—the Madisons/Kauffmans would be destroyed by her hand. An interfering mechanic would be just a minor irritant, a gnat to be squashed against a wall.

What Carlson hadn't counted on was having to eliminate two opponents at the same time. Her attention was divided. That might be their only advantage. Rebecca intended to use it. Nine years of interviewing people in turmoil for newspaper stories had to be good for something. If she could goad Carlson into talking, she might get her to reconsider. Talk was therapeutic. At the very least, it would delay the final act.

Rebecca pressed her forearms on the bleacher, raised up to make eye contact. "Your mother didn't hate you, Elise. You were part of her. She educated you. Gave you a future."

Carlson sighed, shaking her head. "The only reason for my existence was to exact vengeance for the past. Today, I'll do that." She pirouetted, headed for the old man struggling to hold on.

So much for small talk. Rebecca threw herself onto the bench, slid along it, snagged Carlson's ankle. She clutched it one-handed, nails digging into tendons. Yanked backwards.

Carlson tottered but remained upright.

Stretching her other arm, Rebecca gripped Carlson's ankle with both hands. Strained, pulled. Until the rod slashed across her wrists. With a gasp, she recoiled and let go.

Carlson swung again, striking the bleacher. "Revenge begins as a tiny maggot, Rebecca. It writhes and feeds off decaying flesh. It's voracious. Taunting Peyton was satisfying only at first. I gloated watching him squirm as his financial schemes soured, as he felt failure reaching out to pull him under. Brian was a genius at planting rumors and bad tips, at manipulating reporters to print suggestive news items. My cousin thought we were naughty kids playing a game. It was never a game. There was ever only one goal."

"Peyton was—"

"A puffed-up little toad." She went down on one knee. Her face hovered just out of reach. "That night in his motor home, he tried to seduce me. Can you believe it? He was arrogant enough to assume I would succumb. He imagined that having sex with his new partner would give him power over me. That it was good insurance." She sat on the bench. The rod swayed between her knees. "Consider the irony: He thought sex was his tool, his advantage. Instead, it was his undoing. His fumbling brought back my mother's tragedy: sex as a means to survival.

"At that moment, I wanted to kill him." She stilled the rod. "I settled for torturing him. Perhaps a bit longer than necessary, as it turned out."

Rebecca nodded; she understood, wanted to hear more. "How did you lure him to the tent?"

Carlson turned her head. "Are you still with us, Herr Kauffman. Heinrich? Are you listening to your son's gullibility? He was paranoid about his material possessions. A family trait, perhaps? He was so certain the saboteur would try again to destroy the car that he hitched up that silly monitor to listen in on the pits. After we toasted the partnership, he dragged me into the bedroom to show off his cleverness. And to attempt seduction. Even with a willing partner, I can't imagine he was a good lover. What do you think, Heinrich? No offspring. It makes you wonder. Was that one more way in which he failed you?"

Other than a slight sneer, Madison did not respond.

His right forearm lay along the platform, fingers scratching like chicken claws for something to grip. His left hand was turning blue.

Carlson turned back to Rebecca. Grinned. "I think I enjoy having a captive audience. You know how to listen. It is a gift." She crossed one leg over the other, a casual instructor lecturing alfresco.

By her interpretation, Peyton had been annoyed at his lack of success in bedding her. He saw her to the car then went back inside the motor home to sleep off the champagne. She'd remained in the lot, smoked in the dark, quivering with rage. Angry over his advances, but more incensed that she'd even contemplated buying back art her family once owned. By the time her fury subsided, she had a plan. She would give Peyton what he anticipated—an intruder. She drove to the paddock.

"I didn't plan to kill him. I wanted information, and for him to beg. The stage was set for me: spare coveralls, helmets, the battery charger, a large puddle pooled under the car. Even the epoxy. I merely arranged the props and called him like so." She smacked the heel of her boot down on the metal bleacher. Madison cringed at the noise. Rebecca absorbed the reverberation in her arms. "Of course, I used a wrench on the side of a tool chest to sound the alarm. Peyton came running. You know the rest."

She made sure Madison was still hanging, hearing every word. He now clutched the pole with both hands. Elbows braced against the sides of the foot well. The veins in his wrists were bulging. He was growing paler by the minute.

Carlson shook her head, silver hair glistened. "Your son was a disappointment, Heinrich. I played the tape of my mother's final hours. It had no impact other than to confuse him. He never learned German. That was a surprise. He couldn't understand the demented woman crooning over lost masterpieces while she condemned his grandfather, father and all products of their loins to a hell worse than the one she'd known. Still, eventually, he gave me what I needed: assurance that you continued to own my family's art."

She pushed off from the bench and stood. "I'm not a barbarian, Rebecca. I didn't want to make a mistake. There was always a chance that Peyton had sold the Corot on behalf of a third party. But the painting had been his." She swung around, extending the rod in Madison's direction. "When did you realize he'd sold it, Heinrich?"

A groan escaped from Madison. His head lolled back and forth. His arms were quivering from either exhaustion or rage. He couldn't hold on much longer.

Carlson considered him with a cool stare as if she had tired of his existence. Measuring whether a direct kick to the face would release his grip and end it.

Rebecca chanced kneeling on the bleacher. Her legs ached where they had been struck; her neck was tight with tension. She slid sideways, slowly, not to threaten Carlson but enough to reclaim her attention, to keep her talking. "You recognized the Corot when it was offered for sale?"

Carlson almost smiled as she turned her attention away from Madison. "Dreams of recovering the paintings sustained me, as memories of them had sustained my mother. Sophie's bedtime story was a fairy tale based on family wealth, before . . ."

Her voice trailed off, drowned out by the whine of the F1 cars accelerating around the turn. The warm-up lap. The race was about to start. The sound seemed to disorient her. She looked dazed as if she'd lost the thread. The story that had consumed her entire life was coming unraveled.

Behind her, Madison took advantage of the noise, struggled to climb onto the platform. One bony knee was up on the stand, right hand flat on the seat. With the left, he still clung to the upright.

He wetted his lips. He'd listened to Carlson with the panicked air of a child overhearing his parents' plan to put him up for adoption. As Lisa Frankel, her story was inexorably linked with his, but he'd never heard it from her side. Probably never considered it. Even now, he might not digest it. It would take a less egotistical man than he was to accept that the heritage his family claimed was tainted, nearly as abhorrent as the genocide that made it possible.

Carlson faced him, unconcerned that he'd crawled over the edge onto the platform. "You failed to cover your tracks as well as you thought. Don't you want to know how I made the link between Peyton Madison of South Carolina and Heinrich Kauffman, Nazi collaborator? It wasn't just the painting."

Madison swiped away a dollop of spittle, said nothing.

"No?" She raised an eyebrow. "No matter, Rebecca does. She's a curious little cat. So. The chink in Kauffman's armor was Ingrid." At the mention of her name, Madison blinked. Clearly it wasn't what he expected. "Ingrid was Herr Kauffman's first wife. He married her not long after my mother was carted off to Mauthausen. We like to think the marriage was Hilde's doing. Kauffman's mother was rabid on propagating the pure Aryan race for the Fatherland. She would have hand-picked his Fraulein, don't you think? Her son did his part, siring Karl on their wedding night.

"When it looked like the Nazis were going to lose the war, Heinrich, Ingrid and Karl trotted off to Argentina with Heinrich, senior. Two years later, Ingrid and Karl died unexpectedly. Inexplicably."

Carlson swung, stepped closer to Madison. Rebecca inched forward, stopped when Carlson did, tried to look innocent. It was like they were playing the kid's game where you had to freeze when the leader shouted, "Red light." Anyone caught moving was out. In Carlson's version you could be dead.

"Am I boring you, Heinrich? You react badly to being bored, don't you? I suspect that once you and your father had established yourselves in South America— had your well-paid jobs, security within the Aryan enclave—you grew bored. You were, and here I'm guessing, less patriotic than your father and far greedier. You lusted over the works of art he'd hidden away and dreamed of your own company in America. A business not controlled by stagnating Germans unable to forget their former glory. At that point, I imagine Ingrid and Karl's days were numbered."

She whipped around as if trying to catch Rebecca

moving. Almost did. She smiled at seeing her frozen, kneeling on the bench one row below.

Carlson sat, swung her feet up on the bench. Stretching out her legs, she leaned back on one elbow, winked at Rebecca. "What do you think? Did our friend here decide that a pro-Nazi, German wife made him too conspicuous? Did her existence proclaim loudly that he was a German expatriate? Or was he simply tired of her and her simpering offspring?"

Her insouciance was unnerving. Madison had both knees on the platform, both hands wrapped around uprights, yet it didn't phase Carlson. True, his only way down to safety was past her to the stairs. He might risk it. He might make it, unless she'd smuggled a handgun or a knife into the track. From that distance, she couldn't miss.

Rebecca wiggled backward, slid her knees off the bench to standing.

The movement prompted Carlson to sit up, return to the story. "Hindsight. I have no proof, Rebecca. Though the fact that Kauffman worked in the experimental lab at a chemical company is suggestive. Their death certificates read *unknown illness*. Possibly chemically induced? Then there was the speed with which he remarried and left the country. More about that later. We're talking about Ingrid Thierman Kauffman."

She stood, rotated her shoulders, linked her hands behind her back. The rod, held loosely in her fingers, swayed. The pose was too reminiscent of Nazi officers to be coincidental. She was savoring her little drama, hamming it up for her audience, unconcerned about how long the performance would run. That too, was unsettling.

"After my mother's death, I hired an investigator and sent him to South America. He searched for family groups that had arrived from Germany with a young bride, Ingrid, and infant son, Karl. I was optimistic that even if papa Kauffman had changed the surname, he would not think it necessary to erase the faded, and fated, daughter-in-law. He should have.

"Because their deaths were suspicious, the Fraulein and son were remembered, even decades later. An aged interviewee thought the name was Cottman. Close enough for a zealot willing to alter his name for protection, but reluctant to relinquish his Teutonic heritage. The wife and son fit the pattern; the husband was the correct age to have been a young man engaged to my mother in the early forties. And there was an older father who'd arrived with enough collateral to buy a compound for his family. I authorized the investigator to keep digging after Señor Cottman's past. Which brings us to the other woman you married. Both bad choices, Heinrich."

She had strolled almost to Madison. Now she paced back. Keeping both of them within striking range. A cat with two mice. Easy pickings if she didn't rush.

"Did I tell you that when Heinrich remarried, it was to an Argentinian? Teresa. She was supposed to have severed all ties when they came to the States. But when a portrait of the successful Madison family appeared in a national magazine, the proud Teresa just had to send a copy home. She wanted her family, the entire town, to witness her success. The photograph is still in a scrapbook of prominent citizens compiled by a local archivist. So, a minor bit of vanity provided the missing link."

It's the little things that trip us up. Rebecca recalled the blurred photocopy Hagan had shown her of the Madisons in front of their Southern, gracious-living home. It was only human that Teresa had wanted to boast of her good fortune to those she'd left behind.

Madison's face drained of color, a good indication that he'd been unaware of his wife's slipup. Carlson didn't see. She was looking down the stands. Annoyance flitted across her face.

Rebecca heard the banging of feet below her, felt the vibration. Someone was coming to help. She was loathe to take her eyes from Carlson, but risked a quick glance over her shoulder.

She shouldn't have. If she hadn't twisted around, she wouldn't have seen Jasmine racing up the stands, arms pumping, camera smacking her narrow chest, thin legs struggling to mount the steps. Wouldn't have seen her bicolored face burst into a Christmas-morning smile and then collapse in nearly the same instant when she saw Carlson looming over her hero.

If she hadn't turned, she wouldn't have known that the child was grabbing up her camera, fiddling with knobs, rushing headlong into danger.

Rebecca screamed for the girl to stop.

Jasmine either didn't hear or had no intention of obeying. She scrambled up onto the higher bleacher and ran along it, full tilt. Raised her camera at Carlson. Her tiny fingers activated the strobe light.

Flashes of brilliant white burst from it, meant to blind the devil.

Rebecca leapt up to grab the child.

Carlson had anticipated her move. Eyes shut, she lashed out, the rod aimed at the clamor.

The thin baton whirred, connected, slashed Rebecca's arm open. She cried out.

Carlson swung again, higher, going for her voice, her face. She connected with Rebecca's palms. She slashed backhanded, again and again, forcing Rebecca farther away from Jasmine until she heard her stumble. Only then did Carlson open her eyes. Reaching down, she clutched the back of the girl's shirt and yanked her high into the air.

Forty-four

Mick's breathing was ragged; he had a stitch in his side by the time he reached the southeast vista directly below where Madison had dangled over the side. No sign of him on the ground. He must be the bundle cowering close to the edge, not moving. He hoped the old man was still breathing.

As he sucked in air, he considered the possibility of climbing the metal girders up to the stands. Reasoned that even if he could get most of the way up, the outward curve holding the last ten rows afforded no handholds. The lower crossbeams looked liked they'd been planned to exceed a man's reach, say nothing about his grasp. Browning would be encouraged.

Discounting divine intervention, Mick forced himself to move, trotted to the entrance midway along. He prayed Patten was close behind with a posse, not watching the opening laps. No siren yet, but the chief wouldn't really need it, nor would he have wanted to scare the fans.

He ducked into the darkened tunnel, jogged to the end and was once again in bright sun. He pressed himself flat against the front of the stands, shielded his eyes and looked up at the figures forty rows above. Not three combatants, but four.

Shit. Jasmine.

It was a given that she'd wiggle out of the car the minute the guard's back was turned. He'd hoped she'd go north, to the infield following the path taken by the cruiser. Instead, she must have gone in the opposite direction in hope of finding Rebecca first. Planning to search where he wasn't. Probably intended to sneak through the main gate and head for Moore's pits. But something had stopped her before she entered the track.

Had she seen a man dangling from the top of the stands and assumed he was the man Rebecca said was in danger? The smart little kid probably saw the whole thing through her telephoto. Whatever. She'd blundered in where angels feared to tiptoe, aching to help the woman she'd decided to worship. Foolishly, she'd become another pawn in Carlson's game. She and Moore had to be related.

Dropping to a crouch, he started up. Slowed as he neared the crow's nest. One-handed, Carlson was dangling the girl over Moore's head. Her other arm was out of sight at her side. He kept his eyes glued on that arm, searching for any indication of a weapon. He sidled along the row, knees pressed against the sun-baked metal, heading for the last short flight of stairs.

He cursed Patten for not returning his gun. Carlson had the height advantage. She was in front of the highest bleacher, calves braced against it. He wasn't sure whether she'd seen him, but he assumed so. So far, it hadn't spooked her.

Madison had seen him. He was struggling to stand, his back braced against a pole. An elderly man tottering at the edge. Mick made eye contact. Nodded to reassure him, to get him to stay still, not to make any sudden movements.

Carlson twisted a knot of Jasmine's sweatshirt, pulling the cotton taut against the skinny kid, exposing a band of stomach flesh. The skin was smooth brown, delicate belly button, no white blemishes marring its childish vulnerability. Jasmine looked both scared and defiant, confident that her hero would make everything fine.

Moore was probably ready to pass out at the thought of the kid's adoration, her dependence. She said she preferred traveling unencumbered, relished her independence. Truth was, she was a sucker for strays: kids, cats, broken-down old cars, battered men in need of salvation. Walk into her range of vision and Moore would kill herself trying to make your life better. Sometimes she nearly succeeded.

Her back was to him. She was leaning into the lower bleacher, arms akimbo, speaking to Carlson. The drone of race cars masked her words. He inched closer, paused as the whine receded down the front straight.

Moore's clear voice drifted across the deserted rows. Naturally she was pleading for the girl. "Look at her, Elise. She's like you. A survivor."

"A child. Untested."

"A child, yes." Moore shrugged, using the motion to rise up and step on the seat directly in front of Carlson. She was making herself more threatening, more of a target, wrenching Carlson's attention from the girl. "But untested? She's distinctly different. Marked. She hides from crowds, conscious of being judged because of her skin. You grew up hiding, didn't you? Afraid that those safe, happy people around you knew your shame, your mother's guilt."

Carlson remained rigid, the tendons in her wrist taut with strain. "If you had not meddled, the girl would not be here. Blame yourself."

Moore nodded as if she agreed, dropped her arms to her sides. "Show her your scar, Elise. She may be a child, but she can understand."

"Hitler would have considered her trash. A victim of a severe hereditary physical deformity: a candidate for sterilization or death. Would she understand that?"

Moore was like a retriever on point that wouldn't be distracted. She kept her voice even and deliberate. "Like you, Jasmine knew only one parent. Her mother disappeared from home when she was an infant. Her father raised her as long as he could. She's alone now, dependent upon the whims of foster parents. Like you, she's found the strength to adapt and go on. To see the beauty in life, the humor." Moore kept nodding, using the patter to inch laterally away from Carlson, toward the open end of the row.

Mick flashed back to the previous spring. He wondered if she had tried talking to calm the homicidal maniac on the cliff. Had she tried to convince him that he was making a mistake killing her, that her life was worth saving? She hadn't had an audience then. She'd been alone with a can of gasoline facing a madman with a gun.

She continued to move sideways.

He started up the stairs. Prayed Moore wasn't planning something stupid, like putting herself between Carlson and Madison. What good would it do? She had no respect for Madison. But could she, with her conscience, trade him for the girl? No. Moore would want to save his sorry butt as well.

Mick was on the crow's nest, braced on the front railing, six yards away from the action. Close enough to see the muscles in Moore's shoulders tense. She took a breath and continued to creep away from him. There was a chance that she sensed him in back of her and was edging out of his line of sight, to give him room to act. He could hope.

Moore stopped. In a controlled move, she sat on the bench, swung her legs over and stood. Not an aggressive move, but a definite advance on the enemy. Just one row and nine feet separated the two women. Carlson flicked a glance in his direction, registered that he was the third leg of an unequal triangle. She shifted her position to keep Moore in her line of sight. He was betting she didn't have a gun. She would have drawn it by now.

Moore opened her hands, palms up. Body language saying there was nothing for Carlson to worry about, just two girls having a nice chitchat in the full sun over the drone of Ferrari-built engines. When the noise receded, she was talking again. No longer pleading for the girl, critiquing some damn art show. "The paintings were powerful."

Carlson shifted her grip on Jasmine's shirt. "Don't be patronizing."

"I'm not. They were powerful, also disgusting."

"Truly. But so therapeutic. I met Robert Carlson at my showing. We married a short time later. He was older, generous and undemanding."

Moore ignored the digression. "Disturbing, horrific paintings, Elise, but not hateful. When did the rancor begin?"

What was she trying to do with the essay on art appreciation? Her right leg was quivering with the strain of holding it all together. He hoped Carlson was tiring as well. He pulled his gaze away from Moore long enough to check.

He saw it then—a flicker in Carlson's eyes, a flash of doubt, or sorrow. Or pity. Perhaps self-pity. Moore's question had struck a chord. It made Carlson pause. She answered softly, "When my mother died, ranting, screaming for revenge—"

Moore nodded. "The tape you played for—"

"That damn tape." Carlson emitted a guttural bark. The mood shattered.

Shit. Moore, you shouldn't have interrupted.

In a hawk-like swoop, Carlson bent. When she twisted to unsnap a pouch on the leg of her pants, Mick saw the ASP, the expandable baton, pinning the girl tight against her. *What else was in her arsenal? Please, not a gun.*

Before he could charge, Carlson stood, waved a

recorder in her hand. "This tape." She punched the PLAY button with her left thumb, wheeled up the volume. A sibilant hiss erupted as the tape fast-forwarded. It gave way to unearthly keening. Then a woman's voice began muttering alien phrases in German. Garbled, low-pitched, it ranted, then faded off. Only to begin again with renewed force.

"Sprechen sie Deutsche, Heinrich? Listen." Holding it overhead, she wheeled the volume to the max.

Despite his fear, and his anger, Madison was riveted by the voice as it droned on, listing works of art that no doubt resided in his vault. Had he known just which paintings had belonged to his parents' neighbors or hadn't he much cared?

Carlson yelled over the racket. "She taped it as she was dying. She didn't want me to forget one hate-filled word. One second of her pain. It wasn't enough that she'd survived, that I'd made a name for our family, that we had security. That was not enough. She wanted her revenge. She made me promise." The tape ran out.

Moore had moved quickly while Carlson was ranting. She was a scant two yards from Madison, legs apart, arms out forming a shield. "She's dead, Elise. Let the past die with her."

"Why? We're all going to die. I'm just giving God a hand." She dropped the recorder. Gripped Jasmine's shoulder.

Moore tensed. She wanted to jump Carlson, but she was too far past her. Her chest was heaving, but her voice was surprisingly even. "Let her go, Elise. There are mitigating circumstances to explain your assault on Peyton. A jury will be sympathetic when they learn what you and your mother endured. Let us walk away and the law will be lenient. You'll see your art returned and your family avenged. You can start again."

Mick considered it a decent speech, given the circumstances, given that Moore hadn't had negotiation training. Might make a good Christmas present for her, if she planned to keep attracting the mentally unbalanced.

Carlson, though deeply unhinged, wasn't buying it. She was too savvy to believe she'd get away with all she'd done. There were three of them, one of her. If she hadn't been holding the girl, he would have rushed her by now. She was all but cornered, yet she was totally in command. There was nobility in her defiance. At that instant, he couldn't help but admire her resolve and her intelligence. And wonder how she would respond when he played his trump card.

Before he could get her attention, she played one of her own. "Rebecca, you were a reporter in DC."

Moore blinked. She'd made a name writing for the *Post* but was far from a household word.

Carlson smiled. "Don't be flattered. I had you investigated after I arrived here. A female mechanic, you see, made me curious. A reporter made me a bit nervous. I expelled you from the pits so you wouldn't be looking over my shoulder taking notes." She shrugged, dismissing her breach of etiquette. "But, now? Well, I've reconsidered. I want you to tell my story."

Moore stared at Carlson, slow to absorb the implication. Mick could almost see her brain shift gears. A moment ago, she'd envisioned the Holocaust survivor in front of a jury eloquently evoking the pain she and her mother had endured, explaining how it grew into an ugly parasite fueled by blood lust. Now she was being asked to pick up her pen and write the words for her.

The light dawned—Carlson wasn't planning to be around to tell the story herself.

Moore leapt onto the bench separating them, demanded the girl's release.

Carlson closed the negotiations, whipped the baton against Jasmine's throat, grabbed it with both hands and pulled, lifting the girl into the air, her feet scrambling as she hung by her neck.

Moore screamed.

Carlson yelled louder. "Stop. I'll kill her. I have nothing to lose."

That was Mick's cue.

Forty-five

Rebecca froze, her pulse pounding with fear for Jasmine, anger at the situation and at herself.

She'd sensed Hagan's presence on the platform before she saw him. She wasn't positive it was him, only that someone was there: watching, waiting, not interfering. It had given her confidence to stay calm, to keep Carlson distracted, to try to circle around, block Madison. She didn't know how Hagan got there, didn't care. He could be a real pain about lots of things, but he was good in an emergency.

He pounded across the stands, lunged over the bleacher at Carlson.

Carlson backed away. Using the bar as leverage, she lifted Jasmine waist high, swung her behind out of reach. The force propelled the girl's thin legs into the chain link, ripping it loose. The bar at her throat kept her from falling sixty feet to the tarmac below. She couldn't scream, she could barely breathe. Her eyes were huge with terror, her tiny fingers clawed at the rod.

Hagan righted himself, held up a hand, placating. "Elise, don't. So far, you're only suspected of assaulting Peyton. It's a slap-on-the-wrist offense. There are no witnesses. Charges won't even be pressed. Let the girl go. We all walk away. Things will work out."

Carlson smiled as if at a bad pun. "Peyton Madison the third is dead, remember. I killed him."

"You weren't responsible."

"Of course I was. I used the boost on the battery charger to overpower him, jammed him in a race car, continued to shock him pointlessly for answers. I could have stopped as soon as I realized he was ignorant of his family's treachery. I didn't. Do you understand? I felt no remorse, no compassion. He was a bug in my laboratory."

Rebecca checked out Madison. His eyes looked vacant as if all systems had shut down. Listening to his son's killer was draining him. She would have gone to comfort him if she hadn't been afraid of moving. If she'd cared more about his well-being.

She turned back to the stand-off between Hagan and Carlson. She'd missed something. Hagan had sat. His hands were clasped between his knees. Carlson had retreated a yard away, pulling Jasmine back onto the platform. One sneaker had come untied. The girl was gasping and choking, but she was breathing.

Hagan smirked, like a kid with a secret. "Elise, you didn't kill him. I just came from the police station. The chief was at the autopsy. Peyton died from asphyxiation, smothered while in the hospital. Unless a witness can swear that you snuck into his room and held a pillow over his face, there's no way they can convict you of murder."

Rebecca's mouth fell open. Was it possible? Hagan didn't lie about anything important, but he could be spinning a tale to save Jasmine. The kid was endearing; Hagan wasn't immune to charm.

Off to her right, Madison straightened. Disbelief, or rage at hearing of his son's murder, had breathed life into him. He let go of the upright. With creaking slowness he shuffled one step forward and fumbled for the front railing.

Carlson remained still, her body twisted, arms taut from holding Jasmine behind her. Her face was in profile. One emotion after another flicked across it. She didn't want to believe Hagan—that would mean she had failed somehow. But if she hadn't killed Madison, her life might not be forfeited. She could feel Damocles' sword suspended overhead as she swayed between the two, trying to decide which, if either, she wanted to be true.

All Rebecca wanted was to get Jasmine away from her safely. She sent a telepathic message to Hagan, willing him to keep talking, say whatever it took to convince Carlson that she could enjoy a new beginning if only she let the girl live.

Before he got the message, Carlson called his bluff. "If I didn't kill him, who did?"

Forty-six

Mick had chewed on that question on the ride over. Decided that—assuming Carlson hadn't smothered Peyton—he really didn't care who had. His goal was to convince her that she hadn't killed anyone. And prevent her from doing so until Patten arrived.

She waited for his answer.

He bit at the inside of his cheek and shrugged. "His bookie? Peyton was in serious debt, major gambling IOUs. He was behind on payments for the Lotus."

"Nonsense. They'd want him alive to collect."

"But once he'd been assaulted, they might have assumed suspicion would fall on them anyway. Maybe he threatened to blame them. Maybe they thought it would be easier to get payments from his heirs, whomever took over. It's arguable."

He stood. "Or Whitten? He and Madison were too cozy for rivals. They could have been involved in a secret business deal, one that was going south, thanks to

Peyton's losing habits. Whitten might have decided to cut his losses, divest himself of a liability."

Carlson wasn't on board yet, but she was considering. She'd eased her hold on the baton. Jasmine's color looked better; the white side of her face was pinker.

Feeling like a junior congressman at a filibuster, he kept going. "Then there's Browning. He's an odd duck, probably unstable. He was questioned in his sister's death when he was a teenager. Maybe Peyton was blackmailing him and he rebelled. With the boss out of the way, Browning envisioned taking over the team. He didn't know you were stepping in as partner." Mick avoided looking at Moore during the last bit. She would balk at the idea of her race driver having anything shady in his past. Too bad. He was desperate.

Who else? Think.

"Maybe your cousin Franks snuffed him out as a favor to the family? He was going into the hospital as I was leaving."

She scoffed, shook her head at that.

He used his responding shrug to move closer. "Think about it, Elise. There are a half-dozen possible scenarios for your attorney to choose from. All you need is reasonable doubt. Whoever killed Peyton gambled that the assault would be blamed for causing his death. Smothering him in the hospital was the killer's best chance of getting rid of him without attracting attention. If so much hadn't been going wrong with the team that the State Police became suspicious—if the hospital hadn't been so concerned about liability—the medical examiner might not have looked so hard."

He placed his foot on the bench in front. Clasping his hands, he leaned on his knee. His palms were sweating. "It was a murder of opportunity. Not pre-meditated revenge. Come on, Elise, if you'd set out to kill Peyton, you wouldn't have been sloppy. You wouldn't have left anything to chance. You'd have done it right."

"Don't flatter me, Lieutenant." She spit. "Do you think I'm so gullible? You're making up the story to save your friends. After I submit, the medical exam-iner will contradict you, say it was the torture that caused his impaired heart to give out. And I'll be found guilty of manslaughter, at the least."

Mick scowled. "A bad heart? No. The coroner said the liver was a bit shaky, evidence of cirrhosis, but no mention of heart problems. Where'd you hear that?"

Forty-seven

If it had been a film, the screen would have dimmed, the sound track would have muted, action slowed, every nuance of expression captured in stark relief on camera.

What weak heart? Confusion flickered across Hagan's face. He thought he was the bearer of exculpatory news, that Peyton had been smothered. That his death had nothing to do with Carlson's assault.

Carlson was peeved, convinced that Hagan was lying about the asphyxiation. She knew she'd assaulted Peyton. Assumed he'd later died because of a heart condition.

Did Peyton have a weak heart?

His father said so. But not the police. It was possible that the medical examiner had noted it, but hadn't mentioned it to Patten because it wasn't the primary cause of death.

Ian, on the other hand, had raced for Peyton for six

years. He knew of no heart ailment other than stinginess.

Rebecca caught Carlson's eye. In unison, they turned toward Madison. There was a light sheen of perspiration on his face, a tic jumped next to his nose. He'd shuffled another few inches along the railing, but was still precariously near the edge. When he spoke his voice wavered. "Tell me the police are coming. Please. Take me away from this lunatic."

"Lunatic?" Carlson grabbed Jasmine's shirt, slid her across the metal bleacher on her belly. Dragged her like a sack of laundry as she advanced on Madison. "Lunatic is a man who would kill his own son. You did, didn't you? Didn't you? I should have expected it. But it is too heinous. How could you do it? Even my mother refrained."

Her voice was shrill, dissolving as the cars screamed into the turn, their roar sweeping over the empty stands. Madison crouched slightly, eyes darted to Hagan in mute appeal.

Bile rose in Rebecca's throat; one knee quivered. *Had he killed his son?*

The notion bounced like echoes in her brain, too horrific to take root. He'd been patently annoyed when he burst into the hospital room. His anger was directed at her, but his focus had been on Peyton, quaking in the bed. Peyton had been telling her about the voices on the tape. Recounting a harangue in German. He'd mentioned art, the Corot.

Had the old man become so enraged by what he heard that he killed his own son? Her grandmother's picture of the Kauffman family had not been flattering. The mother was a dominating Nazi supporter. The father stole from his Jewish neighbors, then fled the country. The ambitious Madison, once engaged to Sophie Franks, later married two other women apparently as window dressing. Ruthlessness ran in the family.

But murdering your own child?

A clang reached her, a vibration below, moving swiftly, coming nearer. Someone stumbled on the steps. She continued to face front, watching Madison. Hagan glanced laterally and expelled a breath. The person climbing up must be a cop, probably Patten. She hoped he would listen before acting. There was a thread-fine line here between victim and villain.

Ignoring the newcomer, Carlson moved in, totally focused on Madison. Hagan followed, tightening the circle. Like the tableau in a morality play, they waited for direction. Carlson and Madison stood center stage: the principal players, good and evil. Hagan, in the wings, was retribution. Jasmine the sacrificial lamb. That made her the chorus. The observer tasked with enlightening and advancing the action. As in any well-acted tragedy, the tension emanating from them was palpable.

In the silence, Rebecca again heard Carlson's dictum: *I want you to tell my story.* She swallowed. What was the full story? There were so many questions. Could she stomach the answers? How much time did she have before Patten acted?

Rebecca stepped forward. "Madison, what happened to your mother, Hilde?" Her voice cracked, startlingly loud even in her own ears.

His head jerked up. "*Mein Mutter?* Mother?" He snorted. "She was a nationalistic zealot. She stayed behind."

"Really? She allowed her husband, son, daughter-in-law and grandson to emigrate to Argentina with the wealth, while she remained in Germany?"

He shrugged. "You could say that. It was for the best."

His casual dismissal caused her blood to chill. She had no doubt that Hilde had stayed behind in Germany. Not because she chose to, but because she was dead. Murdered by someone in the family. Rebecca wanted to scream, to reach out and throttle the insensitive bastard. Instead she laced her fingers. Forced her hands to remain calm.

"I see. Did your father kill her? Smother her in her sleep, perhaps, then leave her outside in the rubble? Is that where you learned the technique, at your father's side? Then Peyton wasn't the first Kauffman sacrificed to—"

"Shut up. It was necessary."

At last, an outburst. Confirmation.

Carlson whipped her head around, a glint of approval in her eyes, grateful that another person had stepped across the line and was standing on her side. Not just the dead Sophie. A living person, a near-stranger, who comprehended the magnitude of the Kauffmans' villainy. It was validation that she hadn't been wrong in avenging her family. She expelled a long breath, let her shoulders droop. She looked spent, tired of it all, but strangely at peace. "Thank you, Rebecca."

Carlson removed the rod from across Jasmine's neck, lowered it to her side. Laid her hand lightly on the girl's shoulder.

Jasmine squirmed, eyes full of worry and confusion. Rebecca tried to smile. Encouraged by Carlson's softening, she stepped closer to join them.

Hagan stiffened. His hand jerked out, then held.

She stopped, wished like hell she had eyes in the back of her head. Had the cop drawn his gun and was she now standing in the line of fire? Was that what Hagan was signaling about?

She thought she heard more footsteps lower down, but couldn't be sure. Her heart was beating loudly enough to drown out any sound that wasn't obliterated by the race cars. Roughly one minute, twenty seconds a lap to circle the 2.065-mile course. If she'd been paying attention, she could have computed how long they had been standing in the sun bargaining for Jasmine's life, Carlson's soul. It seemed an eternity.

No one moved. No one spoke. Each was waiting for another player to act.

The tension was unnerving.

Rebecca moistened her lips. Uncertain of her role, she did what came naturally, what she'd been trained to do. She faced a man she found abhorrent and calmly questioned him. "Did you kill Peyton because he sold the painting?"

Madison threw back his shoulders. He'd been waiting for this cue. "The painting was mine. They are all mine. I smuggled them out of Germany. My father wanted to turn them over to the authorities. Start fresh, he said. How, with no money? Blithering fool. Without mother he had no backbone. Everything this family has was my doing."

"But Peyton didn't thank you, did he? He took the wealth for granted. When he got in trouble, he stole one of your paintings."

"Yes, my son was a thief. The day I turned my company over to him, I showed him the treasures that made it possible. The spineless coward stole from me and denied it. But I knew. My Corot." A palsied hand shot out toward her. "Then I hear him tell you, a stranger. Plead for your help. Who are you that he should do that?"

A wad of spittle clung to his lip. The tic below his eye twitched out of control. Patches of red flared on his cheeks. He wobbled in place, the venom making him unsteady. "He told you about my paintings. What else would he have revealed? Any more babbling, you would have owned us. Didn't he realize that? He was handing you the power to destroy us. You never give away your power. How could he do that?"

Carlson seemed to have tuned out Madison's tirade. She was bent down to Jasmine's level, holding the child by one arm. Sorrow etched her face; she spoke just loud enough for Rebecca to hear. "I wronged you, child. I discounted you as a person and used you as a tool. I'm sorry if I hurt you, it was not my intent. Can you forgive me?"

Jasmine blinked frantically. Rebecca's pulse quickened. *What was Elise up to? Was she ready to let her go?* She desperately wanted the child away from danger. Hoping she read Elise correctly, she nodded at Jasmine and smiled, *yes.* The girl, in turn, bobbed her head at her captor.

Carlson patted the corn rows then pivoted her away. Jasmine bolted, scurrying along the foot well. She hit Rebecca at a jerky run, nearly knocking her over, welding her arms around her thighs. Elise straightened and regarded the two of them. She shrugged. "Why am I fighting it?" Unburdened, she strode to Madison, stopped less than a yard away.

The old man held his ground. Hagan fidgeted, exchanging tense glances with the reinforcements in the background.

Carlson smiled. "You realize, Kauffman, our families are similar. I'm an embittered woman who refused to have children, fearing I would hate them as my mother hated me. Having allowed herself to be used by the guards, she couldn't forget them when she looked at me. You willingly interbred with an Hispanic and loathed your son as a result, a wastrel who never established the dynasty you craved.

"Or did you want him to? He wasn't Aryan. That was his real crime, wasn't it? Hitler had fought the world and lost your homeland to keep the Aryan race pure. And your son wasn't. Had you always thought him a lesser individual? Did you view killing him as a form of euthanasia? Was his death your *Endlösung,* your final solution?"

The taunt was well-calculated. Whether Carlson believed what she was saying or not, it inflamed

Madison. He launched himself at her, pushed off from the railing, arms outstretched, fingers splayed, talons seeking flesh.

She raised the rod and slashed at him, caught him on the forearm as she circled left. Stepped down level with him. He growled, yanked his arm back and folded it to his chest. Bent over, he charged again, roaring like the bull he resembled.

Carlson was laughing now, circling slowly.

Too late those watching realized what was about to happen.

Hagan lunged. Patten scurried forward. He didn't have a shot even if he'd been certain which one to shoot. Rebecca cradled Jasmine against her, forcing her face between her legs to shield her from seeing.

She would like to have been shielded herself, to close her eyes and pretend it wasn't happening. Rewind the film and choose an ending other than this one. She couldn't, she could only watch as Elise Carlson flung out the baton like a matador's sword, opening her arms wide to Madison as he charged, her face erupting into a grin of triumph.

Almost in slow motion, she whipped the rod behind his neck and caught the other end. With his head locked to her chest, Carlson relaxed her body and let his momentum propel them over the railing and off the edge of the stands.

Forty-eight

"There are no heroes. Still, a tale worth telling."

Those were the last words Elise Carlson spoke as she lay twisted, her body broken on the tarmac. Rebecca was the first to reach her after foisting Jasmine into Hagan's arms and racing, tripping down the stands. Several hours later she learned that Carlson had sustained massive-force trauma hitting the pavement. She died from internal hemorrhaging.

Madison's neck had been broken in the fall. Or before it.

Most of the fans enjoyed the race in ignorance. Spectators around the world listening to Bob Varsha's coverage for Speed Channel never knew. Monday's *Indianapolis Star* carried a small mention of the tragic deaths of two spectators in the southeast vista. Very small. Schumacher won the F1 race, followed by his teammate Barrichello. Another one-two sweep for Ferrari.

The Historic Grand Prix got five inches of coverage

in a side bar. Ian Browning, piloting the Lotus 49C once driven by Austrian legend, Jochen Rindt, snatched the victory when Derek Manning's Brabham spun out on the final lap. Browning was credited with breaking the curse that had hovered over the late Peyton Madison's team during the weeks leading up to the race. Fans were quoted saying that watching the old cars was more exciting than the F1 race—more competitive, more mishaps. The promoters were negotiating to bring it back the following year.

Rebecca was pleased for Ian, proud of the small part she'd played in preparing the car. Glad she'd had the experience of working on the cars and being a part of the races at Indy. Next year she would be content to watch them on television. Or maybe not.

One day she would write Elise Carlson's story. It was worth telling; a lesson worth heeding. The tragedy of Sophie, the concentration camp survivor; Lisa Frankel; and three generations of Heinrich Kauffmans would stay with her for a long, long time. She didn't know in what format or when, but someday she would put the words down. Sprinkled throughout it would be Jasmine's energy and level-headed optimism as a counterpoint to the rigid doctrine that says we must all be alike, that those who are different must be feared. She was willing to bet that Elise had been similar to Jasmine as a child: bright, dauntless, self-contained. Before she was poisoned with unmanageable hatred.

Hagan blamed himself for Carlson's death. Berated himself for not acting more swiftly. Felt that he and Patten should have been able to control the situation. He thought Rebecca had gotten through to Carlson. He wouldn't accept that her suicide was the ending Elise wanted, the one she'd choreographed. That she'd sought a punishment worthy of the guilt that had been saddled on her. If Hagan had reached her, she would have fought him and gone over anyway. She might have taken him with her. Her final struggle would not have been a feeble attempt like her mother's.

He nodded as she spoke the words, but Rebecca could tell he wasn't buying it. For one thing he was unnaturally compliant, agreeing to reschedule his flight so she had time to say good-bye. He didn't carp even when she explained that she would be flying to Boston instead of accompanying him to Maryland.

At eleven o'clock they were attending the memorial service for Peyton Madison. It would give her the chance to congratulate Ian on his victory and wish him luck with the team. Already there were rumors that he would be taking over—assuming that one or both of the cars could be had for a reasonable sum. No doubt Ian would negotiate finances with the family attorney who was flying up to escort the bodies of father and son to South Carolina.

After school, she was taking Jasmine apple picking. She wanted to meet her foster mother, see where the girl lived, assure herself that the girl's spirit would not be eroded by her surroundings. She sighed, flipping the cover of her phone open and shut. Jo often chided her that she couldn't take in every stray that crossed her path. Selfishly, this little one would be so easy to hold on to.

When she told Jasmine that Elise Carlson was dead, the girl had nodded. "I know. She made me stronger."

Rebecca was willing to accept the cryptic statement, but the girl tugged on her arm, wanting to explain. "When a person dies, the energy goes into people close by. Or people they're close to. You don't get it all, just part. That's how kids get to grow and know more. Did you get some, too?"

She hugged her tight. "I hope so."

During the car trip to Dayton, she would call her parents and tell them she was on her way.

Then phone her grandmother with the news of Heinrich Kauffman's death. Dorothea would be intrigued, horrified and energized all at once. Brian Franks was Elise's executor. He promised to deliver Sophie's tape to the U.S. Customs Art Squad in hopes it could be used to reclaim the family's paintings. No doubt Rebecca's grandmother would involve herself in redressing the wrong. Meddling was a family trait.

Her third call would be to Jo. Again. She had to talk to him soon or she'd bite her lip raw from fretting. She needed to apologize for things she'd said or hadn't said. More than that, she needed to know what was bothering him. If she waited until she was on the plane for Boston, Hagan wouldn't be around to listen in if she did reach Jo. Or to gloat silently if she didn't.

Perhaps Jo was taking time off and was at the farm installing bookcases. They'd have a normal, warm conversation. He'd be proud of her decision to face her parents. Amused over the relationship she was forging with her grandmother. Relieved that she was returning to Head Tide.

Perhaps. But it was doubtful.

Frank had found a letter stuffed between the seats of a customer's car. It was addressed simply, *Rebecca*. He recognized Jo's handwriting. No way was he opening it. He'd save it until she returned.

The letter had been curious but not distressing. Panic didn't set in until she called Jo's office, planning to quiz Edna.

Click. "You have reached the law office of Jo Delacroix. The office will be closed until further notice. Legal matters will be handled by Lea Johansson at 202-555-1200. Messages left on this recording will not be returned."

Click.

PERENNIAL DARK ALLEY

Men from Boys: A short story collection featuring some of the true masters of crime fiction, including Dennis Lehane, Lawrence Block, and Michael Connelly.
0-06-076285-3

Fender Benders: From **Bill Fitzhugh** comes the story of three people planning on making a "killing" on Nashville's music row.
0-06-081523-X

Cross Dressing: It'll take nothing short of a miracle to get Dan Steele, counterfeit cleric, out of a sinfully funny jam in this wickedly good tale from **Bill Fitzhugh.**
0-06-081524-8

The Fix: Debut crime novelist **Anthony Lee** tells the story of a young gangster who finds himself caught between honor and necessity.
0-06-059534-5

The Pearl Diver: From **Sujata Massey**, antiques dealer and sometime sleuth Rei Shimura travels to Washington D.C. in search of her missing cousin.
0-06-059790-9

The Blood Price: In this novel by **Jonathan Evans**, international trekker Paul Wood must navigate through the world of international people smugglers.
0-06-078236-6

The Reunion: A group of extremely disfunctional teenagers in a psychiatric hospital are forced to reconnect when two of them die unexpectedly in this thriller by **Sue Walker**.
0-06-083265-7

PERENNIAL
**DARK
ALLEY**

An Imprint of HarperCollinsPublishers
www.harpercollins.com

Visit www.AuthorTracker.com for exclusive information on you favorite HarperCollins authors.

DKA 1105

Sign up for the FREE
HarperCollins monthly
mystery newsletter,

The Scene of the Crime,

and get to know your favorite authors,
win free books, and be the first to learn
about the best new mysteries going on sale.

To register, simply go to www.HarperCollins.com, visit our mystery channel page, and at the bottom of the page, enter your email address where it states "Sign up for our mystery newsletter." Then you can tap into monthly Hot Reads, check out our award nominees, sneak a peek at upcoming titles, and discover the best whodunits each and every month.

*Get to know the magnificent mystery authors
of HarperCollins and sign up today!*

MYN 0205